BORN OF BLOOD & RETRIBUTION

Book Three of the Dark Kiss Trilogy

By Liz Strange

"I know of your studies, Rachel. You are one of the few who has given more than a passing thought to where we come from. I enjoy that about you. I'm sure you could recite a hundred different names I've been known by over the centuries."

"Kali, Hecate, Luna, Balonda, Coatlicue, Lilitu. You have been called Lamia, Upir, Ramanga, Mandurugo, Aswang."

"Yes, yes!" She clapped her hands with delight, mirroring my passion.

"What is the truth?" I demanded, grabbing her about the wrists. We were so close I saw her skin was smooth and flawless, dazzling in its perfection. A fervent desperation gripped me, and my need to understand bordered on madness.

"First we must travel to where it all began. Then I can share with you my story. And my shame."

"Your shame?"

"Yes, for this creature I have become was born of shame and lust. And from that cesspool of evil, my human life was destroyed and the dark gift created. My immortal existence was bought with blood, and fuelled with vengeance. I exist because one man would not accept that he could not have everything he desired, and because I refused to die for his callousness and arrogance. He tried to take what was not his, and paid for it not only with his own life, but condemned his own bother and myself to an existence of eternal darkness."

Her anger smothered me. I fought against it, but to no avail. I would finally have my truth, but the cost might be more than I'd bargained for.

PROLOGUE

Somewhere Along the Mediterranean

The sand felt cool under my bare feet. My gaze wandered out over the dark water as the soft salty breeze tickled along my exposed skin. The warmth from the blood I'd taken earlier lingered, but I still hungered for something only Giovanni could satisfy.

As though he read my thoughts, which he may well have, he appeared along the water's edge, the wind lifting his dark hair. He carried a single long-stemmed red rose in his pale hand. As he approached, he offered it to me, the bloom's aroma gentle and sweet. One tiny thorn pierced my palm and the rose slipped from my fingers to the blanket beneath my body. Giovanni caught my hand in his strong grip, and with deliberate slowness, licked the blood from my skin. His mouth continued up my arm to the hollow of my throat.

I growled as he ripped open the front of my dress. With one clean jerk, he removed my panties and tossed them aside. I was already damp between my legs, eager for his body. I reached forward and lowered the zipper on his pants as he pulled his shirt over his head. The moonlight gleamed off his hard, white form. *Damn, I'm a lucky girl.*

We made love like frenzied animals, lost to the outside world. In our enthusiasm we rolled off the blanket, over the cold sand, until our bodies made contact with the water lapping on the shore. My hair spilled out around me, damp tendrils snaking across my face and between our eager mouths. The sand scraped against my back as Giovanni pounded into me. My entire being throbbed with pleasure, each thrust intensifying the level of physical gratification.

Life was good. There were no worries, nothing dancing in the shadows waiting for its chance to throw us to the wolves. There was only blood, sex, and our connection to one another.

Sometime later, we made our way back to the house. This one was less grand than the one in Greece, but it was secluded and comfortable. We had a private beach, our own dock, and easy access to the larger urban areas of Spain and her neighbours. We had even taken a trip back to Giovanni's homeland to visit places he had not seen for a very long time. It brought home his great age and the life lived long before I was born, and not only the physical, but also the emotional distance he had travelled to come into my life.

The phone rang as we approached the back door. Giovanni rushed ahead, and I heard him speak as I stood shaking the sand from my hair. When he returned, he wore the strangest expression. His brows were knitted as though he worked a difficult scenario over in his mind. His strong arms crossed his torso, which he quickly released when he saw me regarding him so intensely.

"What's going on?" I was not quite ready to become alarmed.

"I'm not sure exactly. That was Charles calling. He said he had a very disturbing conversation this week, and he's coming down to explain everything in person."

"Okay," I responded. "That's rather cryptic."

"I agree. He did say to tell you he has some news that's right up your alley."

"Charles said that?"

"Yes, and he said to expect him and Genevieve in the next few days. He had some other things to check into first."

Charles was well aware of my research into the origins of our kind after the years he had spent with Eli and me. I had passed many nights poring over books and the internet, reading historical and anthropological articles and studies, and contacting authorities of one kind or another. I had even quizzed all the eldest vampires about their knowledge, substantiated or otherwise, during our preparations for the attack on the Desmarais.

Could Charles's call have something to do with that?

"I wonder what's in store for us this time."

"I don't know, my love," he answered softly and took my hand. "But after everything we've been through, I know we can deal with it."

He was right. Together we could survive whatever fate tossed our way.

CHAPTER 1

Harshika

They left me on the damp jungle floor, naked, bloody, and beaten to within an inch of my young life. I'd been cut, burned, whipped, and violated in every possible way, yet something in me was not ready to die. I lay there through the long, hot day, breathing as carefully as I could despite numerous broken ribs, occasionally choking on my own blood and vomit. I willed myself to rise above the pain. My agony was channeled into anger—anger at the indignity of the vicious acts against my body, anger at the men who had done this to me, and most of all, anger at the man who had orchestrated it all. The thought of retribution made me cling to the dimming thread of life and pull myself back from the ease of death. He would pay for what he'd done.

Narsimha, I will have my revenge. You will know the agony and humiliation you have inflicted upon me.

As dusk settled, I became aware of a strange sound. A low, mournful wail filled the vast jungle, crawling along the damp ground and over my exposed skin. It was an animal's cry, but unlike any I'd heard before. With great determination I forced myself to my stomach, and I used my broken hands to crawl along the ground. The sound called to me, its haunting nature luring me to its location for a purpose my mind could not understand, but that my soul embraced without hesitation.

Soon the source came into view. The creature lay on its side, all but hidden under a low-lying branch and a tangle of long grass. Within ten feet of the animal, I realised what it was. The distinctive white-orange coat with its ebony strips was clearly visible from my vantage point. A tiny bit farther and I would be face to face with a mighty tigress, the most noble of creatures.

The animal was now also aware of me. She raised her heavy head and stared with amber eyes. Great pride lurked there, and also terrible pain. She was sick, this mighty creature, as evidenced by her wasted body and the blood-tinged saliva matting the fur about her mouth. The closer I got the more pungent the smell of death became. If it was my time to go, it would be an honour to die alongside the most righteous of all the jungle's wildlife. For some unknown reason, I felt sure this encounter was not simply about my death, but that I was being called to a fate, which would have ramifications beyond my own personal vengeance.

My hand made contact with the rough pads of the tigress's foot then slid over the gritty fur of her lower leg. The animal let out a terrible wail and snapped at the human who dared to touch her. Yet I didn't stop. I was compelled to continue, pushed by an urgent certainty that something momentous was about to happen. My injured body forced forward, demanding something only this sick creature could give me.

The tigress lay her head back down and panted heavily. Her ribs were sharply visible with every intake of breath, and as she exhaled, the air became rank with the stench of the infection ravaging her body. I trembled as the scent hit me, reacting with a strange but undeniable arousal. And hunger. Before I realised what I was doing, my mouth was clamped onto the animal's throat.

A terrible, primal frenzy overtook me, which cast my consciousness out of my damaged body. My spirit hovered nearby, watching with approval as my body tore into the creature and consumed its tainted blood. I had to pull at the flesh with all the strength left in me to inflict a wound deep enough to drink from. The tigress lashed at me with her front legs, heavy claws raking across my already bloodied and damaged flesh. But no more pain could be inflicted on me, as I was then beyond the ability to be hurt or killed. The goddess had heard my prayers and vengeance would be mine. I drank until the creature stilled and there was no blood left in its body.

Awareness slammed back into me and I collapsed against the dry husk of the once-powerful creature's body. What had I done? I had gone mad. The animal's blood was still warm on my face and like nectar in my mouth. It slid down my throat, and hit my stomach to spread a powerful, scurrying warmth throughout my flesh. Soon it coursed along my veins, writhing tendrils of foreign matter surging through my broken body, destroying and somehow replacing my own human blood.

My former all-encompassing agony became a dim memory, replaced by an itching, parasitic influence. The effect of the animal's blood felt both orgasmic and repulsive, and my brain wrestled with the contradiction. My mind swirled, trying to sort out the myriad conflicting effects and sensations invoked by the ingestion of blood. The tigress's life force fused with mine, our conjoined essence bursting past the limits of the natural world.

I panicked and my hands dug at my flesh as though I could let the animal's blood from my body. Bile rose in my throat and froth poured from my mouth. My body bucked with violent convulsions. I tried to scream, but choked, burning, writhing and aching as if being eaten from the inside out. Then darkness overtook me.

The sun had moved a great distance in the sky by the time I awoke again. Still sprawled on top of the wasted corpse of the tigress, I became aware of a foul smell, clawing its way into my troubled mind. My eyes snapped open and I became overwhelmed with not only the stench, but an astonishing pain assaulting every inch of my body. The feeling was even more excruciating than the injuries the king's men had inflicted upon me.

I looked down, amazed to see my once sienna-coloured skin turning black, and when I swatted at my arms a small wisp of smoke trailed out from under my hand. Looking up I realized the sun sat full in the hazy sky, and the horrible reaction was caused by its touch to my skin. It was burning me and the pain was unbearable.

The sensation forced me to my feet, where I began to run, dodging branches and jumping over rocks and other natural obstacles. Despite the pain searing over my skin, I possessed an inner strength and outward nimbleness unknown to humanity, allowing me to run for a thousand miles. A strange tingling began in my brain, as though an internal radar had been tripped, propelling me to an as yet unseen destination.

Soon a small cave appeared, and I rushed inside its welcoming darkness. I didn't stop until I collided with the farthest interior wall of the small space. The rock face was cool and soothing against my injuries. With the pain from my burns dulled, I realised my injuries from the previous day had miraculously healed. I slid to the ground, knowing more change was to come.

As I once again slipped into a deep sleep, I dreamt of Narsimha and the consequences he was about to face.

Eli. San Francisco.

I waited for Micah in the hallway when his class was over. He followed the group of students out of the lecture theater, a black carrier bag full of final assignments slung over one shoulder. Even without the soft touch of me in his mind, and the warm sexual energy that always accompanied my arrival, the gaggle of girls congesting the hallway would have given me away. A shift in the crowd of female admirers allowed him to catch sight of me, and as he did, a huge grin spread across my face.

God, he loves the attention, Micah thought with annoyance. He was right—I did.

Micah stepped past a few pretty young women and caught me by the elbow. When my smile turned his way, and brightened noticeably, all feelings of jealousy and irritation from him vanished. We stood for a few seconds eyeing one another until I cocked my head, curious about his intent.

Screw it, Micah thought, *I'm done here soon, anyway.*

He leaned in and pressed his mouth against my still-smiling lips. Mine were soft and warm, tipping him to the fact I'd recently fed. I felt a brief moment of surprise then I returned the kiss, sliding my arm around his waist. A gentle murmur of surprise then disappointment spread through the surrounding students. The truth was that as many girls who had hopes of going to bed with me, they also had a serious crush on their history professor, my partner. It passed through several of the women's minds how hot it would be to get us *both* in bed. I chuckled and took Micah's hand, leading him away from the group and out to his waiting car.

"What was that about?" I asked as we pulled out of the parking lot.

"I figured it didn't matter anymore. I'm done here in a couple of weeks and then we'll be moving on. Could be fun to leave amid some scandal, don't you agree?" Micah looked at my profile as I drove and slipped his hand up into the hair hanging over the back of my neck. I loved the husky quality to his voice and the way he said my name. His fingers left trails of seductive whispers across my skin.

"Yeah, but you're crushing my rep with the ladies. You could have warned me." A smirk crossed my face, but I kept my eyes on the road. I loved teasing him.

"You're a real ass sometimes, you know that?" Micah pulled his hand back and gave me a playful punch in the arm. He was joking, but part of him remained painfully aware he was the only man I'd ever been with. And the original love of my life was very much a woman: beautiful, smart, and immortal.

Impossible to compete with, Micah thought.

Just as I opened my mouth to address his insecurity, the ring of my cellphone snapped Micah back to reality, interrupting the moment. I pulled the phone from my pocket in a blur, and my lips pursed as I read the caller ID.

"Rachel," I mouthed before answering. "Yes, my lady?"

I paused while listening to Rachel's response. Even with his new preternatural hearing, I could tell Micah strained to catch her words. Out of habit my mental shield snapped shut, so there were no hints from me either. A frown pulled at my lips as I said, "And he didn't tell you what it's about?"

"No," said Rachel

"Okay, we'll be there as soon as possible. Micah has a couple of classes to finish up, though."

"What's going on?" Micah asked, anxiety rising.

I shook my head, continuing to listen to the voice on the

other end. "Yeah, I understand. Must be serious for Charles to have to come and talk to you in person."

"You know how he is," she agreed.

"Okay, yep. See you soon." I felt my frown deepening. "I love you, too." I returned the phone to my pocket.

"Spill it."

"I'm not sure exactly. Something funky is going on. Charles contacted Giovanni yesterday, and he and Genevieve are on their way to see them. Rachel says he didn't specify why, but it's something serious. She's asked that we come, too."

Micah pressed his head back against the seat, thinking before answering. "So, we're going?"

"Of course."

"Why? Because *she* asked you to come?" Micah's voice rose with irritation.

"Micah, what's this about? Not Rachel, come on. You're the one I love. I changed *you*, so we could be together. But Rachel will always be a part of my life. And she and Giovanni want *us* to come." Rachel continued to be a hurdle in our relationship, no matter the many months had passed.

"She said that?"

"Yes, she asked that you and I come as soon as we could— hence why I mentioned you had classes still going on. I wouldn't go without you." I brushed my finger along his jaw line.

"Okay, sorry." He turned away to look out the window, his thoughts so jumbled I imagined he noticed nothing of the dark landscape rushing by. Soon we pulled into the driveway of his modest bungalow. I turned off the engine and pulled him close. My mouth closed over Micah's, and kissed him long and deeply. Despite his concern, the stirrings of arousal began.

"Why don't we go into the house and I'll show you how much I love you," I whispered in his ear, my voice heavy with emotion and desire.

"Deal..." was all he managed to get out before I was already around the car to open his door. As he stood, I pulled him into my arms, licking his throat and whispering all the things I planned on doing to him in his ear.

My hand slid down to the growing bulge in his pants. "I see you like my ideas."

We were barely inside when we pulled at our clothing, letting it fall to a pile on the floor. Once down to his boxers, I grabbed Micah and tossed him in a fireman's lift over my shoulder. My strength was exciting and provocative to him. I carried him down the hallway to our bedroom with a speed Micah always found incredible. The door slammed open with one kick before I tossed Micah on the bed. I pulled his shorts off with a deliciously loud ripping of fabric, and with a smirk, tossed them across the room. Then I was on my knees before the bed and kissed Micah's muscular leg, trailing up to his inner thigh.

Micah moaned when I pleasured him with my hand then my mouth. He closed his eyes and drank in wave after wave of ecstasy, a feeling only I could give him. In my mind I felt his call, his deeply intimate expressions of love and undeniable connection. We were true partners on every level, best friends, and dedicated to fulfilling each other's every need. When I pushed him to climax, he cried out and my fangs enlarged with my own growing excitement.

My face was but an inch away when he opened his eyes. The strain of need was tight on my face and he noticed my lips were smeared with blood—his blood. He licked the sticky residue from my mouth, revelling in the taste and still flying high from his release. He moved himself down my body to reciprocate. His mind, pushed wide open by his raging lust, let me know how beautiful I was to him, so perfect.

I whispered, "I love you," and nothing else mattered.

Afterward, we lay in each other's arms, the darkness softly caressing our intimate moment. I imagined in another part of the world all was not as tranquil.

Rachel. Spain.

"They'll be here in a few days," I said, returning the phone to its base. Giovanni had quietly watched while I paced the room, speaking with Eli. His calmness got on my nerves. "Why aren't you more upset about this?"

"Being upset isn't going to get the answers we need any

faster." His blue gaze was focused directly on me and I couldn't help but melt a little. He knew the effect he had on me. Damn, it was hard to be mad at him sometimes, especially considering how close we'd come to losing each other.

I approached and cupped his chin with my hand. He smiled and his love caressed my skin with phantom fingers. Our lips met and there was no Rachel and Giovanni. There was only us—one love united by darkness, forever unbreakable by time. "You're always the logical one."

"One of us has to be," he responded.

"What do you think is going on?"

He shook his head. "I don't know, Rachel, but Charles, it seems, has changed his ways. I believe, as you do, that he is a friend and ally now."

"Why be so cryptic, though?"

"Again, I don't know and I wouldn't hazard to guess. He'll be here in a few days and we'll know soon enough."

"It's something bad, I know it is." I plunged into that terrible moment when I had witnessed what I believed to be Giovanni's death. Fear's cold hand clenched my heart. Fate could be especially kind, and also cruel and indifferent. I didn't believe because we had escaped the vengeance of the Desmarais that we would never know danger again. The very nature of our existence was dangerous, to the human population and to others of our kind.

"Don't worry yet, my angel. For now, just let us be happy."

"I want to feed." I reached out, and taking his hand, we slipped into the unsuspecting night. When warm with blood we returned to our home. We, too, fell asleep in each other's arms, much like I imagined the lovers in San Francisco to be.

A faint whisper of dread tickled at the back of my mind. My dreams were haunted by the deaths of my loved ones, pain and loss.

CHAPTER 2

Rachel

Nervousness chewed at me as we waited in the airport for Eli and Micah to arrive. I paced the floor of the terminal and shifted my weight from foot to foot when standing. Giovanni took in my actions without comment, though his face hinted at his own worry. His slight smile seemed forced and insincere. A mixture of animosity for the events to come, and discomfort at Eli and I being together again. Though he harboured no ill will toward his pseudo-son, he was still hurt by what had transpired in his absence. I suspected some of the pain would always remain, buried deep, but never completely erased.

Soon the two familiar faces appeared amid a swarm of strangers and my spirits lifted. They both looked wonderful, handsome and strong. Micah was dressed in his unique combination of rock star chic and button-down banality, a look only he could get away with. Eli wore jeans and a form-fitting shirt, his dark hair shaggy about his handsome face. A pang of regret squeezed my heart. As they caught sight of us, they both raised their hands in greeting. Giovanni's arm slipped around my shoulders, and we silently followed the two men to retrieve their luggage.

They both pressed a quick kiss to my cheek and hugged Giovanni before we led them out to our waiting car. As Giovanni drove, I leaned back over my seat to get a better look at the two of them. Of course, I had missed them, Eli especially so, but I hadn't realized just how much until that moment. Eli gave me a sly wink and I couldn't help but laugh. Micah smiled, but there was hesitation in his eyes. His uncertainty and misplaced jealousy called to me before he could get a handle on it. He was young and new to his abilities yet, and even I, with more than two decades of experience under my belt, had a hard time not being too open.

"You both look well," I offered in a neutral tone.

"Yep, we're doing great." Eli looked at Micah with obvious affection. "I've managed to keep him from getting out of control, at least."

"He means he's got me on a short leash."

"Hey now, why are you bringing our sex life into this?" Eli joked, but if he could have, I bet Micah would have blushed. A series of encounters flashed in my mind, a psychic slideshow of more intimate times. The warm caressing energy accompanying the memories gave me a shiver of excitement. Sometimes the emotional feeding off one another gave me amusement and fulfillment. Other times it simply awoke my own simmering lusts.

"Ignore him. He's always thinking with the wrong head these days." Silently Micah felt pleased that even in my presence Eli still thought of him.

"He always did." I chuckled. "God, I've missed you guys."

"We've missed you too, and you, too, old man." Eli looked toward Giovanni as he spoke.

"Thanks, I think." Giovanni said, laughing. "I just wish we called you here under happier circumstances."

"Well, that's Charles for you," said Eli.

"He's proven worthy of being called a friend." Giovanni's voice was gruff, almost angry.

"Yes," I agreed.

The rest of the ride was silent, our tightly held thoughts and stiff postures belying our discomfort. The bustling city soon disappeared, and we continued along the narrow highway to our secluded home far from prying eyes. Loose gravel crunched brightly beneath the car's wheels as we turned into the almost hidden opening to our private lane. Giovanni stopped at the barbwire-topped gate to punch in the code, and the doors whined, swinging inward. Another dark half-mile passed before the house came into view.

Eli stepped from the car and gave an appreciative whistle after a quick perusal of the landscape. The heavy smell of the ocean hung in the air. The beach was just visible from where we parked—a sight I knew well.

"Sure is quiet here," Eli commented.

"And isolated," Micah said.

I gave Giovanni a conspiratorial wink. "Just the way we like it."

"Yeah, I can see the appeal. Maybe this is what we need to be looking for when we head out from San Francisco," Eli said to Micah, who shrugged.

That took me by surprise. "You guys are leaving San Francisco?"

"Yep. Once we're done here, we thought we'd go someplace new. Check out places we've never been before. We've been waiting 'til this semester was done."

"How come you never mentioned anything before?" The words flew from my mouth with vehemence.

Eli picked up on my tone. "Sorry, it wasn't a secret or anything. We haven't even finalised our destinations yet. It's more a work in progress. Anyway, we can always go back. We'll keep the house there and have Danica look after things."

Micah nodded in agreement, and before I could ask something else, Giovanni steered the conversation to a less combustible topic. "Would you guys like the grand tour?"

Eli wisely took up his offer, but not before he snatched Micah's hand and gave him a knowing look. I caught this exchange, and didn't comment. After eight months, the history between us still got under my skin. Giovanni led the way, pointing out the unique features and answering all the questions. I trailed behind like a sullen child.

Less than thirty minutes later, after seeing the house, the guesthouse where Charles and Genevieve stayed, the grounds and the private beach, we settled in the small yet comfortable living room. Giovanni started a fire and threw the French doors wide to allow the salt air to enter, where it mingled with the smoky aroma of the burning wood.

I surveyed the room, trying to project a more light-hearted

front than I felt. It had been less than a year, and Eli and I spoke almost weekly, yet it seemed a lifetime removed from our recent past. We were close on so many levels it chaffed, but also clearly separate on others. It was bittersweet, to say the least.

"So," Eli began, breaking a silence that had settled like a noose about my neck. "The house is beautiful, reminds me of Greece."

"Yes, I loved that house, so many wonderful memories there." I smiled at both Giovanni and Eli as my mind swam through the abundance of colliding images. "And it's wonderful here, too." The last bit sounded too hastily added.

"So how did school go this year?" Giovanni asked Micah.

"Good. Had some dedicated students and some slackers. There was one particularly bright student I've put under the mentorship of a fellow professor. I think she'll really go places in the world of academia. But, like all good things, it's time to end that chapter of my life." Micah smiled, but some unease washed out from him like a soft roll of fog. Eli squeezed his hand then gave me a sharp look.

"Yes, now that you've joined our way of life, there are so many things at your fingertips. It's almost like constant temptation, isn't it? Being able to do and be and have anything you want," Giovanni said.

"Yes, it's certainly overwhelming sometimes. I can understand how new vamps could put themselves in harm's way. It's good to have a guide and supporter through the process." I noticed he and Eli almost always touched one another, for comfort or from nervousness, I couldn't be sure.

Micah unwittingly let out an urgent need to feed, which I picked up on at about the same time as Eli. "I guess everyone caught that?" he asked.

"Loud and clear," I said.

"Charles and Genevieve are already out. That's why they aren't here to greet you guys," explained Giovanni.

"Genevieve is a vampire?" Eli couldn't hide his surprise at my statement. "When did this happen?"

"No, sorry, I didn't mean it like that. It's just that she accompanies him when he goes. She goes for dinner or shops until he gets back. They're quite inseparable, actually. I thought he would have been tired of her by now, or at least changed her, but they seem content with the way things are."

"I never would have imagined Charles being a commitment type of guy. Weird."

We took the men into a nearby town. There Giovanni and I parted ways with Eli and Micah with plans to meet back at the car in about an hour. We strolled to the heart of Alicante's entertainment area, not too far from the beautiful white-sand beaches the area was famous for. The air was warm and electric with life. The nearness of so many humans produced an intoxicating sensation, temptation in every shape and form. The heat and need of the life swirled about, cocooning me with its pleasant energy. I tasted many thoughts, auras fleeting and heavy, before a young man caught my fancy. As I was about to follow him a violent chill struck me. I was sure we were being watched, yet when I turned in the direction I thought the energy came from, nothing was amiss.

Giovanni also stared in the same direction. Suspicion slipped across his face, and pulled his features tight. He scanned the crowd for a few minutes before turning back to me. "That was strange."

"Very. I was sure someone watched us." I gave another quick and fruitless scan across the endless movement of people around us. There was nothing.

"There was something there, something very powerful. Whatever it was that touched us, it wasn't human."

"But who? And why?"

"Perhaps this has something to do with what Charles has come here to tell us." Giovanni's darting gaze stirred up a cold wash of unease, and his closed-off mind indicated he was focused on one thing—protection.

"Maybe. Let's feed quickly and find the guys. I don't like this."

"Me, either."

We hurried through the streets until we encountered a couple of young men in a relatively clear area of town. We persuaded them to accompany us to a spot far from prying eyes, and there satisfied our dark needs. No time for hunting, or games. A few minutes later, we were back where we started, and we both opened our minds in search of the men.

At first there was only the passing blur of random human thoughts, like trawling through radios stations looking for one whose signal was clear. After several minutes of frustration, a familiar tingle sighed its arctic breath in my mind. I reached out toward its vague origin until I felt my call reciprocated. I caught a flicker of the woman from whom Eli fed, a ghostly image I could not hold on to. His annoyance at being interrupted by my psychic search lashed back at me.

"*I'm coming,*" he responded. As I squeezed Giovanni's hand, I knew he felt his presence, too.

About five minutes later, the two men appeared, faces slightly flushed from feeding. I knew their skin would be warm, and I was overcome with a desperate longing to have everyone surround me with their bodies, not in any sexual way, but to have them near and safe.

"What's the matter, Rachel? You look freaked." Micah took Eli's hand, his body language mimicking his partner's verbal sentiment.

Before I could stop myself, I cast a nervous look behind me. When I returned my attention, all three male faces wore similar grim expressions. I shivered from the combined wave of apprehension. "I'm not sure. Giovanni and I picked up on something. It felt as if we were being watched."

Eli looked about. "Are you sure? I didn't feel anything."

"What is going on here?" Micah asked. His uncertainty slithered across my skin.

"I don't know. I think we should head—" I was interrupted by the shrill ring of my cellphone. I saw Charles's number and relief gripped me. "Hi. Where are you?"

"Your place. Where are you? You need to get back here now." That's what I loved about Charles, no beating around the bush.

"We came into town for a bite to eat. The men had a long flight." If anyone overheard our discussion, nothing would seem out of the ordinary.

"Something's going on and it's close. We need to talk now."

"Got it. We're on our way." The line went dead.

We all hurried back to the car, apprehension weaving its sinister web inside all our minds.

CHAPTER 3

"Eli! Micah!" Genevieve called out with her heavy French accent, her love for them a gentle caress of warmth we all tasted. She rushed to embrace them both, her long wheat-coloured hair swaying. After she gave them each a kiss on the cheek, she stepped back to look them the over. "You cut your hair."

Eli smiled, dazzling her. "Yep, trying something new."

"Well, you both look wonderful. And happy."

The men turned their attention to Charles, who had remained silent during the exchange. "I hope you're not expecting a hug from me." The slightest hint of a smile fluttered across his gaunt face, so quick it could have been my imagination.

Genevieve gave him a playful swat, and both Eli and Micah smiled in amusement at the casual, open way she dealt with him. They both laughed when they gave Charles a quick hug, despite his unflinching stiffness. As the men stepped out of the embrace, Genevieve slipped an arm around Charles's waist. The oddness of their pairing never failed to amaze me.

"Well, if we're done with all this lovey-dovey business, can we sit down and talk?" Charles didn't wait for an answer and we all followed him into the sitting room like dutiful children. The fire was reduced to embers, and Giovanni tossed on another log to get it going again. Anticipation swirled its way among us, tickling at fears tucked away in the darkest recesses of all our minds.

Giovanni had barely sat when Charles launched into his explanation. "So, I received a strange call from our friend, Saskia, about two weeks ago. One night as she made her way home, a lone male vampire approached her. He informed her he was seeking her attendance for a meeting with his mistress. He did not offer any explanation or his name. When Saskia attempted to get information, he overcame her with a simple touch of his hand. She said it was like being struck by lightning, instantaneous and incapacitating. She was powerless. He forced her to her knees and probed her mind thoroughly, for what she can't be certain. The vampire informed her he would be in touch soon and then he was simply gone."

Thoughtful silence engulfed the room as we all chewed on the bizarre information. The story aroused fear, doubly powerful from my own personal condition and through the absorption of the feelings of the others around me.

"But there's more to this." Giovanni commented quietly. Charles turned at the sound of his voice.

"Yes. I have received five similar calls in the past week. All from immortals who were either a part of the Desmarais attack, or who had been approached to take part in it. I'm at a loss as to what it could mean."

"You don't think this has something to do with Tatiana?" I spoke with a harsh, rapid tone, remembering with cold vividness the encounter with her, which had nearly cost our friend, Emmaline, her life.

"I can't be certain, but I don't think so. She was not well liked or respected, even among our kind." He paused, careful in choosing his next words. "The thing that bothers me the most is the power this vampire possesses. Saskia herself is almost seven hundred years old. To overcome her with the simple touch of a hand is inconceivable."

"There must be some that are even older than that. Perhaps millennia old. I've read many legends from the far reaches of the world, which clearly describe creatures like us," I said, thinking back on the many tales, legends, and reports I'd scoured in the past twenty plus years.

"Yes, you're quite right, Rachel. I have heard talk of vampires this ancient, but do not know of anyone who has actually met one. Or at least they are not aware they have met one, perhaps is more accurate. To have survived that amount of time, one can only imagine the power they would have acquired." Charles's lips twitched ever so slightly, from fear or awe I couldn't be sure.

"But why now? Why reach out now?" I asked.

"Perhaps our little gathering got someone's attention," Giovanni said.

"Or ruffled some feathers," Eli offered solemnly.

Charles turned his intensity in Eli's direction. "That is hitting the nail on the head, I believe. Our gathering and collective allegiance toward the Desmarais elimination was without precedent. There has never been anything like it before in history. As I have always said and firmly believed until these recent events, vampires are solitary creatures. Couples happen, yes, sometimes for long periods of time, and certainly most progeny stay with their maker for some time, but most interactions are short-lived and superficial. And even those are bent toward some type of gain—money, property, and going back some years perhaps, titles. Even gathering as we are now, the five immortals here, is unusual." His words resonated with me, and I couldn't help but wonder what consequence lay ahead for Giovanni's return.

"Why would any of the elder vampires be angry for what happened? Wasn't what we did for the collective good? I mean, we eliminated a possible threat to all vamps." Micah's thoughts rushed ahead of the words leaving his lips. The ideas were jumbled, most not clearly formed, and pushed past my ability to sort them. Eli looked at him with a pained expression, perhaps encountering the same issue I had.

"I'm not sure, Micah. Perhaps there is more to the hierarchy of the vampire world than I am aware of. I know many vamps, but none more than a thousand years old, and somewhere the makers of these creatures must exist. Even more to the point, somewhere there must be the earliest of our kind. Maybe our actions bothered them in some way."

"Why would they care?"

"Perhaps they did not feel me fit enough to lead their offspring. I simply don't know."

"But you think these visits are at the instigation of some elder vamp?" I asked, feeling through my mind the grim ramifications of such a situation. Had we unknowingly put all who had come to our aid in the middle of an immortal power struggle?

Charles looked me straight in the eye, cutting me to the quick. "I do. I think we should all expect such a visit ourselves in the near future."

"And of the ones who have contacted you, have they offered any suggestions of how they would like to proceed?" I asked.

"They think for now it's best to wait and see what further information is forthcoming. At some point, though, it may be wise to band together, to offer a united front to whoever comes."

This was an ominous statement, but one also completely true. A violent gust of wind rattled the French doors and Genevieve let out a small gasp. Charles placed his hand on top of hers as a show of comfort. The room soured with collective worry.

"And, so, what do you propose for us?" I asked.

"I'm sure I was being watched as I fed tonight, so I think it's best if we stick together," Charles answered in a reserved voice.

"We were being watched as well," Giovanni said as he squeezed my hand.

"Were you?" Charles narrowed his green eyes and tapped a finger to his thin lips. "Interesting."

I watched my loved ones' faces, an inward hysteria at the thought of harm coming to any of them building to a painful level. "Why can't things just settle down and let us go about our business?"

"A good question, my dear. This may come to be nothing, so let's hold our worry in check as best we can." Charles rose, thin body ramrod straight and intimidating as always. Genevieve followed his example, smiling in my direction despite her apprehension. "Let's retire to our room, Genevieve."

The four of us watched as they made their way out of the French doors and across the dark lawn to the nearby guest-house. Irritation itched at me, making my skin feel too tight. Tears threatened to spill, but I would not give in to them. I paced the room with long, angry strides, the men's silence fueling my frustration even further. When I could stand it no longer, I turned to face them. "Well, what do you guys have to say about this?"

"Rachel, can we talk? Alone?" Eli already walked in my direction before I could attempt an answer. Giovanni frowned and his gaze followed us out of the room and down the hall. Once we reached the front foyer, Eli pulled me into a claustrophobic hug. I winced, but didn't attempt to pull away. When he moved back his eyes shone with tears. "What is going on?"

That was it, a cool tear slipped down my cheek. "I don't know any more than what was said in that room. Honest."

He brushed aside the wayward tear with a gentle sweep of his finger. "Funny, after everything that's happened between us, I still feel as if you're the one I can trust above all else."

"You can't erase our connection, no matter what direction life may take us."

"Please don't keep anything from me. I know you think you're an open book, but since I've been around you tonight, I've found you very hard to read."

"Really? Maybe it's just because we've been apart all these months."

"Maybe." His sadness was unmistakable. "I don't want divisions drawn where they shouldn't be. This isn't Micah and me versus you and Giovanni. We're all family here."

"I know. And I promise there will be no secrets."

"Good." He paused, looking at me for so long I squirmed. "I've missed you."

"And I, you." I touched his cheek then snatched it back a little too quickly when a familiar rush of emotion came at me. "Is everything all right with you and Micah?"

"Yes. I love him very much." I didn't detect any deception on his part. In fact, I experienced a soft rustle of love and lust as he uttered his answer.

"Good. Your happiness is very important to me."

This time we regarded each other in the tight and anxious silence. A soft shuffle against the wood floor pulled our attention away from each other. Micah stood about ten feet away, hands clenching and unclenching at his sides. Eli smiled in his direction before he placed a chaste kiss to my cheek. Upon reaching Micah, Eli slid an arm around his body and pressed his lips to his partner's. When he pulled out of the kiss, he nodded in my direction.

"Goodnight, boys." I silently prayed my voice sounded as strong as I meant it to be. God, Eli could still rattle me.

I waited until the two of them disappeared up the stairs to their room then gave myself a mental pause before returning to Giovanni. He was crouched before the hearth with firelight dancing across his ivory skin, and he took a moment before acknowledging my return. "Everything okay then?"

"Yes. He's just a bit upset."

"As we all are."

I took his lead in completely ignoring the fact Eli had needed my private reassurance before moving on. Good choice. "Uh-huh. I think we're safe to assume there's some bumpy sailing ahead."

He patted the spot on the floor next to him and I sat, weary with unknowns. We stayed that way for a long time in a comfortable silence.

Harshika. Turkey.

I sat alone in the dark chamber under the ruins of an ancient city. The night enveloped me in dampness and silence, an ambience from which I drew much comfort. I had no fears of being intruded upon, as the site had been deserted for thousands of years, and remained far off the radar of both tourists and academics. Here I could reflect, think about the recent situation that troubled me, and about my past.

The satellite phone rang, disrupting the eerie quiet, and I cursed out loud in a language long forgotten. I loathed modern technology, but conceded to it being the best way to stay in touch with Achyut as he carried out my wishes.

"Yes," I said by way of a salutation.

I listened as he relayed his progress of the past few days. "Plans are well underway and all the parties have been contacted, mistress."

"Very well."

The phone disappeared into my pocket, hidden in the folds of my long dress. Irritation invaded my contemplation, spoiling the moment like a festering wound. It incensed me that a rag-tag bunch of vampires led by a haughty, self-righteous Englishman thought themselves some type of preternatural alliance. If anyone was a leader of Death's Children it was most certainly me, the first of our kind.

That thought led me back to a time long divorced from the present day, a time before technology and inter-continental travel—a time when my civilisation had been as advanced as any the planet had seen, the center of my world and beliefs. In my time it had been a world ruled by nature, the unbreakable human spirit, and the gods.

Memories of Narsimha also sprang forth as my mind wandered to the past. A beautiful man he had been, strong and intelligent, but also unbelievably cruel. He took what he wanted without thought of pain or discomfort, or the humiliation of others. What did not please him or come to him willingly, he destroyed.

As he had once tried to destroy me.

Rachel. Spain.

My eyes snapped open the next night like the lid of a jack-in-the-box, and for a moment I was confused by the lingering unease of the previous night. I groaned and turned to find Giovanni already awake. He seemed to find my state funny and that did not sit well with me. I don't like to be the butt of any joke, or the source of inadvertent amusement. Don't even get me started on pity.

"Good evening, my love. Not well rested I take it?"

If I didn't love him as much as I did, I would have been tempted to slap the smile off his face. As it was, I cracked a little and gave a snort of laughter. "I've slept better."

"Maybe I can give you something else to think about." His cool lips found mine, and I didn't resist.

As soon as I let myself go with the moment there was a flurry of movement from the upper level of the house, then two sets of feet pounded down the stairs. Giovanni had returned to his side of the bed by the time the knock sounded at our door. He swept across the room and punched in the code to allow access. The door swung open at once and Charles stormed into the space with Eli close on his heels.

"I just received a call from Emmaline. She and Aldous were approached last night by our mystery vampire. The same request—a meeting with his mistress. No details, just a promise to be in touch." Charles spoke in the smooth, neutral tone I'd become accustomed to, but was not completely successful in hiding his concern. One corner of his mouth twitched, almost too quickly to notice.

Giovanni rubbed his fingers across his lips, thoughtful before responding. I rose from the bed to stand behind him. Eli made eye contact with me, his worry plain as day.

"And are we planning to stay here until we receive our invitation?" Eli asked, making the word *invitation* seem like being given the plague.

"What would you propose we do?" Charles was again neutral, but still managed to impart his irritation with a piercing gaze.

"We must be careful here," Giovanni offered. "We don't want to make the matter worse, or incite a dispute where there may not be one."

"Yeah, I agree with Giovanni. No one has been threatened or hurt in any way. Let's wait and see," I said.

Eli shrugged. "Fine. I'll leave it up to you guys."

"Good."

"Now if we're not hiding out or anything, is there any reason Micah and I can't do some sightseeing?" He looked from Giovanni to Charles as he spoke.

"I guess not, as long as you stay nearby and there's a way to contact you at all times. Remember, if nothing else, there may be someone watching us. We don't know for what purpose." Giovanni placed a hand on Eli's shoulder, a fatherly gesture that pulled a guilty twinge from my heart. The two men shared a moment before Eli gave his reassurance and left the room.

"Emmaline and Aldous are on their way down. I thought it

best. I hope I didn't overstep by inviting them without consulting you?" Charles looked at me with eyes as green as fresh grass in a face that held about as much emotion as a blank canvas.

"No worries, we can always make room."

"Should we step up security?" Giovanni asked.

"I don't know that it would make a difference. These aren't human enemies we're talking about."

"And maybe not enemies at all," I reminded them both. "Perhaps we've piqued the interest of some elder or elders with our ability to work together. Maybe there is more of our kind interested in companionship and cooperation."

"I hope you're right." Charles smiled and I stopped myself from shuddering. "Genevieve is waiting." He slipped from the room like a phantom. I closed the door behind him.

Giovanni turned and dropped the clothes he wore in one fluid movement. With unconcealed hunger, I let my gaze wander over his beautiful body. He always knew the best way to distract me from worry.

"Now, where were we?" I asked.

CHAPTER 4

I met Aldous and Emmaline at the train station in Valencia. They had flown to Madrid, and from there continued by rail. Much of the travel in Europe was by train, with easy access to large and small destinations alike. Emmaline's presence whispered to me before I saw either of them. Her aura was akin to putting on a favourite sweater warm from the dryer, the touch gentle and comforting.

Through a slight shift in the teeming crowds, I spotted Aldous. Several other women noticed him as well. I couldn't help but be amused by their admiring looks and received a charge from their wayward sexual thoughts. He was a beauty, solidly built but not too muscular, with eyes like spring skies and close-cropped blond hair. His face couldn't have been more perfect if sculpted by Michelangelo. I felt a little warm under the collar, so I forced my mind in other directions. There were too many attractive men in my life. Really, was that something to complain about?

Aldous saw me and waved. I waved back and made my way to where he stood. He had two suitcases by his side and a huge smile on his face when I reached him. He scooped me into his arms and planted a kiss on each cheek before putting me back on my feet.

"Now that's a greeting I could get used to," I said, meaning it.

"I'm so glad to see you, Rachel." God, I loved that German accent. It made my toes curl.

"Where's your better half?" I asked.

"She went to pick something up she saw in a shop we passed..."

Emmaline jogged up to us, clutching a small bag. Her

waist-length brown hair was loose and wavy, framing her delicate features. "Sorry, I couldn't resist. They had my favourite perfume in a shop back there, and it's not to be found in Wales." She laughed at her own explanation.

"As women, we must do what we must do." I wrapped my arm around her tiny frame and hugged her tightly. "I missed you."

Aldous stepped aside to let us lead the way, taking both suitcases with him. We chatted about everything but the reason of their visit for the entire ride home. The house seemed to watch as we approached, its presence, for the first time, foreboding. I smiled thinly, but neither commented if they picked up on my discomfort. I was filled with an eerie certainty that something bad was going to happen. Soon.

Our extended family was very happy to see the couple arrive. Even Eli was genuinely happy to see "pretty boy" Aldous, and gave him a quick hug. The sitting room had been rearranged, making room for another full-sized sofa. Once again, the fire was crackling and the only other light came from a small lamp near the back of the room. Everyone put their best foot forward, but tensions were high.

Charles broke the silence abruptly and to the point, as was his style. "So now that we have someone here who has actually been approached by this unidentified vampire, I'd like to hear some details."

Emmaline leaned forward, her voice low. "Well, Aldous and I were out feeding. It was a strange night. Several times we felt we were being watched."

Aldous nodded his agreement.

She continued, "On the way home, maybe a mile from our house, a man suddenly appeared before us. There was no hint of anything, he was just there. Of course, we were both caught off guard. He told us his mistress wished an audience with us— that's how he said it, an audience. When we tried to ask a question, he moved forward, and with a light touch of his hands, he had us both on our knees. It completely incapacitated us, we couldn't move, couldn't speak. He said he'd be in touch and then he was gone."

Charles let the explanation sink in before responding. "What did the man look like? Can you remember any details?"

Emmaline and Aldous regarded each other. She shook her head, "Not clearly. It happened so fast, and I cannot explain to you the power this vampire had. I am left with the impression he was quite young when he was changed, and possibly of East Indian or Asian descent. A slight build…. I'm sorry."

"And very soft-spoken," Aldous added.

"Yes, that's right. He had a strange, whispery voice. Very quiet. He spoke English with no discernible accent at all. It was mesmerizing."

"Think about the encounter," Charles instructed. "Maybe we'll be able to pick up on something."

The room slammed into icy silence. The phantom tendrils of Emmaline and Aldous's memory seeped out from their minds, thickening the air to the point where I could almost see it. A soft tickle caught my attention and my eyes slipped closed. A slightly off-kilter overlay of the event as seen from two different points of view melded and came alive in my mind.

The two walked hand-in-hand along a dark path. Varying shades of grey filtered through the landscape, the soft lapping of water distant in the background. They were talking, but just as I focused on the conversation, it was cut short. A man appeared within arm's reach of the couple on the deserted road.

He was small with shaggy, dark hair. His features were indistinct, either from the darkness of the night or some type of glamour he projected over Aldous and Emmaline. A nondescript robe hung over his slight frame, billowing in the intermittent breeze. Yet despite the strange obscurity of his facial features, his eyes were ebony lasers, strangely obvious, and from which it was impossible to look away.

"Emmaline, Aldous. My mistress requests an audience with you." His voice was soft, like a gentle rustling wind through newly fallen leaves.

"Who is yo—" Emmaline's voice cut off as the stranger moved forward to press a hand to each of their shoulders. Immediately, the two fell to their knees, necks strained to maintain eye contact with the vampire before them.

"I will be in touch." He vanished.

Confusion swam through both their minds. The encounter had been intense and alarming, to say the least. I shifted in my seat, looking beside me to gauge Giovanni's reaction. His thoughts came through murky and dark, not fully formed. Micah appeared similarly disturbed, but Charles and Eli keep their impressions locked away from the rest of us. Genevieve was afraid, and her fear masked how affected she was by the projected thoughts, if at all. She leaned into Charles's side for comfort, her face tight.

"Strange how unclear the man's face was, yet the incident was so severe." This came from Charles.

"I agree," said Giovanni. "The whole situation is odd. I don't know what to make of it."

"Then why don't I explain it to you." We turned at the sound of the unfamiliar voice. The French doors stood open, though none of us had noticed a thing, framing the figure of the vampire from Emmaline and Aldous's memory.

He flowed into the room like swiftly running water, and I could not swear with any certainty whether his feet touched the ground. The dark, shapeless cloak about his slight frame covered him from the neck down, hiding his feet. A slight tremor rode my body. I clenched my teeth and focused on keeping my eyes hard. With a strength that heartened and impressed me, though I'd seen it before, Charles rose to his feet.

Once next to Charles, the stranger was even smaller than I initially judged. The top of his head was level with Charles's chest, making him about five foot five. Though he was very pale like all vampires, his skin still held a hint of the warm sienna-colour it must have held in life. Hair, thick and black as coal, hung about the length of his chin. He looked neither happy nor angry, hands clasped loosely before him. Under different circumstances he would have had the appearance of a holy man, a religious leader of some type. There, in our home, his presence didn't speak of enlightenment. It screamed animosity. Charles's face was also devoid of emotion, but his eyes blazed.

"Who are you?" Charles asked through clenched jaws.

"My name is Achyut, and I am here on behalf of my mistress,

Harshika. She wishes to address the vampires assembled here, as well as other of Death's Children." His voice was so light it danced on the air, barely resonating as sound to my ears. It also had an odd, scratchy quality to it, like someone suffering from a lingering bout of laryngitis.

"Death's Children?" Giovanni asked.

"Yes, as my mistress refers to all her progeny."

"Then she is the first?" Charles's voice had resumed its smooth, aristocratic cadence, an effect that has at times been annoying to me, but was now most welcome. He offered an appearance of strength and self-assuredness, which I hoped was more than an act.

"Yes."

"What is it she wishes to discuss with us?"

"That would not be my place to say."

"And if we refuse?" Charles asked.

Achyut chuckled. "That would be most unwise. Please be clear this request is a courtesy. You will attend her three nights from now." He handed Charles a small sheet of paper. "The details are in this note."

As the paper transferred to Charles's hand, Achyut turned to leave.

"Wait! You expect to come here, give no explanation, and we will simply travel to…" Charles looked down at the words on the paper and frowned. "…the middle of nowhere to speak with someone we know nothing of. This is rubbish."

Achyut turned back and raised his hands to shoulder height. His eyes were as black as the night beyond the French doors. The force struck us like a tsunami, as though power leapt from his fingertips. I lost all feeling in my body and slipped from the sofa to the floor with Giovanni right behind me. Emmaline and Aldous also went down while Genevieve appeared to be knocked unconscious. Eli reached for Micah as he fought against the outburst of power. Charles was the only holdout, but even he struggled. His mouth pulled back in a grimace and his hands clenched tightly at his side. Achyut raised an eyebrow and another wave of power lashed out. The force of it made me see stars.

A flurry of images ran through my mind like a movie on fast forward—a beautiful young woman, an ancient palace, a fight, torture, a mighty tiger running through the jungle, and blood. Oceans of blood spilled across fine white stone. Charles dropped to one knee, a sick mockery of a traditional proposal stance. When he could stand it no longer, his other knee touched the floor. Charles shook from head to toe as he tried to resist.

Achyut resumed his departure. As he disappeared into the night, he called back, "Three days."

Once Achyut was gone, Charles sprang to his feet. He came to the couch where Genevieve was sprawled, wheat-coloured hair a halo around her still body. He gently shook her shoulder and called her name.

She stirred, eyes still closed. "Charles," she murmured.

It took me several minutes before I felt well enough to stand. Giovanni regained his composure ahead of me, and held my hand while I gathered my strength. Eli helped Micah to the couch, but showed no signs of lingering effects. Genevieve sat up with Charles's assistance, and it cut me to the quick to see how fragile she was. She pressed into Charles's side, hiding her face against his chest. He wrapped a long arm about her body as he took stock of everyone else's condition.

"Are we all right?" Charles asked.

"What the hell was that?" Eli demanded, his voice rising to such a level I jumped.

"I think we just met one of the most ancient vampires to have ever walked the earth," Charles answered.

"And what does he want? Or his mistress?"

"I don't know, but even more troubling is the fact we seem to be completely defenceless. None of us noted his approach, either physically or mentally, and none could ward off his psychic attack. I have never heard of any vampire being able to control others with his mind like that. Certainly other elders like my maker, Sorcha, can cloak their approach, and even some of the new vamps can easily block their mind like you yourself can, Eli, but this is unheard of!"

"How do we know we aren't being led to our destruction?" Eli demanded.

"We don't," I said quietly.

"What are we going to do?" Micah asked from the couch across from me.

"We are going to meet the mistress, Harshika, and see what she wants of us. At this point I don't think there is any other choice." Charles hugged Genevieve even tighter as he spoke. That simple gesture chilled me to the bone.

If Charles was afraid, we were all in a lot of trouble.

CHAPTER 5

Giovanni slept on the bed beside me. After everyone had settled, and those who needed to feed had done so, we retired to our room. We clung to each other in the darkness, talking and wondering about what lay in store. Every time I closed my eyes my brain churned out endless violent images, both real and imagined. The attack on Giovanni arose, vivid and demanding in my mind, reminding me that possessing the strength and cunning of a vampire does not always conquer all, especially not against an even older and stronger immortal.

What sleep I managed was broken and fitful, scattered with dreams of an unfamiliar young girl. She appeared to be a servant; I witnessed her performing chores, such as setting places for grand meals and laying out clothes for unseen persons of obvious noble rank. The place was strange, like something I had only seen in movies or as ruins in a documentary. The girl herself appeared slight and young, very beautiful despite the troubled expression that never left her face. She seemed constantly afraid.

After a few hours of falling in and out of a restless sleep, I couldn't stand it any longer. Giovanni slumbered, but I remained wide and annoyingly awake. I wandered out to the sitting room, which was now cold. I lay down on the couch, only to immediately flash back to the same mental torture I had endured in bed. I snapped up into a seated position and swiped my arm across the top of the coffee table in frustration. Several items flew across the room, including a glass Genevieve had drunk from earlier. It smashed with a satisfying shriek against the nearby hearth.

"I guess I should remember to clean up after myself while I'm here."

I whirled around at the sound of the voice then felt sheepish for being caught in what amounted to a temper tantrum. Emmaline watched me from the doorway.

"Yeah, nothing burns my buns more than a dirty dish left about," I joked without enthusiasm.

"Seems to me we've met this way before."

"Yes, under other dire circumstances." I didn't have it in me to be lighthearted at that point.

"There was a happy ending there, remember." She took a seat on the sofa opposite me, curling her legs underneath her slight body. She'd pulled her long brown hair back in a ponytail, showing off her heart-shaped face.

True enough. "We planned long and hard for the Desmarais attack, but with this? There's no telling what could happen."

I detected a shadowy nervousness from Emmaline, but she was very strong in holding her emotions in check. That made me wonder about something. "How old are you, Emmaline? I don't think you've ever told me. I'd love to hear your story." The distraction of hearing about her past couldn't be more welcome.

"I was changed in a small town in Wales, in the year eighteen eighty-four. I left home at sixteen to go to London to try my hand at theatre. I was naive, and it didn't take long before I was broke. Luckily a kind family took me in as a housekeeper, preventing me from having to sell my body on the streets. My father was angry when I left. He wanted me to marry and settle down, be a good mother and wife, and he told me if I left, I wouldn't be welcome back."

"Go on."

She smiled, an empty and hollow expression. "So, in my evenings when I was free from my work responsibilities, I went to the theater and the dancehalls, anywhere I thought I might have an opportunity to meet the right type of people. Of course, these kinds of places were always full of life. High society to the common people had their establishments, and I tried my hand at all of them. After several years, I was finally hired on to sing in a chorus in a smaller production. I was over the moon! Finally, I had managed to get my foot in the door. I also managed to attract some attention.

"There was a young man who I noticed came to several of my performances. After a few weeks, I came back to the change room at the end of a show to find a beautiful bouquet of flowers and a note. The young man's name was Jonah Willingdon, a medical student. He asked for me to have dinner with him the following evening, which I quite happily agreed to. I was soon quite in love with the man and even thought we might marry."

She opened her mind more freely and I was flooded with memories of her time there. I saw the faces of the beautiful actresses, the teeming London streets, and much more. This was the fun part of being a vampire, the ability to see and experience things from long before one had been born.

"There was some visiting royalty in town, or so we were all led to believe, an old Eastern European family with lots of money and influence. They came to London, making their residence in a fantastic home in the most exclusive part of the city. They threw lavish parties and, in return, were invited to the *crème de la crème* of social goings-on. Art shows, balls, private parties and, of course, to the theatre. Many times, entire companies were invited back to the house after performances. The artists all wanted to rub shoulders with the rich and elite. No one refused. And this is how I met Samaria.

"She came to town with two of her progeny, one masquerading as her husband and the other as a cousin. The whole bunch enjoyed feeding off the members of high society, both for sex and blood. They sealed many beneficial financial deals in such a way. But Samaria was particularly fond of pretty young flesh. Male or female didn't matter, she only had to like your look. One night, *I* caught her eye.

"I had gone to her home with several of the other girls from the cast. Jonah was busy with work at the hospital. In all honesty I drank far too much and was being an outrageous flirt. I sang and danced with everyone until far past midnight. The guests dwindled and soon there was only a handful of us left.

Samaria approached me and asked that I take a walk with her. How could I refuse the gracious hostess after eating her food and drinking her champagne?

"I noticed one of the girls I came with leaving with the cousin of our hostess and thought 'Good for her.' Little did I know what we were being taken for. I never saw the girl again. I followed Samaria to a part of the house that had been shut off during the party and entered a grand bedroom. It was like nothing I had ever seen before. Everything was gold and silk and mahogany. I was dumbstruck at the beauty and opulence of it all.

"She sat at the edge of the bed and with a crook of her finger called me over to her. With no hesitation at all she put her hands on my body, sliding up the tight bodice of my dress, over my breasts until they rested at my neck, an action both erotic and terrifying. Up close she was even more beautiful than I already thought her to be. She pulled me toward her, brown eyes like liquid pools of desire. I couldn't resist, I would have done anything she wanted me to. I felt her lips on my throat and they were as cold as ice.

"And then she bit me. The pain was horrendous and my hands raked at the arms holding me, but she clung to me like a steel trap. The room swirled and dimmed. I thought I would be sick. Her perfume took on an overpowering stench, choking and blinding me. My body went limp and she laid me on the bed.

"'I would like to keep you with me. Would you like that?' she asked.

"I didn't understand, but I knew if she didn't do something I would die. I blinked, which was the only thing I seemed able to do, and she took that as my answer. She bit her own wrist and brought the wound to my lips. The blood filled my mouth, sliding down my throat before I could even attempt to stop it. I choked and cried and then a wonderful, tingling, powerful feeling pervaded my body. Lightning bolts of pain and ecstasy snapped in my brain, and fire burned in my veins. Then there was darkness."

Her eyes brimmed with tears, locked on mine. "And then

I was a vampire. Samaria and her progeny left soon after, taking me with them. Jonah was left behind without so much as a goodbye. I stayed with her for many years, having the opportunity to interact with Tatiana and others Samaria had turned, until I met Aldous. Soon after that, I left my maker and was on my own until, well, you know what happened."

Samaria's face had been scorched into Emmaline's memory. She possessed classic Slavic features with lovely full lips and eyes so brown they could be mistaken for black. She was much taller than Emmaline, with a fuller, curvaceous figure. I couldn't peg her mortal age at all.

"How do you feel about Samaria now?" I asked after a few minutes of silence.

"Fine, I guess. I'm over being angry, if that's what you mean. Jonah is long dead, as are my parents and siblings. As far as makers go, Samaria was pretty good. She was kind to me, taught me well, protected me, gave me access to money and property. And when I felt it was time to leave her, she let me go with graciousness. We stay in touch still. In fact, she contacted me soon after I returned to Wales. She heard about what happened with Tatiana and wanted to make sure I was all right."

"Why didn't she join us for the attack on the Desmarais?"

"She's very old and does not trust easily. Those close to her are vampires she has made or others she can control. Many of the older vamps are like that."

"I wonder if she's been contacted." A startling thought crossed my mind. How many vampires would be in this audience?

"I can't say. I haven't heard from her since I returned to Wales, but I could try to get a hold of her if you think it's important."

My brain hurt. "I don't know what's important right now and what's not. All I know is this meeting is totally freaking me out."

"I'm worried, too. I don't want any more trouble after everything with the Desmarais and Tatiana. I just want to be with Aldous."

"Yeah, I don't want to talk about the what-ifs anymore, it's too stressful. How have things been with you guys?"

She smiled, her joy like a halo about her small body. "Wonderful. I couldn't be happier." She paused, lost in thoughts of her significant other, then drew herself back into the conversation. "But what about you and Giovanni? You have a more complicated situation with Eli and...well, your history."

I knew she tried to be tactful, but any reference to my relationship with him always rubbed me the wrong way. "Things have been good. Tense at times, but I don't think there's any way to avoid that, considering what's happened. I know Giovanni's forgiven me, and Eli has moved on and is happy with Micah. We have to focus on where we are now."

"It would be nice to have an undo button for life sometimes, wouldn't it?" she asked wistfully, the implication as true for her life as mine.

"I'm glad we've become friends, Emmaline."

"Me, too. It's nice to have another woman to talk with about relationships and those kinds of things."

A familiar tingle swept over me. "The sun is setting."

"Yes. The others will be up soon. I should return to my room." She stood, and a cool gust of wind touched me as she moved to the doorway. Looking back over her shoulder, she said, "Remember, no matter what happens, Aldous and I will stand with you to the end if necessary."

I nodded. I hoped it wouldn't come to that.

CHAPTER 6

Giovanni came out of the steamy bathroom, joining me as I made my way back to our bedroom. I felt Eli and Micah were also awake, moving about their room, but not talking. Farther off I sensed Charles, his cold worry snapping at my awareness like the flick of a light. I didn't like it when he was angry...or nervous. Though I didn't think it was possible, I became even more rattled.

Thirty minutes later, we all gathered in the living room that had become our meeting space. Worry surged high, and we kept conversation to a minimum. Genevieve looked shaken. Dark bags were evident under her eyes and fine beads of perspiration peppered her hairline. Her hands shook in her lap. Charles turned from her to me, and his eyes were hard.

"Well, as we all are aware, we are to meet with Harshika two nights from now. The meeting spot is in a very remote area of Peru."

"Peru?" I asked.

"Yes, she has given us directions to an area in the Junín region. There is a specific meeting place and time where someone will take us to an even more isolated location in the nearby Andes mountain range. It will be difficult, and there will not be anywhere to escape to." He let the comment sink in.

My mind waded through endless possible scenarios, all culminating in something terrible happening to one of my loved ones. A loud knock sounded at the door. I whirled around in surprise, the following silence even more sinister. Eli, Charles, and Giovanni jumped to their feet and, as I was about to join them, Charles raced past me toward the front door.

"Stay there," Giovanni ordered me, before he followed Charles out of the room.

Eli stopped at the doorway, looking back over those remaining in the room. His attention snapped back out into the hallway with the sound of the front door opening. Several people exchanged words, followed by Giovanni's hearty laughter, and the tension drained from the room. Eli smiled as footsteps made their way in our direction.

Charles and Giovanni appeared with two other men following right on their heels. When Kieran and Donovan came into view I jumped to my feet, smiling so wide it hurt my face. Donovan wore a shirt that said *I "heart" Vampires*, and when I read it a slightly maniacal stream of laughter escaped my lips.

"Hey there, chickie. Looking hot as usual!" he said to me. I loved that he could still be his fun, silly self no matter how dire the circumstances. He gave me a hug that felt more like a grope and a sloppy kiss on the lips. There was no sense of boundaries with that guy.

"Rachel. Nice to see you." Kieran had always been more subdued, but I could tell he was pleased to see me again. His smile was genuine, and his touch when he hugged me was comforting.

We all took a few minutes to get reacquainted before returning to our seats. I looked from face to face, pain etching itself in my heart at the idea of losing any one of them.

"I'm assuming you two have received an invitation also?" Charles asked, directing his enquiry to our newest guests. Both men nodded, and no details were necessary. Each wore their fear and worry like a fine mist of perspiration.

"It's just like you said, all of the people involved in the Desmarais attack have been contacted. Perhaps Harshika is not pleased with what happened," Giovanni said.

"Who is Harshika? Has anyone ever heard of her?" Eli asked, his question meeting with a series of shaking heads. No one seemed to know anything about her.

"Even you, Charles? You've never heard of her?" I asked.

"I do not have any idea who she is, Rachel, which is unfortunate for all of us. No one I have spoken with seems to know anything. We are walking into this blind." When Charles was not pleased his eyes glittered like shards of emerald, piercing and cold.

"At least we are coming to this as a unified front. Safety in numbers, as they say," Aldous offered.

"Yes," I agreed. "We can't let anything shake our commitment to one another. Our combined power is something to bargain with."

"That is exactly right. If we stick together it offers not only more bargaining power, but also more safety. We do not know what to expect," Charles said. He paused for a few minutes to allow that statement sink in, before continuing. "So, I will make travel arrangements for all of us to Peru, except Genevieve. I thought perhaps we could have her stay with Danica while we work through this?"

Genevieve's panic shot out from her, her tired gaze flicking between Charles and myself. She pressed her face into his shoulder as I responded. "Of course. She should be far away from this, and Danica is one of the few who knows the truth about us. She's also in the loop with many of our associates, so if she needed to, she would have access to people who can get to her quickly. Or take them into hiding."

My words drew her attention. Genevieve's face was wet with tears and her shoulders slumped. "I don't want to leave you." She didn't need to identify who "you" was. Charles's face twisted with pain at her words, and that was even more heart-wrenching than her tears.

"I won't risk you being hurt, or worse. You are fragile enough in the company you keep now. I might not be able to protect you from whatever it is we are going up against." Charles pulled her into his arms, comforting her as best he could while giving me a knowing look over her shoulder. His expression was hard.

"This is for the best, Genevieve. You are important to us, and none of us wants to see you harmed." Giovanni's voice was soothing and kind, and a look of acquiescence flickered across her face in response. We all understood her reticence. No one present wanted to go to this meeting to which we had been summoned. It seemed a certainty nothing good would come of it.

An icy, hostile silence settled over us. I peered into Giovanni's eyes, wishing I could swim in their brilliance. *It will be all right.* I smiled, feeling far from sure of that sentiment.

Charles stood, and his sharp movements drew my attention. "Rachel, please contact Danica and make the necessary arrangements. I am going to book flights for our group. I imagine we will have to make at least part of our journey in the next few hours." He was gone as soon as the last word left his mouth, not waiting for my response.

I rose, the collective grimness churning like a bad Mexican dinner in my stomach. I retreated to my bedroom, running through different approaches to my conversation with Danica in my head before settling on the blunt, non-diluted truth. The phone rang many times, and I wondered whether she was still teaching, when she finally answered.

"Hello."

The familiarity of her voice warmed me. "Hi Danica, it's Rachel."

"Oh, this is a nice surprise. Haven't heard from you in a while. How are things?"

"Not great."

"What's going on?" I could almost detect the scowl in the tone of her voice.

"I'm not exactly sure, to be honest, but it's definitely not something good." I filled her in on the visits to the other vampires, my personal encounter, and the meeting to which we were headed. "So, Charles would like Genevieve to come and spend some time with you. This situation could be very dangerous, and there are a lot of unknowns. We can't risk her getting hurt."

"Or worse," my niece supplied.

"Or worse," I agreed. "So, you don't mind having a house guest for a while? Can't be specific, because we can't be sure what's going to happen."

"That's fine. It will probably be good for her to have another human who knows her secret. We can talk about things she can't with anyone else."

"Yeah, and she's hasn't been around humans since we found her last year, at least not more than superficially."

"Cool. So, when should I expect her?"

"Sometime tonight or tomorrow. I'll give her your number and she can call you when she's made it there."

"Okay." She paused, and I heard her take a deep breath. "And Rachel?"

"Yes."

"Please be careful. You still owe me a visit to Europe."

I chuckled, knowing her joke was meant to cover her discomfort. "Understood. A marvellous, whirlwind European vacation will be delivered once this all wraps up."

"I'm going to hold you to that. Give my love to Giovanni and the boys. And good luck to all of you."

"Bye, my dear. I'll see you soon." I hung up, my heart feeling as if it weighed a hundred pounds. I stood quietly, hand resting on the phone, and gave myself a few private moments to panic. When I pulled it together again, I marched back to the sitting room with a determined stride. Giovanni raised his eyebrows, but didn't comment on my entrance. I returned to my spot at his side.

"Everything all right?" he asked as I settled beside him.

"Yep." I was thinking about what to say next, when I caught Eli approaching in my peripheral vision. He stopped in front of us, but his gaze drifted to my face.

"So, we're going to head out to feed," he said. "Micah, Kieran, Donovan, and I."

"Okay, just be careful. All of you. We don't know if he's gone, or if there are any more lurking out there. And be back soon. Charles is making arrangements."

"We will." With that, the group of men left through the open French doors.

"And I think we will take the opportunity as well," Aldous said, as he and Emmaline both rose from the sofa.

I watched with cold dread as their forms disappeared from my line of vision. The now deserted sitting room had become too quiet. The unknowns prickled in my brain, making me feel helpless and irritable. Giovanni pursed his lips, contemplating the situation. His thoughts washed in and out at me, some pulling me along their streams. The more serious he became while trying to draw out a logical solution, the harder it was for me to follow. Sometimes his mind was difficult to read, an aftereffect of his torture at the hands of the Desmarais. Stress and other intense emotions only amplified this problem.

I wound my fingers through his, distracting him. As he turned to me, I made a funny face, and he laughed, breaking the tension. Charles soon walked in, and even his sour expression didn't completely wipe the smile from mine. Genevieve followed behind, eyes red-rimmed, but no longer damp from tears.

"I have secured us flights from Madrid to New York. And I have booked us in a secure hotel I have used before. We will fly out from New York tomorrow night. Couldn't get a straight flight, but we will get to our destination."

"And when we get to Peru? I'm assuming there's not a train or other easily accessible way to get to our destination?" Giovanni asked.

"No, there isn't. Harshika has taken care of that. We need to be careful who we talk to and what information we share." Charles sounded confident.

"Agreed. We could be putting others in harm's way, or even ourselves if Harshika feels we have exposed her meeting place." Giovanni frowned.

I nodded.

"We can't let fear pull us apart. Now more than ever, we need to stick together." He turned to Genevieve. "I have booked your flight also. You fly out tomorrow from Madrid. We all go there together tonight, and we part ways once we get to Los Angeles."

She nodded, bottom lip trembling, but she did not cry. "Of course. I'm sorry for my earlier outburst."

Charles's face softened and a grin pulled at his thin lips. "There is no need to be sorry. I'm glad you can and do worry for me." That was the biggest show of emotion from Charles I'd ever witnessed, and I knew better than to comment on it.

She rose on her tiptoes to press a kiss to his lips. "I do worry."

"We should all feed and get ready to go. Let's meet back here in an hour."

Another rushed and unsatisfying feeding later, we returned to the house. Everyone else already waited to depart for the airport. I threw some clothing in a suitcase while Giovanni retrieved money from the small wall-safe in our bedroom. My legs were rubbery and I fumbled with everything I picked up. As I stepped back into the room where my friends and loved ones waited, I knew I needed to get a handle on my fear. They needed me to be strong, as I needed them to do the same for me. Fear lead to indecision and mistakes, and often does. In our situation, mistakes would be deadly.

CHAPTER 7

Less than an hour later we boarded the plane in Madrid. Genevieve would accompany us to New York, then again to Los Angeles, where we would go our separate ways. She would continue to San Francisco to meet Danica, and we would fly to South America. It was for the best, but difficult to leave her behind, all the same.

Our party attracted more than a few lingering and hungry stares, an unconscious response to our collective otherworldly beauty, as we entered the plane and found our seats. A group of immortals as large as we were produced an inescapable effect on the humans near us. I'm sure the other passengers felt equal parts arousal and dread.

Almost eight hours later, we landed in New York. Just enough darkness remained to allow us to get to our hotel safely. The city was vibrant with artificial light, the air heavy with noise and human pollution. Tomorrow evening we would leave immediately after sunset for Los Angeles. From there we would fly into Alejandro Velasco Astete International Airport in Cusco, Peru. An escort would be waiting to take us to our meeting in the nearby jungle.

Harshika. Peru.

I paced in fury along the uneven floor of the low cavern. I'd moved from the temporary residence in the ruins of a now obscure palatial site in remote Turkey to this even more isolated site near the Peruvian-Brazilian border. I often moved from one such ancient site to another, taking pleasure in the knowledge I had known most of these places in their true glory. Many I had walked among during the height of their power and popularity. Now it was their isolation and obscurity I drew comfort from.

For the past few weeks I'd been living in a series of structures long since forgotten by any alive today. These were not easily accessible by either vehicle or foot, and no one but me had ever explored the full extent of their range since their abandonment. Many connecting passages from one open space to another were little wider than two to three feet, and the deeper one entered their depths the more intense the darkness became. No light had penetrated these interiors for hundreds of years, and the only thing living to have touched their damp surfaces were moss and the occasional insect.

I saw perfectly in the solid blackness. Not that there had been much to see at first. But over the past few weeks I'd placed a series of battery-powered lights and torches throughout the maze of caverns to assist my lesser offspring, and brought in several chairs and other necessary items. An ancient throne had been removed from one of the world's largest museums, much to the curator's chagrin, and now sat upon a natural platform. After a series of chairs had been set up in front of it, it was a perfect arrangement to receive my guests.

I would reign with absolute supremacy over my offspring. I would be worshipped as their queen. Each owed me their very existence. If I had not been strong enough to conquer death, then Death's Children would never have existed.

And how dare they band together and form an alliance without my approval or consent? Until now I'd been content to watch silently over my offspring as they moved as individuals and couples, in and about the fringes of humanity. I enjoyed the pain and fear they invoked in those whose paths they crossed. I'd even tolerated their petty in-fighting and vicious destruction of weaker immortals. All of this had brought me pleasure and entertainment. The gathering that had occurred the previous year, and the subsequent unification of a core group of vampires—of that I did not approve.

That the instigation of such a collective force had been for the revenge of one immortal's companion infuriated me beyond reason. It was pathetic, and gifts such as my children had been given shouldn't be wasted on something as inconsequential as love. If I had to, I would destroy all of them, and anyone else who dared to challenge my authority.

Soon.

Soon they would understand the error of their ways.

Rachel. Peru.

The sights and sounds of Peru were pungent and alien to my sensibilities. Even at the late hour we arrived, the streets bustled with vibrant life. With only a short amount of time left until sunrise, we were whisked off to our nearby hotel. Charles had certainly spared no expense, and all four rooms were completely sealed from sunlight, and had an intricate security monitoring system. The type of place at which we stayed had been used to royalty, wealthy businessmen from both sides of the law, and visiting dignitaries. The hotel operators didn't ask questions when unusual requests were made.

Giovanni and I bathed in a tub large enough for several more to have joined us, and relaxed as best we could. Giovanni cradled me against his firm body, his strong legs straddling mine. We soaked in the hot and frothy water scented with lilac bubbles. I swirled my hand around in it absentmindedly, forcing myself from the endless thoughts of doom, which circled in my mind like sharks in a feeding frenzy.

"I haven't been to this part of the world in very long time," Giovanni said after a long stretch of heavy silence.

"Oh?" I replied. I loved the sound of his voice, and any distraction was welcome.

"I was here in the early eighteen hundreds, before Kieran, but after my first visit to North America. The country was under Spanish rule then, and while other South American countries fought for independence, Peru remained loyal. It had the feeling of home to me in many ways. The country had been involved in a series of wars with indigenous peoples against the invading Spanish, all of whom were defeated. There had been much upheaval, but there was thriving trade with countries near and far. I had acquired a great sum of money by then, and I arrived in grand style, bringing my own personal servants and setting up residence in a home once owned by an influential European family. It had been enjoyable to be among people who spoke my native language. I had a wonderful decade here and then moved on."

"And no lady friends?"

"Not that I recall."

I turned around to face him after that comment, and he met me with the most innocent expression I think he had ever mustered before. It didn't last long, though. He broke into a huge grin and I splashed a handful of water into his face. He laughed, and with arms as slippery as an eel's wrapped himself around me and we rolled under the water. We came up soaking wet and coated with bubbles.

Giovanni had broken through the tension and drawn out some of my inner store of contentment. I allowed him to carry me from the tub to the enormous bed and make love to me until the sun started its ascent. As the day arrived, I slipped into a deep sleep, tired and satiated.

The next evening sprang on me, bringing consciousness like a slap to the face. I awoke suddenly, coming to from what felt like a bad dream, though the specifics were hazy. Giovanni was still asleep and from the time on the clock I realised almost an hour until sunset remained. I padded across the luxurious carpet to the bathroom, thinking I might have another bath. I stepped in and caught sight of myself in the mirror. My reflection drew me in, a strange curiosity teasing me as though I had never seen my own likeness before.

I stopped, close enough to touch the glass. A terrible burning hurtled along my skin and I stumbled, landing on my knees. The marble was cool and hard against my legs, and the pain seemed to vanish. My vision swam, then it was not the bathroom any longer, but an unfamiliar setting filled with people from a time many millennia before I had ever existed.

A young girl served some kind of liquid from a large ceramic pitcher while others scurried around offering food, pillows, and cool cloths to keep the heat at bay. Instruments produced music I did not recognize while many voices chatted and sang in a language I could not understand. The ceiling soared far above my head, giving the space an open, magical feeling. Beautiful murals depicting a pantheon of wondrous and fearsome creatures covered all the visible walls, beings I took to be gods the occupants worshipped. The extravagance of it spoke to a home of royalty or other important member of society.

Several key people sat around a table slightly elevated and removed from the rest of those gathered, and the servers and other help were a visible presence to these people's every need. Nearby a group of beautiful brown-skinned young women danced, each trying to catch the eye of an attractive man at the center of this important group. As the young girl who had appeared initially stopped to refill this man's glass, he caught her about her wrist and, with a rough jerk, pulled her toward him. She trembled, but did not pull away. He whispered something in her ear that caused her to pale, then gave a snort of arrogant laughter as he pushed her aside. When he returned his attention to the dancers, the girl scurried away.

The memory—if that's what it was—abruptly switched to a deserted hallway and the sound of the girl's bare feet against the stone floor as she fled from the other room. There were tears now, but no accompanying sobs. When she reached the end, a large door loomed before her. She shifted the weight of the pitcher to allow her other hand to hastily wipe away the tears then pushed through the door. She entered the kitchen. Several men and women cooked and arranged food, cleaning dishes and tending to other domestic chores. No one acknowledged her when she passed through, and she quickly placed her pitcher on a nearby table and left through a smaller door at the rear of the room. This opened onto the outside where the day faded.

After the door closed behind her, she ran. She ran through empty streets, past buildings made of stone and decorated with the highest artistry, and others that were nothing more than dirt-floored shacks. Animals ate and slept in neatly secured pens, ignoring her presence. The girl kept moving until she reached the jungle. There she stopped to rest against a small overhanging tree. She leaned over and vomited. When she was done, she whispered with a shaky voice. The words were spoken in an unfamiliar tongue, which I heard clearly, but in my mind came to understand as, "Not again. Please, not again." I felt her fear and shame so vividly I wished for the earlier burning sensation to return. Anything would be better than the emotional hell this young girl had been trapped in.

The overhead light snapped on and the vision dissipated. I found myself sprawled on the cold bathroom floor, shaking and disoriented. I looked up into Giovanni's concerned face and took the hand he offered. He gently pulled me to my feet and, for a moment, the room swirled around us.

"You all right?" he asked, his voice even.

I nodded. "I'm good now, but what just happened was really weird."

"Tell me." With his arm about my shoulders, he led me out of the bathroom to deposit me at the edge of the bed. He sat beside me and waited for me to regain my composure.

"I woke up and you were still sleeping, so I went to take a bath." His face was serious, eyes intense. "Then it was as if I was in a completely different place.... I don't mean I physically left, but I saw something that wasn't in the bathroom. It seemed like a memory from a place far away from here and from a long time ago. I'm talking like time of the Pharaohs long ago, though this wasn't Egypt. I don't think...it looked more like Asia...I'm not sure exactly." It was like nothing I had ever seen before.

Giovanni didn't speak right away. He considered my words carefully. "This must have something to do with Harshika. That seems the most logical explanation."

"Then it must be deliberate. I think we have established how powerful she is and this was so vivid. It was like being there." A glimpse of the girl's tortured face flashed through my mind.

Rachel, a female with a chilly voice whispered in my mind.

"She's in my head!" I cried.

Her cold presence slithered through my head, smothering my thoughts with her own. A repeat of the scene from the bathroom raced by, but this time the girl seemed to be aware of me.

She cast her gaze back several times and, from my point of view, it was as though she looked me right in the eye. Scattered images popped in and out of my brain—blood, violence, the handsome man laughing, a tiger, the jungle… It went by too quickly to make any kind of sense. But the intensity of it made my head feel as if it was trapped in a vise, being squeezed until there would be nothing left of me. I screamed.

I swam through the vileness of her anger and hatred, ancient memories like razor-sharp nails raking across my brain. The young girl appeared again, eyes round with fear. A group of men, screams, laughter, and a violent struggle. Then the girl's broken body dumped on the jungle floor under a bright yellow moon.

"What is going on, Giovanni?" A flurry of voices and movement sounded about me.

"I don't know! I found her on the bathroom floor and brought her out here. She explained to me what had happened and then screamed 'she' was in her head."

"What's that supposed to mean? Harshika?"

"This is not helping Rachel. Calm down."

The last voice I was sure belonged to Charles.

"I'm okay," I said. "Just give me a sec." I opened my eyes, finding myself flat on my back on the soft cloud of carpet. Charles, Eli, and Micah all peered down at me, and I couldn't help but feel like a spectacle at a carnival sideshow, and I was in my underwear, no less. I sat up.

"Here, let me help you." Giovanni pulled me to my feet.

"Thanks." I took a few shaky steps back to the bed.

Charles leaned down very close to me. He didn't look happy. "Do you think this is Harshika?"

"Yes. I think for whatever reason she's sharing her past with me. She's giving me a glimpse of who she was before the change happened. And whatever happened to her was bad, really violent." I shivered at the thought of her injured body.

"But why?" asked Eli.

"That is a good question," Charles answered. "And not one we will get the answer to unless Harshika chooses to give it. We are very much at her mercy."

"Just the way she wants it," I said.

CHAPTER 8

Thirty minutes later, we all sat in the back of a military-style vehicle, racing along a path through the dense, humid jungle. I used the term path loosely, as it wasn't more than a rut on the jungle floor in the most visible of places. The vehicle was sturdy and fast, made several decades earlier, but had obviously been maintained. Not even a hint of rust existed on the metal exterior, though the seats along the edges of the back compartment were flat and fraying at the seams. I wouldn't even guess at their original colour.

The damp foliage whipped by, slapping against the side of the vehicle and occasionally the occupants. At one time there may have been a canvas cover over the rear compartment. Now there was only the metal frame rising over our heads like the ribcage of some giant, long-dead creature. The driver did not speak a word during the entire ride, and his mind was focused on the task at hand, though some wayward streams of fear and unease slipped away from him. These feelings were as obvious to us as if he had passed gas, a new sensation in the darkness of our alien environment. Around us danced the sounds of the wind and wildlife, and the powerful thunder of the engine. My long hair trailed behind me like a blaze of fire.

We all lurched as the vehicle came to an abrupt stop. The driver leaned out over his seat, looking into the rear compartment where we sat. "Now you walk," he said in awkward English.

Giovanni hopped over the side and offered me his hand. I took it, even though I could have easily scaled the side of the vehicle without assistance. We circled to the driver's side where

Charles attempted to give the man some money for his trouble. He held a thick wad of bills out to the window of the front cab, but the driver vigorously shook his head no. He rattled off a long spiel in a language that apparently none of us understood, as we all either shook our heads or made perplexed expressions, then made a stab at English again. "No take. I paid already." He slammed the vehicle into reverse, turned and sped off the way we had come.

"Now what?" I asked, feeling Giovanni's cool fingers brush my own.

"Now we walk. There are instructions," Charles answered and pulled the slip of paper Achyut had given him out of his pocket. He scanned it briefly then looked off in the direction we had been heading. "We need to keep going for a few miles in the same northeast direction until we come to some ruins. There we will be met and led the rest of the way."

We continued deeper into the tropical forest, our preternatural sight and swiftness allowing us to cover the distance in a few minutes. The feeling was strange, as if we were in another world. Though we were creatures condemned to an existence of eternal night, never had it been so deep and black for me before. No interference from artificial light existed at all, and even the smattering of overhead stars did little to penetrate through the almost-solid canopy of immense trees. The air was pungent with wetness and age, and a heady and primal aroma that engulfed our assembly.

A jumble of ancient structures appeared out of the foliage. At first, they were not discernible as buildings or monuments, but under closer scrutiny it was clear these were not naturally occurring phenomena. They had simply been abandoned for so long the jungle had overtaken them, growing in, around, and over their configuration. Achyut sat atop one of the large structures. His ebony eyes flashed in the darkness as he coldly watched our approach.

He jumped down with effortless grace, landing without sound on the vine-covered earth below. As with our previous encounter, he wore a full-length shift, the edges of which dragged along the ground as he moved. His advance mesmerised me with its fluidity, and also unravelled the tight coil of terror I'd tried to contain. I clutched Giovanni's hand, and instinctively we all moved closer together.

"Good evening, all. I'm glad to see you took your invitation seriously." He had stopped about five feet from where we were gathered. A low, mournful cry filled the air, an animal in distress somewhere in the vast expanse of jungle. The sound crawled along my skin, unnerving me. Achyut didn't flinch. He simply turned and gestured with his finger that we were to follow. And we did.

Within twenty feet, the site where we had encountered Achyut was no longer visible. Looking back, I saw only jungle and darkness as though the place had vanished. How many other sites were lost within the wide and hungry expanse of Amazon jungle, waiting for an accidental discovery to bring their lost beauty back to the world? As I refocused my attention on the task at hand, a new sensation grabbed my attention. We were being watched.

I stopped then, and realising I was no longer in step with him, Giovanni also became still. He turned back to face me and I could just make out his strong features in the thick black night.

"What is it?" he asked.

"I hear them too, Rachel," Charles answered. "There's five of them about thirty feet away."

By now our entire entourage had come to a standstill. Without a sound or hint of movement, Achyut was right before me. He stood so close I smelled his distinctive woodsy scent, and his shift wafted not only at his feet, but over mine as well. The fabric was soft and feathery light. A small sound came from behind Achyut and I knew Giovanni moved toward us.

"It's all right. It is only the Matses. They often follow both the mistress and me when we are in this part of the world. We do not discourage them. In fact, we welcome their interest and worship. We have been known to their ancestors for many centuries, and are even the basis for some of their legends. They are a very dedicated and spiritual people." Achyut almost smiled as he spoke in his terrible, whispery voice, and I imagined the Matses ignorance of his true nature amused him.

"And what do they think you are?"

"They believe us to be the physical manifestation of the jaguar spirit god. In ancient Central and South American civilisations, the jaguar has long been a symbol of strength and power. Many thought the great cat was a communicator between the living and spirit worlds, and that upon death they would be the guides into the afterlife. They are also cunning and fearful hunters, capable of crushing their prey's skulls with their powerful jaws. After a bloody show of our power many millennia ago, a lone black jaguar wandered into the scene and the indigenous people took its appearance as a sign. Now we are forever associated with these creatures in the Matses' minds."

I remembered my many hours poring over books and research articles about various South American cultures—Mayan, Aztec, Moche, Nazca, and many others. What other myths had their terrible power inspired? I tried to imagine the fear experienced by the primitive people as they watched their loved ones being drained of blood until they were nothing more than empty husks. I imagined them trembling at Harshika and Achyut's feet in horrified worship, and the cold delight the mistress must have felt.

"A fitting association in truth, considering what occurred to transform Harshika into the queen of darkness and mother to us all," Achyut said.

I wasn't sure, because of the strange quality of his voice, but it sounded as if the tiniest edge of contempt had crept into his words.

"What do you mean a fitting association?" I asked.

He turned, looking at me as though he had forgotten I was there. Instead of answering my question, he returned to the head of the group.

A soft rustle of wind moved through the jungle, saturated with the scent of the warm-bodied men following our procession. What must they think of this assembly of god-like creatures, crossing their native soil in the dead of night? Achyut resumed walking and we had no choice but to continue to our unknown destination. We travelled for more than an hour, which made me wonder if there would be enough time to get safely back to the hotel before the sun broke on a new day.

About a hundred yards in the distance a soft presence of light appeared. As we neared its source, I noticed a handful of torches illuminating the mouth to a small clearing. As we passed them by, I smelled kerosene. Soon we stepped through an archway of low-slung tree limbs, and I couldn't help but gasp. What appeared before me was so unexpected I couldn't conceal my surprise.

Hidden from human eyes and burdened with centuries of the jungle's maniacal swallowing growth lay the remnants of a once spectacular city. Structures large and small stood, running for miles within an oval-shaped parcel of jungle, the densely packed trees towering over the space like silent sentries. Some of the buildings had been cleared, exposing architectural and artistic wonders for the first time in hundreds of years. Others were huddled silently under layers of vines, grass, and trees. Flowering plants danced over the endless green, vibrant mockeries against the natural, relentless walls of camouflage.

"This is amazing," I managed after several minutes of stunned silence.

I walked forward and ran a tentative hand over the intricately carved reliefs decorating the lower portion of the small structure. The scenes depicted many strange creatures: anthropomorphic beings possessing the attributes of serpents, birds, and all manner of mammals. Very clearly worshipped above all others was the fearsome, vicious-looking jaguar-man who appeared with both human and animal victims clasped in his powerful jaws, while ravaged, broken bodies lay in piles at his feet. I glanced at Achyut's still figure and thought the clothing the jaguar-man wore looked familiar.

I peered behind me, first to the familiar faces, then past them to the dark jungle beyond. As I focused, I clearly discerned several sets of human eyes watching from the mouth of the clearing. Achyut called out a rapid, angry tirade, sounds that made no sense to my ears, but frightened the men back into the depths of the jungle.

He snapped his fingers, the noise like a gunshot in the unnatural quiet. "Come. The mistress is waiting."

CHAPTER 9

Harshika, Peruvian Jungle, Temple Interior.

I smelled their approach from miles away; nine distinct scents invading the weeping dampness of the secret room at the rear of the temple. The room sat deep within the hillside, accessible through the main interior space of the structure. A second secret way in existed, one the priests used in times past to deceive the people into believing they were indeed magical and capable of disappearing from the impenetrable structure. The priests' exit was several miles past the room where I now waited, clear through to the other side of the jagged and foreboding cliffs the temple nestled against, a deliberate plan on their part, obviously, and a convenient means of escape.

Many torches glowed as I entered, though I didn't need the light to see by, and the bitter smoke filtered through the clammy air. It offered me a feeling of tradition and ceremony, something I still held onto despite the more than four thousand years since my human existence ended. Visitors whispered about me and attempted to shield their thoughts, but none were strong enough to rebuff my psychic intrusions.

Pale faces watched in the flickering light, waiting and fearing the reason for their summoning. From the most ancient to the newly changed were in the audience. I kept watch from my perch on the stolen throne, the surface of which was covered with representations of the native people's pantheon of gods, ruling over human kind with their violent, final authority, just like I was going to do with my children.

A series of inscriptions snaked through the terrible scenes

in a style of writing most present had never seen before, let alone understood, except for me. My mind held vivid memories of times in the Peruvian jungle and the series of encounters I'd had with the area's inhabitants over my lengthy existence. I remembered them trembling before me while I gorged myself on the blood of their loved ones. I relived their desperate idolisation and fear of my very existence with pleasure.

Rachel, I thought and smiled.

Rachel. Peruvian Jungle.

Harshika slipped into my mind with frosty ease, knocking aside what little psychic defenses I possessed as easily as one would swat away a pesky insect. Her presence reeked of violence and callousness. Spidery tendrils of her power spread out within my brain, invading my memories and jerking my fear and anger to hyperactive levels. I shook my head as though I could somehow dislodge her presence, and stumbled. Giovanni caught my arm, holding me steady. Achyut watched with thinly veiled irritation.

"What's wrong?" Giovanni asked, his voice little more than a hiss.

"She's in my head again. It's disorienting."

And it was. Her touch felt like a combination of being sick, stoned, and mentally ill, all factions battling for control in a cage match of my brain. It left me queasy, unbalanced, and shaken. What did she want with me? If I got out of here in one piece I really needed to work on my mental shields.

Then she was gone. It wasn't the harsh, aggressive withdrawal like other vamps had been known to do. It was a smooth, seamless exit. One second she was there, the next she was gone, as easy as a soft exhalation of breath. Achyut sensed the difference and resumed his course toward the large temple to the rear of the city. Behind the structure rose an impressive range of cliffs and densely foliaged hills. They stretched as far as my unnatural eyesight would allow, and offered an ominous and dominating presence. Yet despite the abundance of shelter and food, I did not detect any signs of animal life in the immediate vicinity, as though the presence of something so ancient and evil was as palpable as the scent of decay in the air. We were in a literal dead zone where none with any sense would dare to enter of their own freewill.

Achyut ducked into a narrow entrance at the base of the temple, which swallowed his form completely, but his presence still permeated the air about me. We followed in single file with Charles, our unspoken leader, at the head. We moved through a passageway so small it caused claustrophobia, and Charles stooped to keep his head from knocking against the low ceiling. The interior walls were damp and covered with lacy spider webs.

Abruptly the passage ended and dumped us into an immense chamber that raised at least two stories to a ceiling covered with scenes of spiritual awakening and punishment. Even dulled by age and diluted with dust and mould, the images were breathtaking. Depictions of the indigenous people's religious ceremonies showed their animistic beliefs and reverence for the natural world. Some artwork still bore evidence of depiction of the distinctive red face paint and wooden spear-like face piercings of the Matses.

"A superstitious people still," Achyut offered is his feathery voice. "Big believers in consequence." He looked at Giovanni and me at the last part of his comment before turning and gliding to the far side of the chamber where he pressed his long thin fingers to a specific area of the wall. A door-shaped section swung open and the newly revealed space let forth a foul stream of air.

He cocked his head to indicate where we were going, and again we followed. We walked for what seemed like miles, and which may have been the case. The space was barely wider than the width of my shoulders, twisting and snaking its way toward our final destination. The odd vine or other jungle growth had managed to force its way through the stone, upsetting the perfectly laid construction. Every so often a small drop of water would land on my hair or clothing. That the structure had been built by an unsophisticated people with no more than simple tools and sheer will was nothing short of miraculous.

The end of the passage became visible and a soft, shimmery light emerged from the wall of blackness in which we travelled. Packed dirt replaced the stone under my feet, and the musty air within the new space grew bitter. As my eyes adjusted after the long stretch of dark, I realized how enormous the room was. Essentially oval-shaped, it petered off to a narrower end at the opposite side from where we entered. A raised area stood to my right, and encircling it was an endless series of burning torches.

An assembly of immortals, several thousand of them, watched our entrance with interest. Each pale face was expressionless, or as close to it as their individual ages and ability allowed. A handful displayed outright fear. It seemed they waited for our arrival, a deeply unsettling thought. As I let my gaze wander, it passed over a few familiar faces: Saskia, Alessandra, Zhongxing and Mengmei, Jeremy and Sorcha. Alessandra gave a slight nod to Charles, but otherwise there was no acknowledgement from any we considered allies. It wasn't a good sign.

Movement from the raised platform caught my attention, and I knew before I even laid eyes on her that Harshika was present. She sat, small hands clutched on the arms of the throne, her unflinching stare invoking uneasiness among all gathered. She appeared exactly as I had witnessed in my visions.

She was breathtaking, with waist-length waves of ebony hair, delicate features, and a childlike stature. But the look in her eyes was so cold and filled with hate I imagined it worse than meeting death itself. She cared for nothing except control and dominance, and did nothing to conceal this fact. Pain, terror, and remorse were what she expected, and what she never failed to elicit from all who crossed her path. No one was free from her wrath.

She rose and I don't believe she stood five feet tall. A dark, shapeless garment covered her body, not unlike what Achyut wore. Hers came only to her knees, leaving the lower legs bare, and on her feet were delicate camel-coloured sandals. Her skin appeared as white as bleached bone and smooth as glass. Long, raven hair swung about her as she moved to the front of the platform.

"Now we're all here." Her eyes flicked to the door behind us and, without being touched, it slammed shut. Several chairs scraped along the dirt floor as the surprised occupants reacted to the unexpected sound. The construct of the space magnified the sound of movement, upping the level of anxiety.

"Yes, as requested, Mistress Harshika," Charles responded with a bow of his head. His companions followed suit, and all lowered their gazes in forced respect.

"Then take your seats." This was not a gracious offering, but a command. We were not even given the chance to seat ourselves. With the manipulation of her mind, we moved forward and were shoved into waiting chairs. A few started to cry at her display of incredible power.

Achyut came to stand behind and to the left of her. Without realizing I had done so, I found myself grasping Giovanni's hand with all my might. Another hand took my other, and I turned, finding myself seated next to Eli. Beside him sat a terrified Micah.

"I am sure you are all wondering the reason you are here," Harshika began. She spoke with an even tone, cold and devoid of an accent. "For those of you who don't already know, I am Harshika, first vampire and mother to all."

A murmur of voices danced about me. All the immortals tried to contain their minds, but confusing wayward thoughts and memories slipped past, muddling my own brain even more. I shifted in my seat.

"I am aware of the recent...collaboration involving several of you in this room. While it pleases me to see my children working together, I think it is time to be reminded that no matter how strong you think you are, there is always someone stronger. And if anyone is to lead those of our kind, the only possible option is me."

"Lead us in what?" asked a male from the back of the room.

A look of anger flickered across Harshika's face before she recovered. "A fair question, Janos. I think we are all very aware of what could happen if too many, or the wrong person, learns of our existence. We do well to blend in where we can, but let us not forget for one moment that humans are our enemy. They are food, they are a means to money and property, and yes, some-times safety, and that is all. To think anything else is to *delude* yourselves." When she stressed the word, a hot shriek of pain filled my head. The sensation was so violent and sudden I think I blacked out for a few seconds.

As I tried to regain my composure while spots of light flashed before my eyes, I noticed everyone around me acting in a similar fashion. That she possessed the power to affect us all to such an extent astounded and frightened me terribly. What could we do to protect ourselves?

Harshika turned in my direction as the thought passed through my mind. Her gaze bore into me, digging through flesh and bone, and I squirmed in my chair like a child who'd been caught being naughty.

"I understand many of you have human servants or allies of some kind, and that I can tolerate. But those who engage in relationships with humans, lovers, or even more pathetically, friendships, this must stop. It is pointless and even dangerous. You will find yourself lowering your defenses and that will only be to your detriment." This time she gave a pointed look in Charles's direction, but he didn't flinch. Genevieve's face filled my mind.

I couldn't help myself. The thought of Genevieve led to a thought of Danica, with whom she had gone to stay. I caught a dark, conspiratorial look pass between Harshika and Achyut.

"Let me see if I understand," Charles began. "From this point forward, all of our actions will be under scrutiny?"

"Yes."

"Are you implying you are able to know what each and every vampire in existence is doing at any time? And what consequences will there be to interactions that you don't approve of?" Charles walked a fine line between clarity and impudence with his questioning of Harshika, and I wondered if she would take the bait.

"I am always aware of my children on some level," she answered. "As for consequences, it will depend on the severity of the infraction, the number of offenses..." She smiled and I thought I would throw up. "And perhaps my mood."

"So, you would dole out punishments and restrictions at your whimsy? To what end?" *Careful, Charles.*

"To restore order," she thundered. She appeared before us, eyes blazing with anger. Her terrible beauty filled my vision. I wanted to fall to my knees and sob, and it took all of my focus to resist the impulse.

Charles trembled and his lips drew back in a grimace. She inflicted some type of injury to him while he did his best to control the effects. When he fell to his knees before her, my tears could no longer be held in check. They sprang forth, plentiful and urgent, blurring my sight. I swiped a hand across my eyes. Several of the vampires closest to us drew back, leaving only Charles's inner circle before Harshika. A familiar, dreadful tingling appeared at my back and I knew Alessandra had joined us. I almost cheered, not the usual reaction I had when in her presence.

Charles twitched and jerked, lips pulled back in a snarl, while calling on his vast inventory of strength to prevent her from breaking him. Without thinking, I rushed forward and fell to my knees beside him, hands clasped before me as though in prayer. Charles turned, eyes pleading. "Rachel…don't…" he managed to say despite the terrible agony he must have been in.

"Please, Harshika. Explain to us what it is you expect. Let us understand before you punish us!" My voice seemed loud, though my chest was so tight I couldn't believe I was able to emit any sound at all.

"You," she said with a noise crossed between a snort and a laugh. "You seem to stir up a lot of trouble for those around you."

She must have released her hold on Charles, because he relaxed at my side. I made eye contact with him before answering, taking in the small stream of blood trickling from of his ear. "Yes, mistress, I do. Please don't punish others for helping me."

I must have blinked, because Harshika was back on her throne as calm as if the entire encounter had never happened. I still knelt and the dampness of the dirt floor seeped through the thin material of my pants. I hesitated a moment before rising to my feet. I wasn't steady, but I think I hid it well. When I met

Harshika's gaze I found what I'd expected—anger, contempt, and annoyance. But something else lurked in those obsidian pools, something I wasn't prepared for. Madness burned from those eyes, spoiling the illusion of childlike beauty. I was sure her insanity had grown and compounded during her existence, eradicating anything that might have remained of her humanity. She existed as a beguiling shell, containing ancient fury and vengeance, neither of which could ever be satisfied.

"You are quite lovely to look at, but weak. You cling to pointless human emotions and attachments as though they still had meaning for a creature such as yourself. You are a killer, a supernatural being that lives outside the boundaries of life as humans know it," she said in a voice that mimicked a cold tongue slithering along my skin.

"But why must we be this way, mistress? Why can't we have friends and companions? Why must we exist on blood and fear alone?" My voice shook and every fiber of my being thrummed with fear, but I needed to ask.

"Love and friendship all too often end with terrible anguish and consequence. Meeting our needs is all that is real—blood, sex, sanctuary from the sun. These are the things we require and nothing more."

"Harshika—" Achyut began, but she cut him off with a stern look.

A new track sprang to mind. "But what about you, Harshika? Has Achyut not been your companion for countless years?"

With a leap as fluid and powerful as the jaguar to which she had become associated, she landed before me, her tiny hand about my throat. Giovanni rushed to my side and, with a speed to match Harshika's, Achyut interceded his attempt to help. He angled himself between Giovanni and me, stopping my love's momentum without even touching him.

With his hand at a ninety-degree angle to his body, a wave of power burst from him, ending Giovanni's attempt to get to me as surely as if he had struck a brick wall. A low crackling circulated through the damp air as the intense level of Achyut's control held. The phenomenon smoldered against my skin like the sizzling spray of grease from cooking bacon.

"Achyut is not my companion. He is my property."

His hand lowered and the power dissipated, gone like the flick of a light. Giovanni staggered. Achyut nodded to Harshika then moved to his place behind her, his expression unreadable. With a vicious yank she had me off my feet before dropping me again, and I could tell from the immediate tenderness about my neck I would have a black ring of bruising from her contact.

"You are all so weak and pathetic. You have been given the gift of eternal life. You have unparalleled strength and speed. You are cunning and vicious hunters, and yet you are before me worrying about companions and foolishness like love. I am sickened to see what has become of the Children of Darkness. It is time to put things right."

We all returned to our seats. Charles waved off any offers of assistance, wiping away the blood from the side of his face with a movement so quick it was nothing more than a blur.

"You are all to be as true immortals should be, and no other way will be tolerated. I am queen, and the rest of you will fall to the various levels of my hierarchy. Those of you who come to me of your own accord will be given places of honour. These positions come with privilege and my full protection. After this meeting you will be given time to consider your options. You can try to run and hide, but you will be found. The sooner you submit the better it will be for all."

"And if we don't wish to join you?" asked Emmaline, her shoulders hunched.

"Then you will understand what it means to displease me. And any who help these deserters will also face consequences."

"And by consequences, you mean destruction?" Charles asked with undisguised bitterness.

"Not always. I can force you to join me, and there are some fates worse than death. I'm sure your dear friend, Giovanni, is all too familiar with some of these."

Then with a tremendous surge of power, the space between the immortals danced with snaps of static electricity, joining us on a psychic level and bleeding images of Giovanni's torture into our awareness. Moans and screams whirled about me, a flurry of voices refusing to believe the images forced into their minds.

"And no more of our kind are to be made without my express permission." This statement was met with stunned silence.

"Why now? Why this sudden need for control?" Alessandra demanded. She rose to her feet to address Harshika, her icy beauty displayed for all to see. "After all these thousands of years you must have existed where you did nothing to help or guide us, how do you expect us to now agree to this? Many of us have existed for hundreds of years, many longer than that, and we have managed capably without your direction!"

"I agree!" shouted a very large, black-haired male from a few rows behind me.

"We don't need a dictator," shouted another unfamiliar vampire whose skin was so milky white it appeared almost translucent. His eyes were green fire, and burned with indignation and defiance.

A chorus of raucous, incited voices came alive around me. I looked at my companions, who alternated between bewilderment and fury. Most of the assembled had risen to their feet and churned about. A number of times my seat was knocked, almost dumping me to the floor. For several minutes, Harshika sat on her throne as still as stone, watching the display before her. With deliberate slowness she shook her head, her displeasure obvious. Achyut gave a slight shrug, but otherwise did not react.

"Let's get out of here," a male yelled, and a large mass headed toward the door to the passageway.

With the slightest flick of her finger, the group's attempt to flee was halted. As though a silent, invisible tsunami had passed through the room, bodies and chairs were tossed helter-skelter about the damp space. I was pushed from my seat and wisely stayed close to the ground as a mass of immortals sailed over my head. The torches flickered and an awful burning stench assaulted my mouth and nose.

When the commotion seemed to recede, I chanced a look behind me. Splayed about the space upon chairs and in tangles heaped on the dirt floor were the affected immortals. Several had been pressed against the back wall, suspended several feet about the ground with agony stretched across their faces.

A flurry of panic and astonishment bombarded me from all around, fighting to overrun my own tightly held fear.

"You dare to question my power? You dare to defy my word?" I would have expected her to shriek her unhappiness, but her voice sounded low and guttural. Achyut shook his head and, if I wasn't mistaken, chuckled softly to himself.

"I can find each and every one of you no matter where you go or how often you move. Never underestimate what I am capable of!" For just a second, her assertion seemed to falter and her gaze zeroed in on me. Like a parasite, she slipped inside, and her ghostly presence made a brief connection with my own supernatural essence. Then she fled.

Her gaze travelled over the silent crowd, searching, I assumed, for one to be made into an example. Thankfulness embraced me as I realised her fury had passed me by. From the far wall came the horrible gurgling, choking sounds of the victims held by her power. Feet kicked with helpless abandon against the stone, a sound both desperate and unnerving.

"You." Harshika's hand waved in front of her and a male vampire was pulled from the quickly parting mass on the ground. He came to her as if he'd been lassoed, stopping at the edge of the platform. "And you." I felt someone brush against me, but a tight cluster blocked my view of who it was.

"No, no, no!" a male screamed very close to me. I searched for the source and found Aldous attempting to rise to his feet, tears streaming down his face. The crowd shifted and I seized the opportunity to spring to my feet. I looked at the platform and the sight before me caused a spasm of fright to surge through my blood. The long waves of golden-brown hair told me the woman before the mistress was Emmaline.

CHAPTER 10

Aldous pushed his way through the sea of bodies, desperate to get to Emmaline's side. I raced forward, bypassing angry, hostile faces until I caught up with him. I grabbed his arm, and he seemed startled to find me there beside him. "Aldous, don't."

Trails of bloody tears streaked his handsome face, worry radiating like a lighthouse beacon. "I can't leave her."

"Listen to her, Aldous," Harshika said, startling the both of us. She acknowledged us with a brief glance before returning her attention to the shaken assembly. One by one, various vampires were plucked from the crowd until ten individuals stood pressed to the edge of the platform. Then with a flick of her thin arm, a wave of power swept forward, struck the remaining immortals, and smashed us to the back wall. We pressed tightly to the vampires in front and to the back of us. I slipped my hand in Aldous's, as he was still by my side, but there was not enough room to turn my head to look for Giovanni and the others.

"You think I haven't the strength to make you do whatever I wish, even something repulsive to your individual sensibilities?" She smiled and, for a brief moment, I saw she truly was the walking dead. The definition of the bones beneath the tight, pale skin became visible as the alien expression pulled at her face. In a flash of blinding white, her teeth were exposed, her canines as long and sharp as an adult wolf. The vision mesmerised and repulsed.

The first vampire she had pulled from the crowd, a man of medium height and shaggy, blond hair, stepped back and unbuttoned his shirt. Another male turned, one who had been blocked from my line of sight, and came to the side of the first.

All about me thoughts flew, emotions flaring and crashing into one another, whirling like an invisible carousel. The second man turned his face, and once his profile became clear I felt as if I had been punched in the stomach. It was Micah.

Micah came to the other man who still unbuttoned his shirt and ripped it from his body. He pulled his own shirt off over his head and grabbed the man by the hair, forcing him to meet his mouth with his own. *Eli, Eli, Eli. What he must be going through?* Aldous squeezed my hand. I watched in complete horror as Micah removed all the clothing from both the unknown man and himself and forced all manner of indignities upon him. By the end of it, both men were bloody and sobbing. But it didn't end there.

Micah jerked upright from where he had been sprawled on the dirt floor and turned back toward the remaining vampires standing at the platform. A familiar fall of hair swirled as Emmaline turned toward him and walked in Micah's direction. Bile burned like acid in my throat. This was as vile and evil a thing as I had ever witnessed, and there was nothing any of us could do to stop it.

As the two came together, Emmaline had already started crying. She was fully aware of what violations lay ahead for her. As her dress was torn from her body, she shrieked. Her undergarments soon joined her dress on the damp ground. She collapsed to the floor as though strong hands forced her movements, and Micah moved forward until her face was pressed against his groin. She used her beautiful, pouty-lipped mouth to pleasure him while tears streamed down her face.

With awkward, almost-robotic movements Micah pushed her away from his body then struck her with a closed fist. Her head rocked to the side before Micah forced her face down onto the dirt floor. I looked away, unable to watch any more. What savagery I'd already witnessed was too horrific to ever forget. The sounds of Micah's harsh groaning, Harshika's sadistic laughter, and Emmaline's screams for mercy were forever burned into my brain.

The scene, and every type and manner of variation, was played out over and over again with the ten taking on the various roles. The vampires about me cried in anger, and begged for it to stop while we all remained forced to witness every second of the repulsive incident. When it was finished, the victims lay in a heaving, bloodied pile before our queen.

The force that had held the rest of us in place evaporated. The abruptness caused us to stumble forward in a collective mass. Aldous's hand ripped from mine and, before I could react, I was knocked from behind. I was about to hit the ground when someone caught the back of my shirt and jerked me back on my feet. Giovanni stood beside me and I leapt into his arms. "Eli, Aldous," he whispered in my ear.

I didn't need any further explanation or prompting. The crowd had spread out, but most appeared leery of coming too close to the platform. My blood throbbed in my veins, adrenaline burning and blurring my senses. I saw Aldous first on the ground with a naked Emmaline cradled on his lap. I came to them and wrapped my arms about them. My own tears were damp on my cheeks and I choked on the emotion thick in my throat. I removed my coat and handed it to Aldous. "Cover her up." As I stood, I saw the drying blood on her inner thighs and for a moment the room swirled.

Anger replaced my revulsion, bitter and hard, and I knew I would do anything to see Harshika destroyed. I raced past other vampires coming to the aid and comfort of their partners and progeny until I found three men huddled together at the farthest edge of the group. Eli held Micah in his arms, with Micah's face pressed into his shoulder. He shook with the enormity of his sobbing, and Eli's gaze caught me over his lover's shoulder. Micah's flesh had become mottled with angry bruises and furrows of wounds snaked down his back, inflicted by sharp fingernails.

Eli's face was hard. His fury threatened to unleash and, with my mind, I begged him to keep it under control. Giovanni leaned in and pressed a kiss to Micah's bloody cheek, gingerly running a hand over his tangled hair. His gentleness and compassion touched me and it was all I could do not to lose my faculties altogether. Eli came from the other side, sandwiching Micah in the middle, and he now openly cried. I all but collapsed on the floor, crawling on my hand and knees until I joined them. When I touched Micah, I absorbed his shame and agony like a crushing vice.

"Micah, oh Micah," I sobbed.

We were still huddled together when Harshika spoke again. "Enough. You are vampires. You will heal quickly enough."

"You crazy bitch!" screamed one of the male vampires near the platform. He cradled a tall female, his partner obviously, whose blond hair was now crimson with blood. Her head lolled to one side, and I wondered if her neck had been broken. He lowered her gently to the ground before leaping onto the platform. His fury had blinded him, and he raced toward Harshika, arms outstretched as if to throttle her. He never made it.

His body sprang into the air and his legs and arms were snapped back at unnatural angles at the ankles, knees, wrists, and elbows. The sounds of the bones breaking and the tendons ripping were sharp, echoing in the confines of the space. Next his spine broke, bending him backward until he almost folded in half. The entire time he screamed in agony and searing anger for not being able to exact revenge for the attack on his partner. She finished him off by twisting his head one hundred and eighty degrees. I had to duck as his broken body sailed past to land at the feet of the unlucky vampires still pinned against the far wall.

Harshika leapt to her feet and the smile vanished. "You need more encouragement?"

She raised her arm and pointed into the sea of bodies. Several vampires rose above the crowd, dangling over the masses as if suspended on hooks. Several hands reached up in attempts to pull them back to safety, but they didn't budge. The suspended vampires shook, convulsing violently before exploding in a shower of blood and bone. A cool, thick mass struck my back, and when I looked at my side, I found the lower part of a male arm twitching there. I was covered in fluid and gore. A heavy splash of red was visible on Giovanni's pale cheek.

I rose on trembling legs. Various expressions of horror twisted the faces all around me. A second batch of vampires now hung above the crowd, though this time no one dared to try to get them down. As they shook and spasmed I realised the one farthest from where I stood was Donovan.

"Nooo!" I screamed. Time slowed and I was painfully aware of the anguished voices and tears and screams attacking from all sides. I felt Giovanni's grasp on my arm slip. Then Donovan and the others succumbed to the same fate.

I pulled away from Giovanni and, though I could barely see through my tears, I raced toward the spot I thought he had been. The closer I got the slicker the ground beneath my feet became. I slipped and fell with jarring impact on my side, and when I managed to get myself upright again, I had become soaked with blood.

I found him at last. What was left of him, anyway. He had worn his I *"heart" Vampires* t-shirt, and with much difficulty, I managed to pull it from the remains of his torso. Realising I had given my coat to Aldous and as such didn't have a pocket to put the shirt into, I clutched it to my chest like a child with a teddy bear.

"Rachel."

I looked up and Kieran stood before me. He appeared as though he had been showered with blood. Chunks of hair and flesh stuck to his clothing, and he trembled from head to toe. With Donovan's shirt still clutched in my hand, I launched myself into his arms. Giovanni's presence tingled at my back. I pulled slightly out of my embrace with Kieran, enough that I saw his face and held the shirt out to him.

"Take this. Give it to Micah. He needs something to wear."

"Wait." Kieran knelt down and picked up the pants Donavan had worn, turned them waist side down, and with a tight grimace, shook out any remains from inside. When he was satisfied the job was complete, he thrust the pants in Giovanni's direction. "Take these, too."

He took both items without comment. With a blur he disappeared back into the crowd, leaving us in a painful silence. I took one last, sickened glance about me, unable to reconcile the quivering lumps of flesh on the ground with the friend I had lost. I couldn't look anymore.

I reached out in Kieran's direction and he took my hand.

Together we moved to join our friends near the platform. As we approached, I saw Charles, Alessandra, and Saskia had joined Giovanni, Eli, and Micah. Micah wore Donavan's clothes, and the effect was disturbing, but what choice was there? Aldous led Emmaline in the same direction, my coat covering the worst of her injuries, though her traumatised expression would haunt me for years to come. She shuffled slowly, and I knew no matter how many years she might exist, from that night on she would never be the same. Neither would Micah.

Micah caught Emmaline's approach a few seconds after I did. His eyes closed and his jaw line tightened. Eli had his back to her, but he turned after witnessing Micah's reaction. Emmaline came right to him, looking more sad than angry, and didn't stop until she was close enough to touch him. Aldous's eyes were black, but he didn't try to stop her. After a poignant and personal moment passed between Emmaline and Micah, they hugged each other tightly.

"I'm so sorry, so sorry," Micah repeated over and over, lips brushing against Emmaline's ear.

"It's not your fault. I don't blame you." As she stepped back, she saw me and, indicating the coat, said, "Thank you."

"Of course."

So, there we stood, our original group plus Alessandra and Saskia. The confidence their presence had given less than a year before was now a ghost. An urgent murmur circulated through the crowd, and the vampires closest to where we stood moved aside. A small group appeared, marching with determination to the area right before Harshika. She watched in petulant silence, flickers of amusement dancing across her delicate features. At the rear of the group I saw Sorcha, her waves of auburn hair unmistakable, and another vampire who I remembered from my discussion with Emmaline. It was her maker, Samaria.

CHAPTER 11

"Yes?" Harshika said by way of acknowledgement to those assembled before her.

The group knelt, heads lowered, before a Hispanic-looking male with shaggy, black hair spoke. "Mistress Harshika, queen. We come to offer ourselves to you. We are humbled by your show of power, and wish to devote ourselves to your service." The others nodded.

I leaned in close to Emmaline's ear and whispered, "Is that Samaria?"

"Yes," she answered, but didn't offer any further commentary.

"Come, my children." Harshika waved them forward. Slowly the small group assembled at her side, leaving a scowling Achyut standing alone on the other side of the platform. "A wise decision, and one I will not soon forget."

The room buzzed with the explosive reactions from the other immortals. A rapid stream of thoughts, decorated with a multitude of expletives, ran through Charles's mind. He must have been furious, or had let them slip knowingly, as his mind was almost never readable to me.

"Anyone else?" Harshika asked. The room fell silent, ancient eyes watchful and suspicious. A few others joined the group on the platform. Harshika nodded. I didn't recognise any of the new joiners, but I did catch sight of Zhongxing and Mengmei. They stood together, black eyes hard, about twenty feet from me. I stared at them until Mengmei turned her face in my direction and gave an almost imperceptible nod. Her alabaster fist clenched and unclenched at her side. Those two would not join

Harshika's hierarchy without a fight.

"Perhaps, mistress, you could show your children the depths of your compassion with a short reprieve to think things through," Achyut offered.

A murmur of approval circulated the room, but Harshika did not seem to share the sentiment. Her eyes narrowed and her anger coiled, ready to strike. Achyut stood blandly at her side, showing no visible reaction. His stare, directed only at her, was unflinching and I wondered if that was a prompt of some kind. Then, as though her negative reaction had never occurred, it disappeared, replaced with a brittle smile.

"Thirty days," the mistress announced. "You have thirty days to make your decision."

"An excellent idea, mistress," Achyut agreed, acting as though the idea was hers alone.

"Come willingly and you have the chance of maintaining your…relationships. If not, I will not even guarantee your existence. I may allow you to join me, or you may be destroyed. You have enough time to get to the jungle's edge where vehicles will be waiting to return you to town."

A moment of hesitation seized the room before a mass exodus began. Since we were on the opposite side of the room from the exit, we waited until the crowd thinned before moving toward our relative freedom. We watched as the mass of immortals surged forward, knocking, jostling, and slipping in the remains of their fallen brothers and sisters.

Zhongxing and Mengmei had joined our group and, for the first time, I heard Mengmei speak. "There is no way in hell I would join that bitch!" she said, and from the vehemence in her voice I believed her.

She resembled the stereotypical China doll with her porcelain skin, glossy black hair, and chocolate-coloured eyes. She lined them with black and her lips were painted the hue of freshly spilt blood. I knew from personal experience her small body contained an unimaginable force. I'd witnessed her capabilities during the couple's assistance during the Desmarais attack. She and Zhongxing were both stronger than Charles, older and more powerful than Alessandra.

As our group filed past the platform a tight, itchy sensation prickled over my skin. Giovanni and I found ourselves in the middle of the pack, and we slammed into the backs of Charles, Aldous, and Emmaline as they came to a sudden stop. Aldous draped a protective arm around Emmaline's shoulders, then turned back toward me.

"She's stopped us," he explained. "It's as if we've walked into an invisible barrier. Obviously, she still has something on her mind."

We stood still as we watched fleeing immortals disappear through the door. Those remaining had all been a part of the Desmarais attack, save for Donovan who was now a stain on the dirt floor. Remorse licked its cold tongue along my spine. This was going to be bad.

"Not so fast." The pressure holding us in place evaporated and Harshika was before us.

"Yes, mistress," Charles answered.

"I'm sure it has not escaped your attention that the remaining immortals are all the participants in your attack last year." She looked at us each in turn, and none made a sound in response. Her gaze rested on me. "Needless to say, this occurrence brought to a head the problems I had been remiss in dealing with. Now, what to do with you?"

She paced the width of the room, finger pressed to her lips in a mockery of contemplation. No doubt she had already decided upon her plans. Without warning she was inside my mind, swimming without restraint through my fears and thoughts. Then she was gone, and her cold smile appeared again. She moved her hand to my face, and two cold fingertips touched me at the temple. I understood exactly what she meant.

"A tightly knit group this is. You will be hard to break, I should think. I believe it is in my best interest to keep some collateral. That way I can be sure you will come quickly to my way of thinking."

Aldous shot forward as though pulled by an imaginary rope about his waist. He resisted, and the heels of his heavy boots left gouges across the dirt. Next Zhongxing joined Aldous, then Eli, Saskia, and finally me. She left Giovanni, Emmaline,

Charles, Alessandra, Mengmei, Micah, and Kieran standing in a nervous row behind us.

"I'm sure it won't take you long to understand that coming to me willingly is really for the best." She snapped her fingers and Achyut was at her side. He pointed to the platform area, and our line moved forward. I resisted with every ounce of my faculties, but I could not stop myself. At the back of the platform a small door that had not been visible before slid open. "Wait, not Rachel. She and I are going to have a little talk."

My skin crawled as a soulless gaze travelled over the length of my body. I was both cold with dread and hot with fear. Tears burned my eyes. As she turned her attention back to the crowd before her, my feet slid, forcing me to follow, and no matter how hard I resisted I could not stop my forward movement.

Without enough time to form a coherent thought, I was in her arms and at the mouth of the door leading to the long passageway, and eventually the waiting jungle. She paused, "Depart! You have barely enough time to make it to the meeting spot. It would be most uncomfortable to have to pass the day in some cave or under the damp jungle floor." We moved.

Though she did not smile, I felt her pleasure. It slithered along my skin, impossible to ignore. She enjoyed the games she played, and was arrogant with her superiority over her offspring.

"Rachel, no!" I heard Giovanni cry as we plunged into the dark passage. There was a commotion behind us, and I knew Giovanni tried to follow.

"Harshika, please stop. I'll do whatever you want." It was difficult to speak as my face was paralysed, like attempting to communicate with one's jaw wired shut.

"Yes, you will," she agreed.

Then we were no longer in the passageway, or the temple interior. With brain-rattling speed, we burst out into the night. The warm, humid wind rushed by, and the damp aroma of the jungle became vivid against my lack of sight. The hanging vines and tree branches snatched at my body as we sped through the dense fauna. I knew we had travelled a great distance, but time and direction made no sense with the speed at which she moved. When we stopped, I realised I had been carried like a child, clasped in arms as smooth as marble and strong as steel. She placed me on my feet, so close our noses almost touched.

Up close, I saw we were about the same height and very similar in stature. Her power was uncloaked, burning in the space between us. If it were visible, I imagined it, too, encircled her body like a fiery shield. I expected invisible flames to lick out at me, devouring my flesh on contact. But there was no pain.

She stroked my hair, starting at the crown and slowly trailing to the very ends as though she were in awe of the feeling it produced. Bringing a handful of it up to her face, she inhaled and rubbed it against her cheek. Then she dropped her hand as though becoming aware of her actions. It crossed her mind that it had been a very long time since she had been in intimate contact with anyone, at least in a situation that didn't end in the other participant's death. Achyut's company didn't count. The thought passed through my mind as though my own, a chilling and disorienting sensation compounded by my fear.

Giovanni weakly touched my mind, the contact brief, and it unsettled rather than comforted me. Since his return I had made a solemn promise to never leave his side, and here I was alone with the most dangerous creature on earth. My love and cherished friends were either her prisoners, or were about to go very far away from me.

"You must be wondering why I singled you out." Her voice was even, non-confrontational, but I didn't allow myself the privilege of letting my defenses down. She circled about me with quick strides, taking her time to drink in every inch of my body. I bristled with discomfort, but what could I do? I was powerless and she knew it.

"Because it was my need for revenge that brought all of the immortals together, and angered you in the process," I managed to answer without even a hint of shakiness in my voice.

"Yes," she whispered right against my ear, sending spirals of shivers down my spine. "And no."

"Then why?" I asked, and in that intimate moment with her, I desperately wanted the answer.

"There is something unique about you, something that

attracts me. Many times over the years as I tuned my mind to the internal musing of my offspring, your mind has come through clearer than all the rest. Most I touch on only fleetingly, though I can single out any I choose with focus. You—it's as if you're just always there."

I didn't know if I was supposed to be flattered or unnerved. "And does this please you, mistress?"

She giggled, the sound like wind chimes dancing in the night. The laughter swirled about us, hypnotic and surreal. "That's not an easy question to answer, my child. I will say this. For the first time in more than four millennia I wish to share my experiences. I want another of my kind to know what I went through to become as I am now. I want you to understand and know all the wonders I have seen, and then maybe you will truly understand our greatness, and our purpose. You will want to follow me and accept the true way as your own."

"Perhaps you might be open to looking at things in a new light also, mistress." I almost couldn't believe I said this, and I would have done just about anything to suck the words back in, but the damage was done. Boldness was not my best choice of action for that moment.

She didn't answer for several minutes. If I had been able to sweat, I would have been drenched by the time she eventually answered. "I don't think so, child. But stranger things have happened."

Then she grabbed me again and whisked us away through the ebony veil of night in the jungle. We didn't stop until we had reached another lost settlement, indiscernible from the endless expanse of dense greenery battling to take over both the ground and sky. Where there was no obvious entrance, she pushed aside a collection of heavy vines and pulled us inside the dank and bitter interior.

CHAPTER 12

Giovanni. Peruvian Jungle.

My eyes stung and anguished tears were still wet on my face. "Jesus, Charles! We can't leave Rachel behind."

"We have no choice, Giovanni. Believe me this is not something I want to do, either, but the best thing we can do right now is get away from here. We need to regroup and think about how best to proceed. If we act out of fear or anger, it's only putting more of us in danger."

"Charles is right," Emmaline said firmly. "The last thing on earth I want to do is leave Aldous behind, but as we are now, we have no chance of helping any of them." Her face had become puffy and angry bruises rose to the surface of her pale skin. It pained me to look at her, even more to accept she was right.

I took one last furtive look around, then retraced my steps to where the driver had dropped us off earlier. "Let's go." My voice sounded cold and the frustration I felt hissed along the skin of my companions with noticeable reaction.

Alessandra and Charles moved swiftly to the front of the pack, hard, nimble bodies batting against the jungle that fought their escape. The landscape was rugged and the night so dark even creatures as strong as us had to push to make headway. Dawn neared, and no choice existed except to forge ahead as quickly as possible.

The wind rushed by, bringing with it alien scents and tricks of sound. We attempted to move as one, keeping within arm's length of each other, our consciousness of not losing sight of any of the group overt and determined. I kept a close watch on Micah in particular who, as the newest, was also the most vulnerable. When a male cried out, I immediately looked to my right where Micah pushed to keep up with me. Apprehension crawled along my skin. When I saw Micah was not the one in danger, I looked about in confusion. The sound of a body hitting the jungle floor with a heavy thud came from behind. I whirled about and backtracked to see what had happened. Charles appeared at my side.

We walked forward tentatively, gazes scouring the dark and jumbled landscape for the source of the disturbance. Charles stumbled and almost went down. He grabbed my arm to steady himself. As my eyes adjusted, only then was I clearly able to discern Kieran's prone shape on the jungle floor. His face was frozen into a mask of agony, his body deathly still. A small, thin object protruded from the side of his neck. Just as I bent down to investigate further, something light and fast brushed along the side of my face.

"I got it," Charles spat out before he disappeared into the darkness. The jungle was then eerily quiet.

I dropped to my knees and my fingers found the object still lodged in Kieran's flesh. I pulled it out, careful to not inflict any further injury. As I squinted in the solid darkness, I took in the beautifully handcrafted dart, the end as sharp and precise as a modern ampoule. As I looked down again at my offspring's motionless form, understanding snapped alive in my brain. *Poison.*

I heard a rustle, the sound startling close and I was immediately on my feet. The others closed rank behind me, but knew better than to draw any more attention by talking unnecessarily. When Charles appeared, relief flooded me. The others moved a bit closer, and as Charles joined them, it became obvious he was not alone.

The man's heart beat a furious rhythm in his chest and his scent was hot and acrid to all non-humans. He was conscious, but frozen with fear. From his position under Charles's arm, his wide eyes stared at the immortal faces, arms dangling flaccidly.

"I caught this one. The other two got away, but I don't think they'll be back."

"What are you going to do with him?" asked Mengmei. She licked her lips with unabashed hunger.

"I'm going to find out what's in that dart and then you're welcome to him." Charles's voice was razor sharp and the man twitched.

Charles dropped him to the ground in an unceremonious heap and, quicker than the blink of an eye, landed on top of him. He stared into the man's face, instantly catching his mind. Charles didn't have to exert much effort, or even speak, and a flood of information poured from the man's lips. Unfortunately, none of the immortals understood his language.

"How is this going to help us, Charles? We don't know what he's saying," Alessandra said with irritation.

"Use your mind. Remember the images associated with his words and the sounds of his language. We can find some way to figure out what he's talking about," I said.

"Exactly," Charles agreed. "And we will take the dart from Kieran back to Genevieve, and maybe she can figure out what it is."

"He's not dead, just paralysed." Emmaline knelt at Kieran's side, looking into his wide eyes. "I can feel him trying to communicate, but it's hazy."

I hauled Kieran to his feet, flipping him over my shoulder. "We have to go now. We'll figure out the rest later." I handed the dart to Charles, who was careful not to touch the poisoned end. "Take this."

We made it to the rendezvous spot with minutes to spare, the wasted body of the Matses man left for the jungle scavengers. A different driver waited as we emerged, an older man with a pockmarked face and waist-length hair. He watched as we appeared, leaning lazily against a large extended truck. Without comment he hopped into the driver's seat, and the crew of immortals piled into the back. He tore away from the meeting spot before Alessandra was even seated, and drove at breakneck speed through the winding, arduous path back to town. My face twisted in anger as I stared out the back of the vehicle. I scanned the dark landscape, tears slipping down my cheeks.

Rachel, I'm so sorry.

Rachel. Somewhere in the Jungle.

Achyut arrived a few moments after we went inside. Harshika
had pulled me along behind her by the hand, making me
feel childish and weak. I trusted she saw well enough as we
ploughed along at a tremendous speed, though I could make
out nothing in the blur of shadow and blackness. The narrow
passageway opened abruptly into a larger chamber.

Inside were several cots, a table and chairs, and an abundance of modern and expensive-looking electronics. I recognised some of the equipment—fax machine and generator—but
the rest was foreign and beyond my capability to use. Much like
the building where we had met earlier, the walls were adorned
with pictographs—images of war, celebration, and spirituality.
I noticed the sinister-looking jaguar-man again and, this time,
a female counterpart. I made a close examination of the faded
figures, taking in the familiar clothing and, when I looked up
again, Harshika watched me.

"Yes, that's us. Achyut and I," she said. A moment from a
time long forgotten filled my mind with breathtaking detail
before being snatched away, leaving Harshika and Achyut the
only two privy to that experience. "There was a time we were
worshipped as gods here. We kept the most beautiful pair of
jaguars in this place." She motioned with her hand to indicate
the space in which we now stood. "I have a powerful affinity
with all the great cats—jaguars, lions, tigers."

"Yes, the tiger," Achyut agreed.

I startled, as he had been so quiet it slipped my mind he was
present.

"But more of that another time." She gave him a stern look
and he did not speak again.

Her body stiffened when she spoke to him, her projection
of authority over him one layer in the silent way with which
they communicated. I was dying to know their history. That
he was subservient to her was obvious, but there was more to
it. He had a regal, formidable quality to his presence, making it
easy to presume he was of privileged birth. Harshika seemed

somehow cruder by comparison, less eloquent than her companion. I realised, as her eyes grew hard and angry, she'd caught my observation. Achyut did not react in any way, though surely he had not missed my thoughts.

"They've reached the driver," Harshika said to no one in particular. "Giovanni is most upset at having to leave you behind." She cocked her head as though she had caught something amusing. "A pretty one he is. Very lovely."

When I saw her licking her lips over the image of my love, a flash of pure hatred seethed through my body. My blood boiled at the thought of this hideous creature touching my Giovanni, of him being forced to submit to her vile and malicious whims. My teeth clenched so hard I bit my tongue. The shock of the taste of blood in my mouth distracted me, and when I refocused, she giggled.

"So easy to read, my child. Everything in your mind always comes back to Giovanni. Only in the grips of blood lust is your mind ever completely free of him. Are you aware of that?" Her dark eyes twinkled with amusement, but her words surprised me.

"That's because I love him. He is everything I exist for."

"And what about your desire for blood? Or your need for fear? Is that as much of what you are as your *love* for Giovanni?" She spat out the word as one might expel a mouthful of phlegm.

"Yes," I answered. "It is a part of me by nature of what I am, by what I had to become to be with Giovanni. I embrace my nature. I accept I am a killer, a liar. We are all parasites on humanity, but I am still capable of love, compassion, and even remorse."

With a snarl and a flash of fangs she landed on top of me. The back of my head smashed onto the ground with such force an explosion of stars danced before my eyes. The trail of blood from my tongue spilled over my bottom lip and filled my mouth with thick copper. Her face hovered above mine.

"Parasites? Not a very flattering term for creatures as powerful and wondrous as we are." She pulled me up to a sitting position with an abrupt yank on the front of my shirt, and a mouthful of blood sloshed down my face. She traced a finger through the wetness and brought the stained flesh to her lips. Her tongue licked away all traces before she returned her attention to me. "Why do you continue to hang on to human ways and feelings? You are so much more than that."

She released me and flowed to the other side of the room. Achyut sat on a narrow cot, watching. His expressive was bored, posture impossibly straight. When she reached him, the change to her demeanor was immediate. Her posture became aggressive and her tone sharp. The sounds that came from her mouth made no sense to my ears, but the rapid-fire release of dialogue hypnotised me. Achyut answered with the same strange cadence, his feathery voice loud in the cavernous space.

After several minutes of exchange between the two, I rose from the floor to shaky legs. Fright and worry assaulted me, my body weary to the bone. I only wanted to sleep, and find myself in a place where I could see Giovanni's face. "May I lie down on one of the cots?"

They both turned at the sound of my voice. Harshika nodded then continued talking. Achyut didn't acknowledge me with words, but I noticed his attention drifting in my direction several times throughout the conversation.

My eyes were heavy, and the call of sleep impossible to ignore with my cheek pressed against the rough canvas cot. I spoke without being aware my brain had decided to. "What language are you speaking?" As if at that moment it made any difference at all.

Harshika seemed surprised at the question. "A dead one."

Intrigued, I coaxed my eyes open again, despite my exhaustion. "From where?"

"From what your modern scholars refer to as the Indus Valley. In what is now Southern Pakistan. There are people there who speak a bastardised version of our language, the Brahui."

My eyes slipped closed again and I remembered the dream from the hotel with a human Harshika and the strange surroundings. "And you lived in a palace?" I asked, uncertain of the correct term to describe the place I'd witnessed.

"I did, in Mohenjo-daro. I had been brought there as a young girl to work. My family was of the poorer working class and it was not uncommon for families to give their children to the rulers to work in homes, citadels, businesses. For some reason I struck the fancy of one of the high priest's men, and my family had no choice but to hand me over to them. He took me to the home of the royal family where I was to work in the kitchen and perform duties as requested by the family. If I pleased them, then my family would be protected and rewarded."

I slipped over the edge of consciousness when she said, "And that's where Narsimha Rajaneesh stole my life."

CHAPTER 13

Giovanni. Peru.

Charles and I made an awkward entrance into the hotel with Kieran sandwiched between us. Our group offered the illusion of returning from a wild night out, resplendent with raucous laughter and overly loud conversation. To the very few souls we passed, our comrade would have appeared to have drunk a bit too much and paid the consequences of his reckless behaviour. The truth would never be suspected.

Once past the front lobby and into the elevator, we were comfortable the ruse had been successful. The door swooshed open onto a silent but too-bright hallway, where we hurried to our rooms at the farthest end to beat the immanent sunrise. Its arrival snapped at our heels like an angry dog. Only Charles, Mengmei, and Alessandra were strong enough to withstand its effects, and even then it was for but a short while.

"I'll take him with me," I said to Charles as we paused outside my door. Kieran's body was still stiff and immobile, but his mind had begun to free itself of the poison. He was aware of what happened and where we now were.

"Yes. I think he'll be okay. It's just a matter of time for the poison's effects to wear off."

"Tomorrow?" I asked.

"We get out of here as quickly as possible." He turned to address the rest of the group. "As soon as the sun is down, we are out of here. Understood?"

They agreed in a murmur of voices. Emmaline gave us a look that would break the hardest of hearts and entered her room without another word. As Charles helped me get Kieran to the bed, Mengmei and Alessandra disappeared into their own rooms. Only Micah lingered in the hallway, fear and uncertainty escaping his shaken mind like soft perfume. His longing for Eli was terrible and his heart sick with shame at what Harshika's influence had caused. Charles gave me a look that assured me he would take care of Micah. I saw him lead the man away, an awkward arm about his shoulders. I engaged the security system with rapid dexterity.

Kieran appeared as a corpse in the grips of rigor mortis on top of the heavy duvet. It was a harsh reminder of how vulnerable we all were. I slipped off his muddy shoes and removed his jacket. The room had already been set up with window covers impenetrable by sunlight and bullets, and my rational self knew we were safe, but I felt more rattled than I could ever remember being. Even the fact that Charles had some of the most highly trained and physically fit people in the world watching their rooms and the hotel didn't alleviate my apprehension. This was even worse than when I was being held by the Desmarais. They had been only human, after all.

Harshika was something else entirely.

I sat on the edge of the bed and lowered my face to my hands, not realising how badly they shook until that moment. My eyes ached from crying. I was filthy, covered with blood and drying mud from the ruckus inside the temple, and the voyage to and from the meeting place, but I couldn't have cared less. As I leaned back and the sun rose, sleep overtook me.

Rachel. The Jungle.

When I opened my eyes the next night, both Harshika and Achyut were already up and about. It took a moment to rouse myself from the disorientation of waking in a foreign place, but as cold dread curdled my stomach on recognition of my two guardians, I was soon wide awake. They were seated several feet away at a table filled with equipment. To my surprise they were both dressed in modern clothing, unlike the previous evening, and Harshika had even pulled her long tresses back in a tight ponytail at her nape. Her exposed skin was aberrant perfection, almost too dazzling to look at. But I knew from personal experience her touch was ice and her skin uncomfortably firm.

She pointed to the chair beside her, and I took her action to mean I should sit. Neither one addressed me as I obeyed. Instead they resumed their conversation in their dead language. After several minutes, Achyut stood and, with a brief nod in my direction, marched out of the chamber. Being alone with Harshika was even more terrifying.

"So now it's just the two of us." She fiddled with something that looked like a very large cellphone for a brief moment then turned her full attention on me. I wished she hadn't. Her gaze travelled over my body, imparting the sensation of a slimy residue slathered on my skin like the trail of a slug. Her psychic gaze made a sudden dive into my mind, shocking and blinding me. My chair rattled and I grabbed at the table's edge to stabilise myself.

"Sorry," she said, though it was clear she was not. "I forget how fragile your mind is. I'll try to be gentler in the future."

"If you want to know something, why don't you ask me? Why do you always have to rummage in my brain like that?" I managed to check my tone on the last few words, but her intrusions were painful and disorienting.

She snickered at my response. "I don't know what it is about you.... I'd almost say I was starting to like you." I must have made a strange face, because her giggling turned to outright laughter. "Don't worry. Interest or attraction doesn't have a lasting effect for me. I could still kill you without a second thought."

That is comforting. "I'll keep that in mind."

"Now we need to be on our way. I've made arrangements for us, and a plane will be arriving soon."

"What plans? What about Achyut?"

"He has his own agenda," she answered. She did seem to enjoy her petty games, being cryptic one moment and a fountain of information the next, and there was nothing I could do about it. And there was no way to know if she spoke the truth.

"So where are we off to?"

"Many places. First stop—Egypt."

"Why Egypt?" I asked, my surprise genuine. I wondered at the purpose for taking us there.

"Because after my homeland, it's the first place I stayed with any permanence. I reigned over the people there for many years, leading them, controlling them, and feeding off their need to be dominated. I'm going to show you how the immortals of the world should be thought of, and how far and deep my influence has been throughout the world. Humans might not understand or accept the truth of what we are—blood-drinking undead that exist by stealing their virtues and life. But on some instinctive level they are aware there is more to the world than can be easily explained and substantiated. They yearn for something bigger and stronger than themselves to worship. Humans, like my children, have lost their way and no longer understand their place. I am going to share with you the truth."

"Egypt?" I asked out loud more to myself than for any clarification. The word brought to mind many things—power, intellect, spirituality. As my mind wandered Harshika's image appeared. Not the Harshika who stood before me now in the twenty-first century, but as she was then, millennia ago. She was dressed in draped red silk, eyes heavy with kohl, her neck adorned with gold and jewels. At her feet lay a beautiful lioness, and small cats of every shape and colour. She was a god.

"I was known then as Sekhmet, daughter of Ra."

She drew me into memories so vivid, so sharp, I couldn't help but smile. I heard voices speaking in a strange language, distinct from the one she shared with Achyut. I smelled perfume, food, animals, and my eyes burned from the smoky haze of lamps lit several thousands of years before. I tentatively raised my hands before me, walking deeper into Harshika's reminiscence and, perhaps, deeper into her madness.

She was naked and glorious. As the young and beautiful temple girls washed her with scented water, the sensation was mirrored on my own body. I shivered at the touch of phantom fingers and warm water cascading over my skin. The scent enveloped me, both wonderful and strange. Heavy combs worked through my hair as the girls prepared Harshika for the intricate plaiting they would execute before adorning it with fixative wax and jewels.

When the vision ended abruptly, I stood with my arms wrapped about myself, and it was Harshika's cold hand on my hair, not those of the long-dead temple girls. Up close, I couldn't help but be drawn into the black pools of her eyes. Death and pain haunted them. I wanted to look away, but I drowned, losing myself.

"Rachel," she said in a delicate voice, and the phenomenon was gone.

My gaze dropped to the floor. "Yes, mistress."

"It's time to go."

She took my hand and led me outside. The night was warm and damp, the air heavy with silence. My eyes were still adjusting to the complete darkness only found in places far from modern life when she scooped me up with impossibly strong arms and tore into the jungle. I could do nothing but hang on to her thin frame and think of Giovanni. The speed at which we moved caused tears to stream from the corners of my eyes, and the unnatural wind created from Harshika's movement screamed in my ear.

Giovanni, please help me. I remembered his face as the snow swirled about us on the night we'd committed ourselves to each other. The taste of his lips came alive against my own. I choked on my fear and my desperate need for him.

Then in a final indignity, his face blurred in my mind. My memories of him slipped, and I knew it was Harshika attempting to steal them from me. My brain ached and throbbed as I fought with everything in me to hang onto him. Her laughter thundered in response, graying reality and making it impossible for coherent thoughts to form. My blood was ice, my desperation bright.

"You are mine now, Rachel. Mine to do with as I please, and that means there is no room for anyone else." Her words were lashings, violent furrows tattooed on my deepest understanding.

Giovanni, please.

CHAPTER 14

Giovanni. Peru.

They were immortals. I had no doubt about that. I spotted them as soon as the elevator doors slid open and, even if I hadn't, I would have picked up on their supernatural energy, which all immortals emit to varying degrees. Sometimes it's a whisper or vague hint, and with others it's a screaming beacon. Not many are able to maintain a completely nil presence in the company of other vampires—only the very few with natural-born abilities, or those who have existed for so long they have acquired the skill. Of the many vampires I knew personally, Sorcha had been the only one I'd ever encountered who could cloak her presence, until Harshika and Achyut. Even Charles and Alessandra slipped up now and again.

There were two of them, a pleasant-looking young man who appeared to have been changed in his mid-twenties, and a young woman. No, girl was the more accurate word. She stood above average height for a woman, but her body had been forever trapped on the cusp of maturity. Her chestnut hair was worn long and loose, and warm golden eyes peeked out from its protective veil. She held the young man's hand and, upon closer inspection, there were some distinct physical similarities between the two. Both had high cheekbones and wide mouths, dark hair, their body shapes lean and graceful.

The man made eye contact immediately and watched as we approached. "Can we speak?" he asked when we were within arm's reach of each other.

I nodded to the girl before addressing her partner. "Of course."

"Stay here, Clellia," he instructed, and followed me into the deserted lounge.

A quick perusal of the room satisfied me we were alone. I sat at a small table where the man joined me, extending his hand across the table. I took it and gave it a firm shake. When our hands touched, I absorbed a powerful sensation that seemed to encompass the entirety of the stranger's being—guilt.

"My name is Daniel," he said, and I noticed for the first time how sad his eyes were. I suspected it was more than the current situation that had brought this condition to the man's existence. This seemed something that clung to him with quiet persistence.

"Nice to meet you, Daniel. I'm Giovanni."

"Yes, I know who you are. I heard of the attack against the Desmarais last year. I'm sorry I didn't become aware of it in time to assist you." He held his gaze steady as he spoke and appeared sincere.

"That's all right, Daniel. Things worked out for the best. And we are certainly glad to have your assistance now. I assume that's why you are here, to help?"

"Yes. Clellia and I have been through enough. I can't even imagine what it would be like to be under that creature's thumb for the rest of time."

"Me, either. It seems to me we have all done well enough without her guidance or opinion, for the most part, anyway." The memory of Tatiana passed through my mind.

"Then my cousin and I can join you?"

"Of course. We are leaving now, heading back to my home in San Francisco, and you're welcome to come along."

Daniel's relief seemed inappropriate as he glanced over his shoulder in the direction of the hallway. It was then I understood how tightly he hung onto his thoughts—almost completely blocking any escape of memory or feeling. His mind was burdened with one thing only. Clellia.

Rachel. Unknown.

When we emerged from the sweaty jungle after more than an

hour of travel, a new and expensive-looking SUV waited for us on the edge of a dirt road. Harshika pulled me into the back seat with her and, after a quick exchange with the driver, we were on our way to a waiting plane.

Soon we approached a small, private airstrip. A sleek black plane awaited our arrival, the crew focused on meeting my captor's every need. Driven by both fear and greed, each human met her with downcast eyes and an almost psychotic attention to detail. We took our seats in a cosy interior room equipped with a gigantic viewing screen and state-of-the-art sound system. The butter-coloured leather seats were so soft it bordered on eeriness. I curled up on one, and waited.

Harshika conferred with several people about what I couldn't be positive as they spoke Spanish, and I did not have fluency in the language. When she had been satisfied, the door to our area shut and she set up the equipment to watch a movie. As the opening credits of *Gone with the Wind* filled the screen, I was surprised by her choice.

She was still standing when she said, "You must be hungry."

I was, but not painfully so. I could go one to two days without feeding if needed, and I didn't want to ask her for anything. Without another word she opened a small door in the walnut paneling and withdrew a familiar-looking object. She poured the contents from the medical bag into a small container, which it turned out was a portable warming device someone might use to heat a baby's bottle. She handed the contents to me and settled into her own chair.

I raised the container to my mouth, not surprised to find the blood at almost exact body temperature. I sighed then consumed the rest in two greedy gulps. She whisked the empty container away without comment then turned her attention to the movie. The engines started with a soft rumble and, as we headed down the laneway, panic gave me a tight squeeze. As we soared into the dark sky, so did my certainty I wasn't going to get away from Harshika, not in one piece at least.

Eli. Peruvian Jungle.

I opened my eyes. It was dark, the floor cold and damp. I felt Aldous beside me, our bodies touching lightly, but there was nothing comforting about it. It was a stark reminder of our current circumstances. I also picked up on the fact that Zhongxing and Saskia had already awoken. Aldous stirred, then sat up. The events of the previous night shot through his mind, reaching the rest of us with jarring vividness.

"Sorry," he snapped, his irritation with himself and the situation touching as a harsh jab to the brain.

I touched Aldous's arm. "It's fine. We're all pissed."

The four of us were in a dank ten-by-ten-foot room with a dirt floor and no source of light or ventilation. Not that the group incarcerated here needed oxygen, and all had decent night vision to varying degrees. It was the helplessness and claustrophobia triggered by the confined space. This added on to our collective anger and worry for our loved ones.

"What are we going to do?" Saskia asked.

"What can we do? We're trapped in a locked room inside a stone temple in the middle of the jungle. There're not too many options here." I tried not to take my frustration out on her. I closed my eyes and concentrated on finding any of those close to me. For a fleeting moment I thought I picked up on Giovanni's, then Charles's psychic auras, but the sensation was so faint it could have been my imagination. There was nothing of Micah at all.

Then, like a radio snapped to full volume, I received a stream of consciousness loud and clear. *Giovanni, help me.*

The thought of Rachel alone with Harshika killed me. My lover was gone, I hoped under the protection of my friends, but considering what they were up against, that did little to assuage the dread holding tight to my heart. All I wanted was to be far away from this place, holding Micah in my arms. I needed to know Rachel was unharmed.

I'd never felt so helpless or scared in my life.

Giovanni. San Francisco.

Charles had barely walked through the door when Genevieve jumped into his arms. Danica watched from the bottom of the grand staircase as the group entered, scanning one face after another. When the one she looked for didn't appear, she crossed the foyer toward me and looked me right in the eye.

"Where's Rachel?" she demanded.

"It's complicated."

"I'm sure it is," she snapped. "Give me the Coles notes version." I was momentarily confused until she clarified. "An overview."

"The first vampire is pissed. She wants to control all of the immortals and she's holding some of us as ransom."

"And Rachel's one of the some?" Her expression begged me to correct her.

"Yes," I answered.

Charles stepped in and touched Danica's arm. She flinched. "We're going to get her back."

"And we're going to kill that bitch!" Emmaline's voice dripped with venom.

Genevieve looked around at everyone gathered. "Eli's gone, too. And Aldous and Donovan. And you have strangers with you."

"Donovan was killed." Kieran grimaced at the memory and from the shock on Genevieve's face. "There's lots to tell you."

Daniel moved toward the two humans, hand outstretched. "I'm Daniel. This is my cousin, Clellia."

"Nice to meet you," Danica said, though the shock of the news was apparent in her grim expression.

"Let's go to the backroom and figure out what's going on." I said.

As everyone walked toward the back of the house, Charles caught Genevieve by the elbow. She looked at him quizzically. "Wait," he said.

Noticing they were not coming with the group, I called back to them, "What's going on?"

"You guys go ahead. I want Gen to start working on this dart right away. I think I know a way we can use it to our advantage."

I accepted his explanation and followed the others. Most were seated, waiting for us to join them, but Daniel was out on the back patio, staring over the dark landscape. Off in the distance the city's lights danced and the ocean offered its distinctive aroma.

"Alessandra, fill the ladies in," I said in passing.

I joined Daniel in silence, letting the moment unfold without pressure. After a few minutes, he turned to me, smiling, though his eyes still held a twinge of despondency. There were soft memories open to me of an unfamiliar place. I saw the ocean and long stretches of desert. An image of the Sydney Opera House flashed, and I understood.

"Reminds me of home," Daniel said. "The lights and the ocean, the climate."

"You're from Australia?"

"Originally. We've moved around as we all do. We were back about fifteen years ago, but it had been ages before that."

When Daniel spoke, my skin tingled with a warm, almost sensual feeling. It was an odd sensation, and not one I'd known from another immortal before. There was always some effect from being close to another of our kind, but this was unique. It wasn't unpleasant, or even unwelcome, just strange. Daniel looked out over the backyard again and the feeling subsided but didn't disappear altogether. Curious.

"Is there something you want to tell me, Daniel?" I asked.

"I suppose there is." He indicated toward the patio set, and walked over to take a seat. The chair scraped along the flagstone surface as it was pulled out. I took the seat opposite him and waited.

"I think you have the right to know my background after taking us into your life like this. Perhaps we...I should say I, as Clellia is completely innocent of any wrong-doing. Until she was changed that is. I'm sorry, this isn't making any sense. It's still hard to talk about."

"Just start at the beginning."

"Clellia and I were living in Australia as you guessed earlier. It was the nineteen-twenties when our change came about. Our mothers were sisters, though there was almost fifteen years between them. They came from a family of twelve, my mother being the oldest and Clellia's being the youngest. Most of the siblings stayed in the same area, buying land and starting farms and cattle ranches. A few moved to the larger urban areas that were springing up, but for the most part we were country folk. Of course, Clellia and I grew up together, our parents' farms backed onto one another and we often spent time together." He paused, deep in a memory of his human past. I became aware of an odd combination of emotions—wistfulness, sadness, and desire. Brief sparks of images occurred, but nothing coherent.

"So, when I was a teen, I began to develop these terrible... urges, I guess you would call them. The first time it happened I was about thirteen and I was just finishing up with some chores, thinking of taking a swim before going to bed. I headed to a nearby pond, accidentally stumbling onto my older sister, Clair, and one of our stable hands. You can imagine what they were doing. I hid and watched, finding their excitement fed my own. I didn't get caught, so I kept doing it. I spied not only on my sister, but others as well. I would sneak out at night and go into the nearest town, peeping into windows. I broke into a few homes, stealing ladies' undergarments and other things I found arousing. Soon looking wasn't enough.

"Then it progressed. In a few years time I visited prostitutes in town. I had stolen money to pay for their services, and I learned many things under their direction. And what I learned I took with me and used on my victims. My first assault happened when I was seventeen. She was a lovely girl from a farm several miles away from my family's. Her name was Juliet. I had made advances to her, hinting at a relationship, until finally convincing her to sneak out and meet me one night." He looked me right in the eye before continuing. "I hurt her badly. She ended up getting an infection from her injuries and died about a week later. She never told anyone what happened, so I got away with it.

"This went on for years. Sometimes it was just touching,

sometimes more. Sometimes I was able to stave off my impulses with visits to the city, but it never lasted. When I was twenty, I finally got caught.

"There was a community picnic where people from miles around came to socialise, eat, and take a break from their hard lives. There were so many people it was impossible to control myself. I walked about, looking for a victim, so confident in my power. And then I saw her, a girl I did not recognise. She was standing off by herself, looking uncomfortable and lost. She appeared to be about my age and wore her waist-length auburn hair unfettered. I introduced myself and after a half hour of small talk, I asked her to take a walk with me. She wanted to let her parents know where she was going, but I assured her everything was fine. I didn't know it then, but my mother had seen us leaving together. I also didn't know my mother had suspected the truth about me.

"Now, I knew the area like the back of my hand. I led her to a very remote spot where we wouldn't be stumbled onto accidentally. I sat down and she joined me. I didn't even give her a chance. I pushed her back and clamped a hand over her mouth. Her eyes were huge with fear, and that only excited me more. I pushed her dress up, careful not to rip it, because that would be hard to explain when we returned to the picnic."

"She was crying, and her tears were hot as they streamed over my hand. Slowly I pulled my hand from her mouth. 'Please don't hurt me. Please,' she said.

"'You just lie there and let me do what I want to do and I won't hurt you. And when I'm done, you're going to go back to the picnic and act like nothing happened. And you're not going to tell anyone, or I *will* hurt you. And your whole family.'

"She went silent, simply nodding. I'd never attempted an attack in broad daylight before and that made the encounter even more enticing. I was starting to undo my belt when something smashed me in the back of the head. I fell down, grabbing it and when I pulled my hands back, they were covered with blood. The girl jumped up, started to run and then stopped. Everything was blurry and my head was throbbing. I heard someone talking, a female's voice. 'I'm going to take care of this.

Put your underwear back on and go back to the picnic. Don't leave your parents' sight again, okay?'

"I heard the sound of someone running away and then a face appeared right above my own. I blinked, trying to focus on the features. When my vision cleared, it was my mother looking down at me. She slapped me with all her strength and spat in my face. She tossed the rock she'd hit me with to the ground.

"'You're a disgrace. You make me sick. I knew something was going on. And I know you've been sneaking off in the night, and now I guess I know what you've been doing.'

"I was sick with shame, let me tell you, but I was also pissed. Nothing was going to be the same after that. She yanked me up on my feet, and brought me back to the picnic. She told my father I had fallen and we needed to go home. Once there she told him the truth, and he beat me to within an inch of my life. It took two weeks lying in bed before I could walk again. By that time, they'd arranged for me to go into the care of a ministry training programme where I would be watched closely. And I was. Bed at seven with a locked door. Chores where I was never alone, communal bathing. And the private counselling to help me with my demons never seemed to end. I spent two years there without leaving, and my family never visited me once.

"When the church was satisfied I'd been cured and that my training was complete, I was assigned to a small community where I would be assisted by an older more experienced minister. I had started to settle in when Clellia came into my life again.

"During the years I was away her father had passed and her mother remarried. The new husband owned a shop in the town where I was relocated. They started attending our church, and one day my aunt recognised me. She didn't know the truth of why I had gone away. As far as anyone but my parents were concerned, I'd left because of a calling by God. It was a nicer and easier explanation than what had actually happened. She of course invited me for dinner, which I accepted. And there I saw Clellia.

"She was the oldest, sixteen by that time, with several younger siblings. I'd honestly thought I'd managed to get control of my urges, that I was better, but one look at her and they came back with a vengeance. I did nothing that night, but when I got back to my room, I couldn't stop thinking about her. I came for dinner every Sunday, and my aunt was so proud to have a member of the church in her home and as part of her family. I recruited Clellia to help around the church and with the children's groups. And she seemed to like the attention I gave her, which only spurred me on.

"Then one evening when she was there helping to clean up after a youth event, we found ourselves alone. I used the opportunity to start playing with her mind. I needed to set the stage for the plans I had. The more attached she became to me, the easier it would be. She trusted me so much and wanted my approval. It was repulsive what I was doing.

"Months later we found ourselves in a similar situation, a different event, and we were the last ones left. Clellia's parents always trusted me to escort her home, so proud she was so involved with the church. And that's when we were changed."

Daniel had opened his mind as his story unfolded, allowing me to journey with him through his remembrance of abuse and broken trust. Now there was much shame associated with his actions, but back then he had been sick with inappropriate and uncontrollable lust. That this was his own flesh and blood, so innocent and trusting, made the circumstance even more distasteful. Clellia as a human girl had been stunning with childish beauty, but was a child nonetheless. And because of Daniel, she would remain one forever.

"And how did you come to be vampires?" I asked, waiting to pass judgment.

"Well, I planned to attack her there in the church. I didn't have time to follow through on my disgusting plans, though, as I myself was attacked. Someone jumped me from behind, knocking me across the floor and into the podium. My attacker came over to me, grabbed me by the front of my clerical robes, and all but shook the life out of me. I was vaguely aware of a female form and long brown hair. Clellia was hysterical by then.

"Then I was dropped to the floor and I must have passed out. When I came to, Clellia was quiet, lying a few feet away from me on the floor. She looked so peaceful, but pale. The woman was seated at the front pew, waiting for me to wake up. When I tried to raise myself, she was on me.

"She was beautiful, clear, pale skin and warm brown eyes. Her hair was dark and thick, worn loose the way I liked it. She wore a simple navy dress, fitting with the fashion of the day. Her lips were so red as she leaned into me. 'Who are you?' I asked.

"'My name is Johanna.'

"'Why are you here?'

"'Helping myself.'

"'I don't understand.'

"'I'm here to take your blood,' she said matter-of-factly. 'And have some fun.'

"'Some fun?'

"'Oh, yes. I've been watching you for a while now. I've been aware of your thoughts, naughty and perverted as they are. And I've been watching you with this sweet cousin of yours.' She had a touch of amusement in her voice, though the situation was far from funny. 'I think it will be quite fitting to have the two of you trapped in this moment for all eternity. Your cousin forever the sweet, young girl, and you forced to see her every day as this child who will never grow and never age. You have damned the both of you to remain as you are now forever.'

"And then she bit me and drained my blood. She forced her own blood on me in my weakened state as she must have also done with Clellia, and then took us to her hideaway. She spent a few weeks with us, teaching us how to hunt and protect ourselves, and then she was gone. Clellia and I have been together ever since, alone."

"And you never saw this Johanna again?"

"Not until last night. She was there among the crowd. She made eye contact, but didn't approach me."

The chair creaked as I leaned back, thoughtful before speaking next. I didn't know how I felt about the whole thing. As a human man I would have been incensed and repulsed, but now it was not so clear-cut. I didn't feel any dishonesty or hidden agenda from Daniel, and I did not pick up on any memories of an inappropriate nature with Clellia since the night of their change.

"And what is your relationship now."

"As family. More like a father and daughter. That's how we tend to represent ourselves if we settle for any amount of time. It's believable with the resemblance."

"And you haven't forced yourself on her, or hurt her in any way since Johanna crossed your path?"

"Not at all. I protect her at all costs." His eyes were wide and serious, haunted by a past he could never escape.

"So, in essence you have both been punished for your sins."

"Yes." He broke eye contact. "Clellia more than me, if we're being honest. I have trapped her in eternal limbo, not a child and also not yet a woman. And forced to rely on her abuser for protection? How sick is that? My guilt is nothing to the hurt I have caused her."

"Has she ever attempted to leave you?"

"Never. Certainly, she has the power and the money to exist on her own, but because of her appearance it's harder to blend in. Sometime she can pass for eighteen, but it's usually the result of forcing the acceptance on the human party, and it's exhausting having to maintain that."

"I imagine it is," I agreed.

"Perhaps when all is said and done, she might find an immortal closer to her age that she would prefer to be with? We haven't had the opportunity to meet many others of our kind, and certainly not any interested in our particular circumstance."

"Giovanni?" Alessandra called, poking her head out of the patio doors.

"Yes, we're almost done. A few more minutes."

She nodded and disappeared back inside the house.

"Maybe by helping others of your kind you can find some peace yourself. It might be a new beginning for both of you." I stood and offered my hand to the other man.

Daniel looked at the outstretched hand as if it might explode in his face. When he realised I was serious, and offered friendship with that simple gesture, he accepted. We shook hands, sealing the unspoken deal.

Together we walked back to the house, our friends and allies gathered within. Plans needed to be made to rescue our loved ones. Their absence was a relentless burden on our minds. Sometimes pain and fear brings factions together like no other motivation can.

And there was the matter of taking down the oldest and most powerful immortal to have ever walked the face of the earth, if such a thing were even possible.

CHAPTER 15

Rachel. Egypt.

The plane skipped across the world with ease, touching down at a private airstrip just outside of Cairo. We were received by a group of men reeking of wealth garbed in traditional Muslim head scarves and dress, with warm sienna skin and dark eyes. Harshika greeted them with calculated respect and her voiced carried a warmth with which I was not familiar. I remained quiet as she conducted her business. Though I'd changed and scrubbed myself on the plane, I wasn't exactly presentable.

As the men made noises as though they were about to depart, the eldest of the group dropped to his knee. Harshika offered her tiny hand, which the man took and pressed to his lips. I took in the shudder the man experienced at the contact with her cool skin without comment, but found the moment curious. Fear accompanied his gesture certainly, but also admiration. I would have to press her for details when a chance arose.

The men left in an impressive black limousine and we followed shortly thereafter in an SUV-type vehicle. I've never been a great car enthusiast, but Harshika's tastes obviously ran to the new and very expensive. The driver was a young man with a fresh sprinkling of acne across his cheeks. He didn't smile and only spoke when something was asked of him. He drove with determined focus, navigating the hectic streets without incident. Soon the vehicle pulled up in front of a small but posh hotel, built in Moorish style, which highlighted the use of grand arches and glazed tile.

Egypt was everything I ever imagined it to be. Even though I viewed it through the veil of darkness and not under the harsh, unrelenting sun, it was still glorious. The mishmash of ancient and modern could be seen at every turn. Every style and economic class blended in with the shifting sea of tourists who had come from every corner of the earth. Voices and various languages swam through each other in the narrow streets. The heavy air smelled of spice, pollution, and blood. All about the grand mecca that Cairo had become were the restless, shifting desert sands, waiting to reclaim the land that now held this thriving city.

The bellboy took Harshika's luggage, pocketing the handful of bills she placed in his hand with grace. He made brief eye contact as a show of respect and thanked her for her generosity. It was an action perfected over time as he catered to the wealthy and influential. Then he charged ahead, his immortal guests following in his wake. Alone in the elevator with us, his temperature rose in kind with his unease. Our presence affected him deeply, but he continued to fight to hang on to his dignity and professionalism. He had no clear reason for his discomfort, and his thoughts about us were neither bad nor good. We were both attractive to him, but unsettling.

He couldn't get out of our room fast enough, though he did stop to thank us for our patronage and wished us a pleasant stay.

As the door closed, Harshika brought one of the bags to the bed. She snapped it open and turned back to me with some clothing in her hand. "Take this. Shower and dress so we may depart."

I took the clothes, thought about protesting, then kept my mouth shut. I did feel grimy and rumpled. Since my own clothing had most likely returned to the States with Giovanni, I wasn't in a position to argue. The water was warm and the pressure decent. I scrubbed at my skin and lathered my hair twice with a flowery-scented shampoo. Refreshed and clean, I dressed in the articles Harshika had given me. The underwear was still in the package, but there was no bra. The outfit consisted of a pair of loose cotton pants and a long tunic. When I caught sight of myself in the mirror, I did a double take, unaccustomed to dressing in such a way.

"Rachel, open the door," Harshika called form the bedroom.

I did as instructed. She pointed at the toilet and told me, "Take a seat."

Then without a hint of modesty, she dropped her own clothing to the floor and ran a bath. Apparently not letting me out of her sight was a literal statement. My cheeks warmed as I took in her naked body lowering into the water. She flicked a look my way. She knew how perfect and beautiful she was. Harshika's effect on me was not lost on her, and that made me angry with myself.

"There's no use fighting it," she said. Her voice was calm and smooth, irritating me to no end. "I have this effect on everyone, whether they want it or not. It doesn't matter if you like me, or how strong your fear is, you'll still want me." Her words dripped with condescension.

The thought of wanting her was not the least bit attractive to me, and far from comforting. But she was right. My gaze kept drifting to her, drinking in her naked form. My fear remained, my wariness only having had its edge taken off, but my attraction to her continued to grow. Her presence breathed over me, caressing and seductive. I had to fight to keep myself from reaching out to touch her hair, which cascaded over the edge of the tub. My anger raged, burning me from the inside out. How could I feel anything but hate for such a loathsome creature?

Again, my sense of time and place was stolen in an abrupt assault, and I was swallowed by the urgency of her memories. She used her psychic prowess to hurtle us beyond time and space, travelling to a land where the cold consumed everything, and the dark landscape was draped in ice and snow. Here Harshika resided in a hidden cave high in the peaks of a treacherous mountain pass. The bitter air nipped at my skin and the moon reflected off the white landscape with impressive strength, mimicking the early morning light.

Deep inside the cave, past a series of cramped tunnels, she had been surrounded by young maidens of Nordic descent with crude shrines erected to her worship. Her dark hair was covered with a shimmery white material, giving the illusion of fairness to her hidden tresses. She had been dressed entirely in white as were the young girls and women in her attendance. She appeared delicate, ethereal, belying the truth of the monster she really was.

About the space swarmed a multitude of domesticated felines, sleeping, eating, and lounging on every surface. At Harshika's feet were sprawled two majestic black cats similar to the jaguars of South America. Yet these cats were slightly smaller and, up close, their black coats appeared to have a pattern of small spots. The term *black panther* flared out and, knowing these were not creatures indigenous to the area, I assumed Harshika had brought them with her.

Several young women approached where Harshika lounged, their arms raised before her. I watched in horror as a young man, clean and dressed in the finest materials, was brought to her. The women stepped back as Harshika came to the man who stood, fighting against the bindings that held him. His wild eyes showed his fear, but he did not cry out.

The women chanted and sang, and the only word I could clearly make out was "Freya." They backed away, leaving Harshika and the man alone in the space. I trembled, trying to pull away from the image my brain had been tricked into experiencing, but it was no use. Shock fought with anger as I in turn fought to hide from this memory. Her fangs sank into the man's soft flesh, and I could taste the blood as Harshika drained his life away. God help me, it was glorious and sweet.

I was sucked back to reality with the taste of blood still warm on my tongue. Harshika stood before me, towel wrapped about her lithe frame. I slipped and she caught me, easing me back into a seated position. I wiped my hand across my mouth, half expecting it to come back streaked with blood. Of course, there was none, but my hunger had been awakened. I had already drunk blood on the plane. I shouldn't be thirsting as I was. I felt certain this physical reaction was of her influence over me, as contrived as the game she'd played with my mind.

I closed my eyes and latched onto an image of Giovanni. I returned to our home in Spain, joining him on the cool sand of the beach before our house. He smiled at me, leaning in to press his lips against mine...so close I could almost taste him. Then the image vanished.

Harshika was even closer, her arm held out in offering. Bright spots of blood beaded at her wrist where she had opened the vein. The smell of it taunted me, begged me to have a taste. I licked my lips, then with no conscious decision I was aware of, I found my mouth pressed to her flesh. Her blood burned down my throat, but in a most welcome way. Her power licked along my veins, whispering and imprinting her terrible past on my own awareness. She'd bound me to her in a way I feared could not be broken, but I had no will to stop drinking.

Gently she pulled her arm away. I licked at the liquid on my lips, instantly filled with shame. "You should feel the effects right away, increased strength and control, better ability to be in touch with our kind."

"Why would you want me to have these things? Aren't you afraid I'll use them against you?"

She laughed, a throaty, warm sound. "Afraid of you? I am afraid of nothing."

"Then why?"

"I should like to keep you close when all this is done. And those in my inner circle must be strong." Several faces appeared as she thought about those she had already chosen and those she would like to have with or without force. I didn't recognise any of them except for Sorcha and Samaria.

"I don't want to join you," I snapped and jumped to my feet.

The next thing I knew I smashed into the mirror about ten feet away. The glass shattered and tore at my skin. I hit the vanity top then tumbled to the floor. I looked up, stunned. Harshika had not moved an inch. Blood poured from my head and face, pooling underneath me on the tile floor. Tiny feet appeared in my line of vision. I raised my face as she knelt. Her lips pursed, but she didn't seem particularly angry. With a quick jerk, she removed a fist-sized chunk of glass from my scalp.

A sluggish flow of blood dampened my hair and spilled onto my shoulders. Harshika pressed her mouth to the wound and it closed instantly. The other damage also healed, as if it had never happened at all.

"You'd best learn some respect," she said, and the matter was closed.

She walked out of the bathroom, leaving me in a pool of blood and frustration. I counted to ten then stood. The blood washed from my face, but there was nothing I could do about the tunic. She must have caught my thought, because just as I turned to join her in the bedroom she appeared at my side with a fresh garment.

She had already dressed in a modernised version of an Indian sari. The colour was a soft orange, and complemented her dark hair and eyes. With a quick rake of the brush I pulled my hair into a ponytail and followed her out to the hall.

The desk clerk watched us leave the elevator and travel to the front door. Not another soul could be seen. There wasn't much time left before sunrise, and it was not a time for tourists to be milling about, especially unescorted women.

"Be careful, ladies," the clerk called out.

The door swooshed closed behind us. I felt the clerk watching us until we were out of sight. Harshika led me to a desolate area that seemed to have some significance for her, but didn't offer an explanation. We stood there for several minutes, looking out over the harsh and empty landscape, until she grabbed my hand. Without comment or explanation, she led me back, stopping to take blood from an elderly homeless man before returning us to our hotel.

We lay on the bathroom floor behind the locked door. I fell asleep with Harshika pressed tight at my side. My dreams were hers, filled with times long past, dominated by pain and blood.

CHAPTER 16

Giovanni. San Francisco.

I bolted awake, erupting from the fog of sleep like a gunshot. I reached for Rachel's hand like I always do, and finding nothing but an empty bed, crashed back to harsh reality. Rachel was gone, held captive by a vicious and remorseless monster. I punched the bed in frustration before throwing on some clothes and heading downstairs.

My foot had barely touched the top step when voices from one of the upstairs bedrooms piqued my interest. I followed the sound, recognising both speakers as I neared. I opened the door without knocking and was met with stares from two sets of eyes—one human, one vampire.

"Good, I'm glad you're up," Charles said as I entered.

I acknowledged my maker with a small nod then surveyed the changes the room had undergone during the daylight hours. All the furniture had been removed and the table from the kitchen was now in the middle of the space. A desk from Rachel's office had been dragged in, as well as another table that was not familiar. All surfaces were covered with equipment, books, and papers. Genevieve sat in a dishevelled mess at the heart of it. Dark bags under her eyes showed how tired she was, and I could taste her frustration.

"What's going on here?" I asked.

"Genevieve has isolated the components of the dart's poison," Charles answered briskly, nodding toward some of the equipment on the desk.

Genevieve tucked a section of hair behind her ear that had

escaped from her lopsided ponytail and peered up at me. She looked so fragile and lovely, but underneath the gentle exterior was a firecracker of personality and brilliance. "Ingenious buggers. Excellent use of natural resources. The curare plant, or *Chondrodendron tomentosum* is the main component of *ampi*, which is what the natives call this poison. I pity the poor bastards who were the test subjects for this stuff." I tasted her exhaustion, but her mind felt oddly energised by her discovery. It reminded me of Rachel's excitement at studying ancient texts and poring over academic papers, something I'd always been blasé about. I experienced a poignant wash of guilt at not having shown more enthusiasm, promising myself to be more involved with her interests when I got her back.

"And this is to our advantage?" I asked.

"As long as I can get my hands on my research," Genevieve answered and turned her attention back to the items before her.

"I've already made arrangements for it to be shipped here. It will arrive sometime tomorrow." Charles returned her irritation with a soft voice, something that still surprised me about him. He could be so gentle and kind when it came to Genevieve.

Danica came to the door, giving a light knock before entering. At the sight of me, tears filled her eyes and her worry for Rachel wafted from her like fog. Various images floated from her to me with her anguish, of both her childhood and of their reclaimed relationship as adults. I went to where she stood and pulled her into an embrace. She resisted at first then melted against my chest.

Her form reminded me of Rachel's, though she was too warm and soft. Her hair was slightly thicker too, I noticed, as I ran my hand along it, and she didn't have the right scent. With Danica held in my arms, I understood how Rachel could have come to be with Eli. I'd never fully allowed myself to be in her shoes before, my jealousy always barring the way. The pain I felt without her now was unbearable and unrelenting. I couldn't go on without her.

I pulled away, leaving my arm about her shoulders, and forced myself to smile. "Let's go downstairs and wait for the others. I can hear them milling about."

"Yes, I need to eat and so does Genevieve."

She looked at Genevieve for agreement, but she peered at something under a microscope. When she didn't acknowledge her, Charles nodded and we left the room.

Downstairs Alessandra was in the kitchen, her white-blond hair shining, her pale blue eyes missing nothing. She gave a smile with a lot of fang before returning to what she was doing. I was surprised to see her making coffee, which under other circumstances would be a completely normal activity. But these weren't normal conditions, and Alessandra was a powerful immortal who catered to no one, let alone did domestic chores. But for some reason she seemed quite pleased with herself.

A comment about the absurdity of the situation was on the tip of my tongue when Charles swept into the kitchen. His brow furrowed as he took in what Alessandra was doing, and he gave me a brief smirk. "Alessandra, why don't you let Danica finish up and join the rest of us in the back room? We have things to discuss."

"Of course." She handed the coffee container to Danica. "Let's go then."

We followed her to where the others waited. Mengmei and Kieran were seated on the couch, looking rested and focused. Micah was a mess. His mind screamed anger and fear, and he could barely keep it together. He was so worried about Eli, his thoughts swirling in a dizzying frenzy, and I knew I'd have to keep an eye on him. In his state he could be a serious liability, to himself and others. His supernatural abilities were so new they had yet to be tested while under duress. I couldn't bear what it would do to Eli if he were hurt, or worse.

Clellia and Daniel sat on the loveseat. When I greeted them, Daniel met my gaze with surety and respect, but Clellia kept hers downcast. This seemed to be a habit of hers, hiding in Daniel's shadow as though she had no identity of her own. It was a sad way for an immortal to live, and a waste of power most could only dream of possessing. Something needed to be done about it, but more pressing matters were at hand.

Emmaline paced before the French doors, but she stopped as Charles and I entered and perched on the arm of the sofa next to Kieran. He patted her hand on her lap, and a small smile appeared. Kieran had a calm nature about him that appealed to both humans and other immortals. I remembered it well from the years we'd spent together. I had always been sorry our time together had been so brief, and that I'd left so abruptly. He would be a good choice for Emmaline to lean on while we fought to reunite with our loved ones. I took the empty place next to Mengmei, leaving Charles to address the group. Alessandra took a seat at his side.

"Well, this is a new night and the time for us to focus on what we need to do now, not what has already happened. We cannot let our worry and our anger get the better of us. Harshika will detect every weakness and use it to her advantage. There will be time for grieving and remorse later."

He paused to look over the room, taking in each immortal for a sense of agreement. "Genevieve is upstairs working on something I brought to her. This will be a part of our final plan, but this brings us to another issue. Harshika warned us she is able to reach any of our minds at any time, and though I think this is only partially true at best, we should err on the side of caution. The details of what we are working on will remain between Giovanni, Alessandra, Mengmei, and me. We are the oldest and of the strongest mental abilities here. The less the rest of you know the less chance Harshika might become privy to our plan. We do want you to know we are not going into this confrontation unprepared. Needless to say, we must all be diligent. Do your best to keep your mental shields up and take stock of what is going on often. Harshika will not be easy on us."

"And in the meantime, what would you have us do?" Emmaline asked. Her anger was controlled, but simmered near the surface. Most of her wounds had healed, but a shadow of bruising lingered about her jaw line and under one eye. I knew from experience the deepest injuries, the emotional pain, would be hardest to heal.

"I think we should all reach out to any immortals who left Peru that we know, no matter how superficial the relationship, and ask they come to join us. Their leaving makes it likely they feel the same way we do. There is safety in numbers, as the saying goes. I imagine Harshika will be doing the same, or perhaps Achyut will be doing the dirty work for her."

"That seems likely," Mengmei commented.

"Should we all feed before attempting to recruit allies?" Daniel asked.

I stood and nodded with enthusiasm. "That's a wonderful idea. We all need to be in top form before entering into possible tricky negotiations with other immortals. And perhaps we might also take the opportunity to better acquaint ourselves with our newer friends here." An idea had jumped into my mind and I wanted to act on it.

I looked at Charles, who regarded me with curiosity. "Alessandra, why don't you take Clellia, and perhaps Kieran and Daniel could go with Micah. Emmaline and Mengmei, could the two of you go together? Charles and I have a couple of things to discuss still."

For the first time, Clellia raised her head and looked directly at me. Her shock and worry couldn't have been more evident if she'd outright refused, but the others seemed to take my direction in stride. Daniel tried to sooth Clellia, who at that moment seemed every bit the child she had been when she died. Her eyes were wide and her mouth set in a tight line. She spoke with her cousin in hushed whispers as Alessandra approached. She offered her hand, which Clellia took after a moment's pause. She looked back over her shoulder at Daniel as the two walked by.

"This had better be good," Alessandra whispered in my ear as they passed.

The others departed in their small groups, leaving Charles and me alone. The aromas of garlic and oregano filtered in from the kitchen, tickling at an old memory.

"What was that about?" Charles asked.

I filled him in on Daniel and Clellia's past. "I thought it might help Clellia to have a female influence, and one who is strong and smart."

"I see. But Alessandra? She's not exactly the motherly type."

"No, but she is formidable. And if anyone could help this

poor soul make a clean break, and feel capable and self-reliant, it's Alessandra. And the rest of us can help fill in the pieces."

"And if she doesn't want to leave Daniel?"

"Then we tried. It may simply be a case that they have never known any different. Who knows who may turn up on our doorstep to offer their assistance? There may not only be allegiances formed, but perhaps new friendships also."

"Giovanni, you let your emotions rule you." Charles's tone was light and teasing, but also implied understanding. A lot had changed between us in a few short years. I'd have never thought it possible, but we truly were friends.

"Forever is a long time to be without love and companionship, Charles," I said. Rachel's face flashed, driving a stake of desperation through my chest.

"I know it well."

Several hours later, after all had returned from feeding and attended to their various responsibilities, Alessandra cornered me in my room. She entered without knocking, but I was not surprised as I'd felt her icy presence a full minute before she appeared.

She glided across the space, a not unhappy expression on her face, and perched herself on the gold chaise across from the bed. I watched, cellphone in hand, deciding it best to let her begin the conversation.

"That's one very messed-up vampire. She's practically scared of her own shadow." Her annoyance trickled out from her, chaffing against my skin and electrifying the air.

"Can you help her?"

"Of course I can help her," she snapped. "The question is why would I want to?"

"All right then. Do you want to help her?" I dropped the phone on the bed and gave Alessandra my undivided attention.

"Yes, but not because you want me to. Your cuteness doesn't work on me." Then she was on me with her hand about my throat. She traced a finger along the side of my face and licked her lips. "There are more entertaining things I could be doing." As she let down her guard, she laughed. Her hand fell away. "It's awful. I can't stand to see one of our kind so cowed. She's survived for almost a hundred years, so there's some strength and tenacity in there somewhere. I just need to coax it out."

"And convince her she can survive without Daniel."

Alessandra's eyes flashed with hatred at the sound of the man's name. "Don't even get me started on him. What I wouldn't do to get my hands on him."

"But you won't?"

"Of course not. This is not the time, nor place. We need all the bodies we can get. But when things are done, all bets are off."

"He is sorry, Alessandra. And he has never touched her since their change."

"I know."

"Clellia told you?"

"No. I got the information on my own." Inwardly, I cringed. I knew *how* she got the information. Poor girl. "But once she understood I was aware, there seemed to be some relief for her."

"Good," I said

Alessandra stood in a sudden, startling move, and left the room without another comment. "Thank you," I called after her.

I managed to contact two immortals who had been a part of the Desmarais attack. One agreed to come immediately, the other needed time to consider his options.

It was a start.

CHAPTER 17

Rachel. Egypt. Three Days in.

The next night breathed over me with a sigh of relief, releasing me from my restless slumber. The proximity to Harshika had made the memories invading my dreams so intense I woke feeling as though I hadn't rested at all. My hunger burned with an urgency I hadn't experienced in many years. The longer I was in Harshika's presence, the more unravelled I became, growing more dependent yet more repulsed with every passing second.

Harshika had already awoken. The bathroom door stood ajar, and I saw her legs hanging over the side of the bed closest to the bathroom. I rolled onto my elbow, my body stiff and mind strained. I ran cold water into the sink and splashed it onto my face, hoping to help revive myself somewhat. My reflection stared back at me, uncertain and worn. To the human eye I would still be lovely, seductive, but to my immortal sense I saw the effects of my ordeal.

Harshika snapped her phone shut as I entered the room. As usual her beauty stunned me. She'd dressed in yet another Asian-inspired outfit, this one a cool blue. My own had been rumpled from sleeping, but I declined her offer to change. I didn't care what I looked like. Nothing seemed to matter if the rest of my eternity was to be relegated to the status of Harshika's personal slave. I remembered Donovan's death with sudden vividness, and remorse squeezed at my already aching heart. I missed Giovanni with every fiber of my being. I missed Eli and Micah, Charles and Genevieve. I longed to see their faces and hear their voices...

"Your friends have been very busy," Harshika said, an obvious reference to what I had been thinking. "They are back in San Francisco, having picked up a couple of new allies in Peru. They are contacting all the immortals they know, as if that could make any difference." She spoke with a grating bravado, which stung as much as she meant it to. There was as light hesitation in her focus, and I experienced the change in her demeanour like a shift in temperature. Her warm confidence chilled and her lips pursed ever so slightly.

"What's the matter, mistress?" I asked.

She turned her attention at the sound of my voice, and her eyes were now hard with anger. "Oh, that Charles, such a crafty one."

"What's Charles doing that has you so worried?"

"Nothing has me worried, child, and Charles is no longer any of your concern. He'll get what's coming to him, something I understand you would have enjoyed inflicting yourself until very recently."

So, she had been keeping tabs. Until the last few years, Charles had been *numero uno* on my mental hit list. Now he was a most trusted friend, not someone I would stand by and allow to come to harm. The thought of any of my friends meeting an end like Donavan had was a knife through my heart. My fangs enlarged with my flood of anger.

She smiled and that made me loathe her even more. "Let's go. I have much to show you tonight."

She didn't wait for my answer. I was grabbed by the arm and escorted from the room. This night, since it was still early, the lobby was busy and loud. The same desk clerk eyed us as we departed the elevator. He thought how beautiful we were and wondered whether we were lesbians. His thoughts leapt from his mind to my own with a clarity I'd never experienced before. He could have been speaking directly in my ear, or inside my brain. Harshika hadn't kidded when she said I'd notice the effects of her blood right away.

A car waited for us at the curb. This time the driver was an older man who seemed to speak no English. Harshika conversed with him briefly before he peeled away from the hotel.

He took us from the city and pulled over along the edge of a remote stretch of road at Harshika's instruction. He seemed reluctant to leave us there, but also happy to be rid of us. He snatched the money she offered and turned his back on us as we left the vehicle. There wasn't another soul for miles.

Once the car was gone, Harshika grabbed me in her arms and ran. To me it looked as though we barrelled headlong into an endless expanse of desert, but I knew there had to be a specific destination in mind. If nothing else, Harshika was methodical and focused. The wind blew hot and dry, whipping through my long, loose hair and stinging my eyes.

We ran for a very long time before anything appeared in the dark, forlorn landscape. Then, like a proverbial oasis, a site half swallowed by the desert appeared. The sand shifted restlessly, wanting to reclaim what had been lost for so many years. The stone had dulled, the sand and sun having eaten away the layers of plaster and paint, but the site was still unbelievably gorgeous. Harshika set me down in the middle of a wide courtyard where columns of limestone towered over our presence. The ghosts of a once-grand people danced in the shadows, hungry for our admiration and worship.

She led me to a section of the wall where an enormous relief of a female form with the head of a vicious lioness had been carved. Below her were the remains of the people on whom she had passed judgment. Pressing against the lower sections on the lion-woman's body, she revealed a hidden door. The stone protested its release, and had to be forced wide enough to allow us entry. She yanked me inside, meeting a hot and impenetrable darkness.

My head smashed against a stone outcropping and I swore a blue streak. There was blood when I drew my hand back. Harshika's giggle did nothing to make me feel better. Slowly my eyes adjusted and I could at least make out shapes and discern changes in height. I followed her though a long series of twisting corridors until the space opened onto a wide room. I heard her fiddling about, then the distinctive sound of a match being lit. Several torches hanging from the wall were lit, the smell acrid.

I looked around me, taking in a bath the size of a small pool, a throne set back in the room on a raised platform, and strange anthropomorphic statues as well as other carvings. It took me several minutes before I realised this was the room from her memory of being bathed by the temple girls. I remembered the room as it was then, alive with colour and aromas and beautiful women. Harshika had been their goddess, basking in their worship and fear. Now everything lay under a soft blanket of sand.

She lounged on her throne now, its beauty weakened by time, relishing the memories of an era long forgotten. She twirled her long, dark hair around her finger, a dreamy expression softening her usually harsh demeanor. With a wave of her hand, her power seized me and I walked toward her. The only thing I saw was Harshika in all her terrible, haunting glory.

I knelt before the throne, as I knew I was expected to, but I could not break my stare from her face. The room spun, shaking, the air around me writhing with a need to absorb me. Hot, urgent demands bombarded my senses, begging me to relent. The longing was terrible, excruciating, but I couldn't decide if it was for blood or sex. In that moment, I would have gladly killed for either.

When I came to my senses, I was cradled in Harshika's arms and her cool lips were pressed to mine. I tasted blood in her kiss, thick and lovely. I lingered for a moment, before realising I was being a passive participant. I turned my head, feeling her mouth slide across my cheek. I struggled, but it was no use. I would be free only when she chose to release me. A bright throbbing in my throat rose above my other sensations and emotions, and I knew without a doubt where the blood had come from.

"What are you doing?" I managed to get out through my tightly clenched teeth. Revulsion stung like bile in the back of my throat.

"Comforting you. I forget sometimes how powerful my influence can be. Lesser immortals have been left mad after contact with me. Or worse." She smiled, and I believed her intent was to be calming, but it had the exact opposite effect. Her hand smoothed my hair, unnerving me.

Her comment was a backhanded compliment if I'd ever

heard one, and did nothing to make me feel any more at ease. "I'm good."

"Perfect. Then come on a voyage with me. I'll show you the splendour of Egypt at the peak of its power. You'll see how the people worshipped me as a god." Her voice dripped honey, sultry and hypnotic. This time my fall back with her into the ocean of her memories came gently. Time swirled around us, pulling us deeper with sweet caresses and an urgent, hungry need to be shared. Then we were there.

Like my first taste of Harshika's life in ancient Egypt, the memory had colour, sound, aromas, and texture. The mistress sat on a gold-leafed bench before a dark wood table, the surface of which was filled with bottles of cosmetics and perfume, hair accessories and jewellery. A strange mirror-like object was mounted on the wall above the table, offering a slightly distorted version of Harshika's beauty. A pair of dark, short-haired cats lounged on a bed covered with silk and furs. One eyed me with cold detachment as I hesitated behind where Harshika sat.

"Come, Rachel," she said in response to my appearance.

"How are you doing this?" I demanded. "This isn't real. I was never here at this time. This is your past."

"You have no idea the things I'm capable of," she said.

She turned about on the bench to face me, and offered her hand. As much as I didn't want to take it, I so wanted to see what only she could show me. I longed to see the art and structures in their perfection, colours bright. I wanted to see the people, their clothing, their homes. I wanted to touch, taste, and hear languages no longer spoken. She knew the lure was too strong for me to refuse. I loathed her for being able to make my wildest dreams a reality.

I slipped my hand into hers and she nodded. As she passed the bed, she ran a hand along the back of the cat closest to her. It responded immediately, rubbing its body against her side and purring loudly. Then we stepped from Harshika's private chamber into the outer space, a room that on some level I knew our physical selves were in, in the present time, but it looked nothing like the faded, gloomy chamber we'd entered. This was a place full of life, splendour, and magic.

"Remember," she reminded me, "I am known as Sekhmet here."

The statues and intricate wall carvings were a glorious mimic of life. Faces stared back from heavily kohled eyes, lips the colour of fresh blood. Gorgeous silks and stretched leather covered all the sitting surfaces and furs were scattered about the stone floor. A multitude of lamps filled the space with hazy, soft light. Incense burned, adding to the mystical atmosphere and permeating the air with its musky scent. The temple girls attended to fires and food, and a trio sat playing instruments I thought were a lyre and a sistrum, the other a more recognisable harp.

I was not dressed in the borrowed clothing of my reality, but in a white, draped garment similar to Harshika's. My arms were bare save for several heavy gold bracelets about my wrists. My hair felt tight, and my neck strained. I raised my hand to touch the coarse wig and heavy headpiece atop it. My sensitive fingers found carved metal, and a sheet of textured fabric that fell down the back of my head and over the artificial tresses disguising my real hair. On my feet were leather sandals and I discovered more gold bands about my ankles.

I smiled despite myself, but I couldn't help it. Excitement coursed through my veins. I wandered about the room, touching everything, overcome with an emotional rapture I couldn't control. The longer I lingered there, the less I cared it was Harshika who shared this experience with me. There was only one word to describe what consumed me: awe.

When I found a table filled with papyrus scrolls, books, and other written documents, I almost fainted with joy. *Can I?* I thought, to which Harshika nodded from her throne across the room. Two very young girls rubbed oils into her hands and feet, an honour they understood to their core.

I sat, trembling with anticipation. My mouth was dry and my skin warm, reminiscent of the false heat a vampire takes on after feeding. I pored over line after line of beautiful, intricate script, diagrams, and maps. Tears of happiness welled in my eyes. I could understand some of what I read, but most was incomprehensible. How I would have loved to take those documents back with me and have them translated and preserved.

A small sound came from my left, and I turned, startled to find an older, severe-looking man standing so near me. A beak-like nose dominated his face and his eyes were black and hostile. He was bald, though a soft shadow showed his hair would have been dark had he not shaved it. He wore an ankle-length dark robe and a large metal collar that hung down in a half circle of gold almost as wide as his substantial shoulders. Under one arm he carried a bundle of new scrolls. He did not seem pleased to see me.

Harshika appeared at his back, leaving the startled temple girls to clean the oil that spilled with the suddenness of her movement. The man stiffened, sensing her there, then lowered to his knees as he turned, scrolls still held tightly under his arm. I remembered from my studies that scribes, as obviously this man was, were highly regarded members of Egyptian society. They were in charge of writing magical texts, issuing royal decrees, keeping and recording the funerary rites, specifically within the Book of the Dead, and keeping records vital to the bureaucracy of ancient Egypt. It was most likely a great taboo for me to have been touching his documents.

I left the table with reluctance and took my place at Harshika's side. The scribe raised his head, meeting her gaze briefly before looking in my direction. He understood I was more than human, but also not of the same caliber of power as "Sekhmet." He did not speak, but remained on his knees until we departed.

We followed the same corridors out, this time lit with burning torches and lined with colourful scenes of war, worship, and daily life. The night was cool, but strong with the aroma of life. In the once-barren courtyard, soldiers and priests, servants and others mingled. I wanted to stay and observe, soak in as much as I could to hang onto once the memory vanished, but Harshika had other plans. She pulled me along with her.

We wandered away from the buildings at the heart of the city's business and religious center toward the humble dwellings of the working class. There the streets were busy and dirty and loud. Laughter and arguments sounded about us, merriment and sorrow. I could still smell the meals recently consumed, and the underlying stench of human waste and sickness. Thriving, vibrant hearts pounded around me, rushing blood like a siren's call to my dark needs.

Harshika showed me everything. I saw homes, schools, farms, and the papyrus reed boats choking the shores of the mighty Nile. Their distinctive square sails flapped in the intermittent breeze. She allowed me access to the most sacred of places—tombs, burial preparation chambers, and even the current pharaoh's home.

The people bowed in fear and reverence as we passed. Some offered gifts of gold and food, others animal sacrifices and even their own blood. Harshika drank it all in like the egomaniac she was. How disappointing it must be for her now, hiding in the shadows, demoted to the realms of fairy tales and myth.

We came full circle, ending in the inner chamber where our supernatural journey had started. The temple girls had fallen asleep and the scribe was gone. The room shimmered as we entered, the hurtling sensation seized me, and sudden, complete blackness erased the ancient beauty I'd been fortunate enough to experience.

This time Harshika sat on the stone floor and I sprawled across her lap. My face was damp with tears and my chest ached with loss. Gently she brushed the hair away from my face, waiting for me to regain my composure.

I pulled myself up to a seated position, pressing my back into the bottom of the short staircase leading to the platform that once held Harshika's ebony and ivory laden throne. My reaction amused her.

"You were here for a long time?" I asked when I could finally speak.

"Hundreds of years. I've come back many times, allowing my identity to mimic the changing religious views. I have inspired many stories and schools of thought."

"Tell me," I said with more enthusiasm than I meant.

"One story from this land speaks of my supposed creation in a time when men conspired against their creator, Ra. After considering the matter, Ra decided to send his Eye in the form of a lioness to chastise the insurgents. Sekhmet, me, wrought havoc and would have devoured all humanity had not Ra, stricken with regret, then had the ground covered with red-dyed beer in place of blood so that Sekhmet, deceived by the colour, drank up the liquid, became drunk and fell asleep, thus sparing mankind. That's why I am often represented as a lioness-headed deity as you have seen for yourself. Silly humans." She ended the story with peals of girlish laughter.

"Another," I begged.

"Well, as the stories were influenced by the passing of time, it was believed I was a dual personality, representing the realms of light and dark. In my light personification I was called Bast, and I reigned over fertility, the protector of children, and all cats. Sekhmet came to be viewed as the goddess of war and pestilence."

"Why cats?"

"I have a natural affinity with them. They are drawn to my power."

"Achyut said this had something to do with the way you were turned, how you became as you are?"

"Yes," she agreed, a hint of anger in her tone. "But we are not getting in to that just yet. And the stories and accounts my existence has inspired do not always involve cats. I have often been blamed for plagues, hauntings, and other atrocities. My effects are often attributed to the interference of Lucifer and other assorted demons. Though in all the thousands of years I have moved across this earth I have witnessed and experienced many strange things, but I have never come across either God or the Devil. In fact, the closest thing to an all-powerful being I have ever known is me."

"I've read so many things since my own change. I have tried to find some kernel of truth, something to lead me to the beginning of our kind. I beg you to tell me before you destroy me."

"I know of your studies, Rachel. You are one of the few who has given more than a passing thought to where we come from. I enjoy that about you. I'm sure you could recite a hundred different names I've been known by over the centuries."

"Kali, Hecate, Luna, Balonda, Coatlicue, Lilitu. You have

been called Lamia, Upir, Ramanga, Mandurugo, Aswang."

"Yes, yes!" She clapped her hands with delight, mirroring my passion.

"What is the truth?" I demanded, grabbing her about the wrists. We were so close I saw her skin was smooth and flawless, dazzling in its perfection. A fervent desperation gripped me, and my need to understand bordered on madness.

"First we must travel to where it all began. Then I can share with you my story. And my shame."

"Your shame?"

"Yes, for this creature I have become was born of shame and lust. And from that cesspool of evil, my human life was destroyed and the dark gift created. My immortal existence was bought with blood, and fuelled with vengeance. I exist because one man would not accept that he could not have everything he desired, and because I refused to die for his callousness and arrogance. He tried to take what was not his, and paid for it not only with his own life, but condemned his own bother and myself to an existence of eternal darkness."

Her anger smothered me. I fought against it, but to no avail. I would finally have my truth, but the cost might be more than I'd bargained for.

CHAPTER 18

Eli. Peru. Fifteen Days in.

We'd been sitting in the darkness without feeding for several days. Only twice had anyone appeared, throwing into the cell several bags of blood before locking us back in the blackness. The air was still and dank. There was no sound except for our movements and voices. Collectively we were a strong group of immortals, with Saskia and Zhongxing being two of the oldest I'd ever met. I knew if I had to, I could control the hunger for at least another few days, but after that the need would be too great. I would lose to the bloodlust and the madness brought on by starvation. My mind seized on the image of Giovanni as we had found him in that concrete box in the Desmarais compound. I knew I didn't have the strength to survive such an ordeal, not even for Micah.

The room that held us felt like a tomb and I prayed it wouldn't become our final resting place. We'd all adjusted to the severity of the blackness within the room, but that did little to assuage the suffocating claustrophobia brought on by the four of us in such a small space. Every inch of the area had been examined and tested for weakness and none could be found. The walls, floor, and ceiling were all solid stone, and the door was steel at least a foot thick. Even the seams where the metal met stone had been prodded and dug at, but our efforts were in vain. We were trapped.

Saskia and Zhongxing spoke little and offered next to nil in the way of mental communication. The odd time their anger or frustration gave an external flare, breathing over Aldous and me like fire, but it was always short-lived. They seemed almost to shut down, but I think it was a coping mechanism and a way to be ready for escape should the chance present itself. Aldous, however, shared much of himself.

Our emotions often collided and mingled, and memories leapt from one to another. I left my mind open, allowing more than I usually did, in a need to have some contact and comfort. I allowed him to see my years as a child, growing up with Rachel and Giovanni. I shared with him my change and the years following Giovanni's supposed death. I did my best to allow him to absorb the heat and joy that came from my thoughts of Micah, which in turn pulled at similar emotions he associated with Emmaline. Any wayward memories of Tatiana that escaped were quickly drawn back and hidden behind locked doors.

Gruesome events and powerful shame from his time in the war lived with particular vividness in Aldous's memory. Those years haunted him still and, in a strange way, softened me toward him. I remembered my jealousy when he had come to Rachel for help at the house in England. Since that moment I'd held myself off from getting to know him, or even considering liking him. In truth, he was a smart guy, solid and powerfully in love with Emmaline. His thoughts of her were fire and roses, so intense his emotions rode through me like a jolt of electricity. For him, if there wasn't Emmaline, there was nothing. It made me realise how desperate and artificial my feelings for Rachel had been, and how genuine the ones for Micah were.

We never talked about what had happened between Micah and Emmaline. We both knew it was nothing that would ever have occurred without Harshika's involvement. We were all friends, and none of us would ever willingly shame or disrespect another as they had been forced to do. The encounter had been seared into my mind and it hurt as much now to think about it as it had to witness it. Aldous was as torn about the incident as I, and we both were livid about our inability to protect our respective loved ones.

Fuck! Fuck! Fuck! Fuck!

I jumped to my feet and paced for about the hundredth time.

I pushed aside everything else around me but my own thoughts. I concentrated on filling my mind with Micah's image. I thought about his shaggy dark hair, the way his eyes crinkled at the corners when he smiled, his crooked front tooth. I recalled in detail the tattoos covering his arms and back, reliving nights I'd traced my finger along every line. I remembered his smell, the tightness in my chest I experienced every time I saw him. I felt his hands on my body and his lips against my throat.

He was my true love, my other half. Why had I denied that to myself for so long? Why had I hurt him time and time again, mooning over Rachel and a love that could never be? Of course, my feelings for Rachel were strong, and my bond to her was unbreakable, but I had never been in her heart as Giovanni was. And even after I knew Micah wanted me and, more importantly, loved me, I had chased after her. I had pushed her to love me in a way we both knew she couldn't. I had betrayed the only father I'd ever known. And I'd hurt Rachel, who had never been anything but loving and protective of me.

Stop! Guilt was not going to help. I needed to stay focused, strong. We needed to get out of this place. Harshika must be stopped. Jesus Christ, a year was not enough time with Micah.

A sudden sound outside of the door interrupted my thoughts. Silence filled the room for a few seconds before my fellow captives rose to their feet. My body tensed in anticipation. *Good luck*, Aldous said inside my mind.

The door pulled open and a slight figure stood in the doorway, illuminated by a lantern held in one hand. I recognised the scent and commanding presence even before I saw the person's features.

Achyut.

Giovanni. San Francisco. Seventeen days in.

I saw a woman with long red hair walking with a confident stride through a busy downtown street. She had a strong aura about her, full of *joie de vivre* and a healthy sexuality. Her presence spurred me, taunted me. I wanted her blood.

I fell in step beside her and she turned to see whose

attention she had attracted this time. She was used to strange men approaching her and she was armed with a stinging rebuttal that never passed her lips. She was stunning, but there was a hardness to her that ate away at the facade of her beauty. And she was strong. It took a few minutes before I fully captured her mind. Even then she struggled mentally, trying to pull away from my influence. Rachel had been like that in the beginning, but she also had an ingrained gentleness always at odds with her darker desires.

Rachel. The fact Rachel had been taken from me clawed a ragged, seeping wound within my chest, filling me with an ever-present and inescapable agony. The pain of our separation shattered and danced about inside me, turning everything it touched black. Endless pangs of worry and fear surged through my blood, intensified by my hunger for her and my frustration with being unable to keep her safe. Harshika had better not harm one hair on her head. My body tensed with rage and I had to force the thoughts away.

I returned my attention to the stranger at my side, still walking with me, her internal fight growing less with each step we took. If I were to remain strong for Rachel I needed to feed regularly. I led the woman to my car parked a few blocks away and drove us to a secluded area. Her blood was sweet on my tongue, its substance burning fire through my veins, and I did feel stronger, more focused. I left her alive, but just barely. It had been difficult to stop, but I did. Many of us fed in the area and would for the next few weeks. It was best to keep the unexplained deaths to a minimum.

I left her on the side of the road with a false memory of drinks with a strange man, a false name, and casual sex. She would be confused when she woke and most likely embarrassed and angry with herself for acting so foolishly.

Two unfamiliar cars were parked in the driveway when I pulled up in front of the house. They must have been allowed through, as security was tight and the house full of immortals on high alert for anything suspicious. I reached out with my mind and touched a wall of coldness and death. There were already a few new immortals inside. I also became aware of a third warm-blooded body in addition to Danica and Genevieve's familiar qualities. Each human gave a slightly different sensation, one that became ingrained with repeated exposure. Without knowing it, each person emitted waves of personality and affection—strong, sick, soft, enticing. After a moment I realised I had touched this third presence before. Her energy was bright and joyful, impossible to ignore.

I punched in my code and the door opened. I relocked it and followed the intermingling of human and immortal auras to the back room, which had become our unofficial meeting place. Several of the dining room chairs had been brought in, and three unfamiliar immortals and one old ally occupied them.

Jeremiah, a Native American man who'd been changed in his early thirties, raised his hand in salute when I entered the room. For some inexplicable reason his presence filled me with hope. He might not be one of the oldest or strongest of the vampires known to us, but he was a formidable presence, smart and cunning, a lot like Charles in that regard. He could think on his feet and would rather die than show a lack of bravery. I'd learned before he left England after my rescue that his original Algonquin name had been Makkapitew, which meant "he has large teeth." Fate had a twisted sense of humour sometimes.

The other three sat clustered together, one man and two women. The man was of average height and solidly built, giving me the impression he'd done some kind of heavy, manual labour in is human life. His kept his brown hair closely cropped and his large hands were clasped on his lap. He wore dark jeans and a button-up shirt, easily passing as a regular guy, but to my sensitive faculties he hummed with power and desire. He gave me his attention and the power flashed, making me feel as though I'd been dipped in boiling water. He withdrew, but the sting of his touch lingered.

I stuck my hand out. "Hello. I'm Giovanni."

He stood and took my hand with an iron grip, just as I'd expected. "David."

"Nice to meet you."

"And this is Lucy and Solange." He indicated the two females.

They both rose and shook my hand. I sensed immediately neither woman had been turned by David. Lucy was younger, her mind told me she'd only been a vampire for about fifty years. She had a lovely full face with chin-length blond hair and pale blue eyes. She wore her nervousness like a scarlet letter, and was not confident in her ability to assist us.

Solange was far older than Lucy by at least a few centuries. She held her origins close to her heart, only making me privy to the longevity of her immortal condition. Thick ebony hair fell to her waist and her eyes flashed like chips of onyx. Her figure was full and voluptuous, her ample chest all but spilling out of her low-cut blouse. Raw, unbridled sexuality oozed from every pore. This was a powerful weapon for her and one she used to her full advantage. Her gift seeped forth, warming over me and tingling my body in a way I wasn't receptive to.

She smiled in my direction, fully aware of the effect she had. "A great pleasure to meet you, Giovanni. I heard much about you and your companions from Tatiana, before her untimely demise, that is." Then she chuckled, and it wasn't a happy sound.

Charles came to stand beside me. "And you considered Tatiana a friend of yours?"

Solange laughed again and, this time, it had a note of real humour. "God, of course not. Who was actually friends with that wretched creature? I tolerated her, because sometimes she could be useful, but she was also a lunatic."

Out of the corner of my eye I took in Emmaline's reaction. She clenched her fists and there was a slight tremble to her lithe frame. The night of Tatiana's attack jumped into her thoughts, poking at the raw wound of Aldous's absence. I understood her pain, which ran as deep as my own.

"Well, we're pleased and thankful to have you here. Has everyone been introduced?" I looked about the room.

There was a murmur of agreement. I noticed Clellia sat beside Alessandra, and Daniel was on the opposite side of the room with Micah and Kieran. I didn't comment, but Alessandra gave me a look that said everything.

"We have information to share," David said after he reclaimed his chair.

"Please," I said.

"Yes, we stayed in Peru for a few days after the summoning. We watched the site where we met and spoke with several other immortals who had returned to the city. Harshika left Peru the next night with Rachel. Achyut also left, but apparently on his own and to a different location. The ones who pledged themselves to Harshika's service were split up into small groups who then departed in several directions. Essentially, they have been turned into her goon squad. They are contacting immortals, pressing them to join her. There have been several skirmishes already and a few deaths."

"It's as we suspected," Charles said, his voice cold but thoughtful.

"I wouldn't be surprised if someone came calling at this house. It would be quite a scoop to acquire the group here," I said.

"Agreed," Solange said.

"Can I ask who the humans in the kitchen are? The ones we are all so aware of, yet are acting as if they aren't here?" David asked.

Charles tensed. "My partner, Genevieve, Rachel's niece, Danica, and a mutual friend named Mary-Jane."

"And you live in close proximity with humans like this on a regular basis?" He couldn't keep the skepticism out of his voice.

"Like I said, Genevieve is my partner, so yes I am in close proximity with her. Every night." His tone implied he didn't enjoy this line of questioning.

"We see Danica and Mary-Jane often, as well as other human friends and associates."

"And you're never tempted to feed from them?" asked Solange.

"It's always tempting when humans are around," I answered. "But to those we've befriended, we never cross the line, not even for a small taste. This is a choice we've made."

"And how do you make the distinction between those you feed from and those you have relationships with?" David pushed. The word *relationship* came out of his mouth with a sneer as though the very idea of it left a bitter taste.

"I don't know that I could explain it to your satisfaction. It's something you simply feel."

"I see," he said, though his tone suggested otherwise.

As I was about to attempt some clarification, David's expression changed, became tighter, almost pained. The women also expressed some discomfort. Lucy pressed her lips together and her eyes drooped shut. Solange shifted in her seat.

A cold, spidery presence crawled into the room. It slithered along my spine, licking its icy tongue over each vertebra, slinking closer to my skull where I knew it would bore into my brain. Everyone in the room displayed effects to varying degrees, with Micah and Lucy taking the hardest blow. My body tensed, shaking as though trying to ward off the phantom attacker. I drew on every ounce of my unnatural strength to keep the presence at bay.

"Harshika is listening," Charles said.

"Yes," I answered as the stinging, freezing numbness travelled through my arms and legs. "Pull together everyone!"

There was a collective surge of energy—hard and urgent and angry. For a moment Harshika's force dissipated and it was like being slapped with a hot rush of desert air. Then she lashed out and my mind exploded in a shower of agony and blackness. I fell to my knees, dimly aware of others crying out. I imagined a dropping bomb, forcing my own internal power to mimic the course of its surging destruction, pushing out in waves against Harshika's intrusion. Our energies collided. I recoiled, the impact plowing through my body, taking my consciousness with it.

Rachel!

CHAPTER 19

Rachel. Southern Pakistan. Eighteen days in.

Harshika moved us from place to place, across borders, oceans, and time. She exposed me and forced me to relive many different eras of her life, witnessing things I'd have never imagined. Though I learned much about her through these experiences, I didn't come any closer to the truth of her miraculous transformation. She kept insisting she would only share that particular story on her terms, and only when she finally brought us to the homeland of her human existence.

Now we were here. I knew from previous conversations she came from what the world now referred to as the Indus Valley Civilisation. I had vague recollections of reading about this place during my many nights of research, and knew it had flourished in a time when Egypt and Mesopotamia ruled as the most advanced urban cultures on earth. I knew geographically it had been located on the Indian subcontinent and centered on the Indus River basin. In recent years, majestic structures and domestic and religious artifacts had been uncovered, but for the academics there were still more questions than answers. It was a people and time locked in mystery, all but forgotten to the modern world.

In all the time we had been together, Achyut had not reappeared. I knew she spoke with him almost nightly, as I often overheard their conversations, but I never knew the content. All communication took place in their secret language and Harshika was too smart to slip up and give away anything with her emotions or mind. I remained completely at her mercy. She controlled where we went, how I dressed, when I fed. And when the time came, she would make the ultimate decision: whether I would live or be destroyed.

We travelled into Pakistan via India, where we had examined in-depth the effect of her existence on the culture and religious beliefs of the inhabitants. We found the worship of Kali still strong, her image adorning temples and other sites all about the country. We stopped at several shrines dedicated to her worship, and observed the reverence with which her honour was attended. If the people could only understand how even more monstrous the real Kali was.

We made our way to the ancient site of Mohenjo-daro, now a Unesco World Heritage Site. It had been partially excavated, and every attempt had been made to preserve the site and the treasures held within. What had been exposed showed a marvel of the ancient world, a perfectly planned city with streets laid out in a grid-like fashion, and buildings constructed of sun-dried bricks of mud and burnt wood. Its public buildings included a granary, great hall, public bath, marketplace, temples for worship, and defensive towers. There were fertile lands for farming, and access to the nearby Indian Ocean established it as an important place for trading.

As we stole over the deserted landscape, Harshika shared with me the amazing scientific and industrial advances her people had made, centuries ahead of other communities around them. They had irrigation, sanitation systems, extensive linguistic and measuring systems, and buildings with underground heating. A proud and capable people they'd been, with lives dedicated to family, societal well-being, and spiritual fulfillment.

Without warning the settlement appeared. An abrupt change in Harshika's demeanour came over her, which I experienced like a slap to the face. Her steady, heavy-handed control over me dipped, her usual cold assuredness replaced with unease. I'd been travelling with her, swallowed in her power and unable to act of my own accord for so long the sudden change was disorienting. Her domination was absolute, smothering all other intrusions and sensations. Like an invisible but undeniable force, she had me blanketed, cornered, unable to rely on my own feelings and abilities.

Though the few infusions of her blood had increased my strength and speed, allowing me to keep up with her instead of being dragged along behind like a bag of garbage, it had also given her a more intimate knowledge of my inner musings and control of my body. She had imprinted herself on me and drawn me into her depraved mind. I absorbed her contempt and hatred, ever charging through my veins and hardening my heart. I'd always known my nature was dark, evil even, but I'd never felt so black before. Even after my change I'd been capable of love, compassion, empathy. Her vileness slowly stole that away from me, and I loathed her for it. Yet some part of me felt a burgeoning acceptance.

With her psychic shields lowered by her distress at being at Mohenjo-daro again, I seized the opportunity to push to the forefront the horrific images of the assaults on Micah and Emmaline, as well as Donovan's death. That seemed to further dilute any connection or inappropriate affection I felt for her and, for the first time in many days, my mind cleared. I used all my power, now greatly amplified by Harshika's blood, and reached out to Giovanni.

"Giovanni. Help me, help me. We're in Pakis—"

Then she had me again. She'd regained her composure, her volcanic anger firmly back in place. She struck me with a granite fist and I crumpled to the ground. Her dark eyes blazed, her madness unleashed. I cowered at her feet, begging her not to destroy me. A familiar tingle attempted to connect with me, but was wiped away with Harshika's fury.

"Remember, one word from me and Achyut will destroy your precious Giovanni and all your other so-called friends. Don't try that again."

"I'm sorry, mistress," I croaked, my throat tight with fear.

The cold, controlled persona returned. One strong hand hauled me to my feet and with the other she pointed to a remote area just within my field of vision. Anticipation, like an electric current, travelled from her body to mine. My blood coursed through my veins, rich with ancient memories and secrets.

"So, this is where it happened. Or where it began, I should say." Her voice was quiet, wistful.

The tingling began, first at the base of my skull, surging along my spine and out to my extremities. My fingers became ice, much colder than my natural state, stiff and awkward. Then I slipped inside her memory, spiralling and careening through countless centuries, back to a time as foreign as a distant planet. It was a vacuum of sound and sight. There existed nothing but touch, a spinning sensation. Time nipped at me, pulled, caressed, twisted me through the dark, frozen void.

At some level I knew we had physically gone nowhere, that the feelings evoked by this mental excursion were nothing more than tricks against my faculties. It was difficult making sense of what Harshika was doing to me. There was a dim burning, a tearing like a slow bleed in my brain that seemed to amplify with each experience. No matter what the outcome, my time with the mistress would leave a permanent imprint on my existence thereafter. Of that I was certain.

"Here's where I was born." She indicated a humble single-floor residence in a rural area outside of the city. At first there appeared only darkness, but as the words escaped her lips, the structure took shape before my eyes. I smelled cattle, damp earth, and smoke.

"My family raised cows and goats. I helped my father and brothers grow barley and millet. Other farms grew peas, wheat, or cotton."

I could now clearly make out the enclosures for the animals and smelled the manure and feed. The air was heavy with aromas, both sweet and pungent. I scanned about me, taking in the fields beyond the house and, farther away still, the creeping jungle. We were in a valley with rolling hills, dense with trees and other plant life. I closed my eyes and concentrated, barely picking up the sound of a nearby body of water.

"Come inside." She ducked into the brick house.

I followed. Inside, the main room served as kitchen, dining, and family space. There were several sectioned-off spaces at the rear that led to bedrooms. The bathing and toilet area was outside in a separate building. We looked in at sleeping forms—Harshika's parents and several children at various stages of development. One room held five children, all cramped together on grass-filled mattresses on the floor. If the sight of her family affected her, she made no indication. Instead she turned and pulled me outside again.

We raced along the hard-packed dirt road, following the path as it twisted by other farms and homes until we were at the mouth of the eastern entrance to the city. A large tower rose before us, a formidable presence in the dark and silent night. We passed by like thieves, our movements too quick to track and too quiet to be detected by human ears. We travelled a series of narrow streets, running straight and parallel through the surprisingly large settlement. Harshika pointed out places of interest such as the citadel, the granary, the public bath, and assembly halls.

She showed me the structure that held the town officials and religious leaders. The outsides of the buildings were covered with a beautiful and mysterious script and murals full of strange beings and animals as vivid as life. There were the grand homes of the artisans and traders, and the humbler homes of the working class—the butchers, builders, fishermen, and the cotton spinners. The courtyards bore the signs of personal touches, painted furniture, plants, and even children's toys. A repeated theme appeared in much of the art—a round, womanly figure Harshika explained was the mother goddess the town's people worshipped, to be looked upon for fertility in both human life and crops.

Then she led me to a large, multi-story building with a gated entrance. The stone wall was at least two stories high with a series of life-sized engravings surrounding the entire structure. A difference to the quality of the air presented itself here, a tension and urgency that pressed along my body. Harshika took my hand.

"This is where I worked. My parents gave me to the priests as a young girl, and I was trained to serve the king's family. I learned to prepare food, to dance and sing, the proper way to dress, how to style a woman's hair and makeup. It was a great honour, you see, to be picked to serve the royal family. It meant there would always be food for your family and protection, and an honoured place in the afterworld." She smirked at the last part of her speech, the irony not lost on her.

"It's beautiful. Amazing that a culture this advanced and organised existed at this time, and how sad that it ended and its wonder lost for so long."

Harshika wasn't listening to me. She stared at the wall, tracing the lines of a male figure's face with her hand. An assault of images careened through her mind, slipping to me in angry bursts, but making no sense at all. The flashes of faces and locations I understood, but the words accompanying them were foreign. It happened more and more as we progressed through this specific time in Harshika's life, as though she fell back into old habits. When she mentioned things such as the royal family and king, there were other words associated with these items in the background, as if explaining to me in relatable terms.

Narsimha.

The name sprang out of her thoughts, urgent and harsh. His name screamed angry red and bitter violence. Her reaction exploded in my chest and her hatred boiled in my blood. An image of his face appeared—strong, handsome, and arrogant. I realised the figure she had been touching on the wall was a representation of him and that from his dress, I could deduce he was a member of nobility, perhaps even the king. Understanding rushed to me and the pieces began to fall into place. This had been the man who had made advances on Harshika as she performed her servant duties in the great hall, the one she had run from crying into the jungle.

"Yes," Harshika confirmed. "Narsimha is the reason for all of this. He was a selfish and cruel man. Not at all like his brother."

"His brother?" I asked.

"Yes, his brother, my friend, the only one who cared and tried to protect me. But that will come. I must tell this story the proper way. Come." She waved me over to the wall.

We scaled the walls easily, falling to the soft grass below. Guards were at the gate entrance and walking the perimeter of the building, at least in this memory-state there were, but we slipped past them with ease. Harshika led us to a deserted servants' door, and after eliminating the lock, pulled us into a dark storage area. It was cool, and as my eyes adjusted, I took in the bags of grain and stores of food. Barrels of wine and other liquids lined an entire wall. Like phantoms we passed through to a door on the other end of the space.

This one opened onto a dim, narrow hallway. The smells of the last meal lingered and the space suffocated with unrelenting heat. She led me along, the diligent tour guide who pointed out everything that might be of interest. We moved through room after room, too quickly to really absorb the uniqueness and proud beauty, but enough to make me wish I would have more time there.

In one dank hallway, off the building's main food preparation area, was where Harshika and several other servants had their sleeping areas. The small room held two beds and a small wooden box to keep clothing and personal effects. There was barely enough space to fit the three items in the small space. Harshika made a strange noise beside me, quiet but audible to my ears, and it took me a moment to understand what had prompted the response. On the bed closest to the door, lost in the shadow of sleep, was Harshika as she had been in her human days. She closed the door again.

"He would come here sometimes," she said, and she didn't need to clarify who "he" was. "Usually drunk, always cold and vulgar, he forced me to do awful things, though until *that* night I was able to save myself from complete humiliation." A flash of blood and the looming jungle, a bone-chilling scream heard only in my mind made me stumble. The second-hand memories overwhelmed and confused me.

She turned and yanked me off in another direction. Pointing out the majestic baths, the private worship areas, and the royal family's personal rooms intensified her anger. "This was his room," she whispered as she stopped outside an oversized wooden door. I thought she would enter, but instead she retraced her steps.

Then we turned into a new hallway, one we hadn't yet travelled, and by far the most opulent of any we'd seen. The ceiling stretched to the skies above our heads and a hundred people could have comfortably filled the space. Gorgeous scenes of the royal family and interpretations of their divine origin adorned the towering walls. There were accents of gold and jewels, and beautiful handmade tiles covered the floor. Not a speck of dirt could be seen, not a thing was out of place.

At the end of the space loomed giant hand-carved doors inlaid with gold. The handles alone were bigger than my arm. Harshika's body stiffened and, for a split second, the vision she had me trapped in faded. The experience was similar to a television channel that was momentarily eaten by static. The ground beneath my feet quivered and the air about me chilled. That strange, soft prickling began at the base of my skull then my *unreality* snapped back into place.

"I can take you no farther like this," she said in a distant, icy voice. "Neither one of us can remain in this time, not in the conditions I have created. There can be no Rachel here, nor immortal Harshika. As this unfolds, we can only watch and hear. There will be no interaction or influence. This is not our place to participate."

I was about to ask what she meant when faster than the blink of an eye, everything changed. I became a disembodied spirit hovering in the cold darkness. Though I could not touch or call out, I knew I was not alone. The mistress stayed with me, watching as her own mortal life ended and a vampire came into being. I heard her strained words and watched with my mind's eye as the terrible events unfolded.

Harshika. Mohenjo-daro.

A large delegation would soon arrive, and every servant in the house was overworked. The cooks had been preparing for days, the musicians and dancers practicing nonstop. Every inch of the house and grounds had been cleaned, repaired, and decorated. My hands were raw and my body ached with an exhaustion I'd never felt before.

Leaders from distant lands and important merchants came to feast with the king and his family, and nothing short of perfection would be acceptable. It was a chance for the royal family to impress their subjects and allies alike, and also a time to formally introduce the new king before his wedding. Narsimha had recently taken over after the death of his father, and he needed to show he was just as capable and fit as his predecessor. He was glorious, handsome, twenty-six years old, and eager for power.

I was twenty years old by that time, having been in servitude to the family since about the age of thirteen. As I'd matured, I'd grown into quite a lovely young woman with a lithe yet strong body and thick, glossy hair. I'd caught lustful stares from many of the men with business in that house and felt the sting of jealousy from the other female servants. If I'd been of higher birth I would have been trained as an official dancer, expected to perform for religious ceremonies and other celebrations. As it turned out, my lot in life consisted of menial chores and manual labour. The only bright spot in all of it was that I helped the noble ladies of the house bathe and dress. There I handled the beautiful materials of their clothing and smelled the perfumes. I touched jewels as dazzling as the sun in the sky.

That night, even the servant girls were dressed in new outfits, and were instructed to bathe with expensive oils and prepare our hair. I felt so beautiful. And because of one man my appearance would change the course of history.

I spent hours arranging tables and chairs, filling rooms with freshly cut flowers. I passed Narsimha many times that day, and with each encounter his gaze grew hungrier. I knew he wanted me. He'd been forcing himself on me for many years, preying on both my physical weakness and my duty to serve his family. I prayed every night he'd tire of me, and though he might turn his interests to other places, he always came back to me.

No one knew about this except for Narsimha, me, and Achyut, for Achyut was Narsimha's younger brother, you see, and my only friend. Narsimha bullied Achyut as much as he forced himself upon me, and we commiserated in our shame. He had tended me one evening after a particularly brutal episode. He cleaned me up and held me as I cried. He talked to me and, best of all, he listened to what I had to say. We met as often as possible, usually at night on the grounds, or we'd wander to the outskirts of town, even the jungle. He never touched me or disrespected me in any way. He treated me as his equal, even teaching me to read. I knew he loved me and wanted me as his wife, and that love made my life tolerable.

Achyut possessed a kindness Narsimha could never understand, and his intelligence far exceeded that of his vain and impulsive brother. But his place was firmly second, and his youth and frailty kept him at a distinct disadvantage. He looked at things in ways no one else did. He would have been a wonderful ruler, but that was not meant to be.

That night Achyut came to me when I worked and pressed something wrapped in cloth into my palm. "Wear this tonight," he said, and left before I had a chance to answer. I let the cloth slip open, revealing a gorgeous figurine on a fine metal chain. It was too lovely for a servant girl to have, but I didn't want to hurt him by not wearing it. So, when the time came to dress, I proudly put it on, and found myself unconsciously fingering it throughout the evening.

The people came in hordes, filling the house to a capacity that verged on uncomfortable, requiring the servants to be on constant alert for furniture to be moved and guests to be accommodated. We had to make sure no one was without food and drink, or entertainment. We showed them to the privies and private areas for the men and woman to have their hair and face paint retouched. It was chaotic, yet magical. Achyut caught my gaze many times, and made goofy faces at me or simply smiled. Narsimha also watched me, but his gaze made me feel dirty and afraid.

One time as I cleared his table, he grabbed me about my wrist and pulled me to him. His breath reeked of alcohol as he pressed his mouth against my ear. "Tonight I will come for you, and when I'm done you'll be lucky if you can walk back to your room. I will have whatever I want. You will serve your king."

His words made my dinner churn in my stomach, and terror pounded in furious tempo through my blood. A cold sweat broke out on my skin, dampening my clothes. The vileness of his touch lingered. That encounter triggered a flood of past indignities. I remembered every word, every forced kiss, every tearful, humiliating encounter with such vividness I had to bite my lip to keep from screaming. I pulled my arm away and left as quickly as I could without drawing attention from the guests. Of course, Achyut had seen what happened.

I ran to the kitchen and out the back of the palace. I ran down the passage leading to the city and beyond. I ran until my lungs screamed in protest, but I didn't stop until I reached the jungle. There I collapsed and was violently sick. I howled with anger as tears burned and streamed down my face.

Then I heard footsteps. I turned to flee farther into the jungle when a familiar male called out. "Harshika. It's Achyut. I know you're here somewhere."

I called to him and he appeared, scooping me into his arms. He dried my tears and rocked me until my breathing returned to normal. His warm hands stroked my hair. Over and over he whispered how beautiful I was and how he would do everything he could to protect me.

Eventually, when I was calm, he said, "I want to marry you. Tomorrow I will go to my mother and talk with her and, if she will not consent, then I will run away with you."

His words stunned me. I knew he was serious; I could tell by the look in his eyes and the fierceness in his voice. His love warmed me, but it was not something I could return. I cared for Achyut deeply, but I did not love him. But I knew he would look after me, and there was no better option for a woman in my situation.

"Yes, I'll marry you," I said. Then, for the first time in all our years of friendship, he kissed me. It was soft and gentle, everything his brother's wasn't. There was no anger, no force, no choking tongues and he did not push for anything more.

We stayed in the jungle for many hours, waiting until enough time had passed so those who would be leaving left, and those staying would have retired to bed. We stole back into the place grounds, sealing our plans with a final kiss before parting ways.

Then the life I should have had was stolen from me.

Narsimha and a small group of guards came from around

the side of the building almost as though they waited for us. The sneer on Narsimha's face pulled bile into the back of my throat. Fear shook me from head to toe. I looked at Achyut for reassurance, but found only uncertainty.

"What exactly is going on here, little brother?" the king demanded as he reached us. Two guards grabbed my arms and I cried out.

"Stop that! You're hurting her," Achyut said.

"She's a servant. Property. I can treat her any way I please."

The men were all drunk and spurred on by the king's volatility and lust. Without warning he struck me across the face and, had it not been for the men holding onto my arms, I would have crumpled to the ground. Achyut lunged at his brother, a sudden and surprising move, managing to get in one good punch to the side of his brother's face before some of the other guards seized him.

Narsimha rubbed his jaw when he instructed the men to take us inside. The guards forced us into one of the underground storage areas where no one would hear our screams or interrupt what was about to happen. Dumped to the ground, I could do nothing but watch as Achyut was dragged screaming from the room. A vicious struggle ensued and it was several minutes before the men who'd removed Achyut returned. One of the guards had blood on his hands, which he callously wiped on the edge of his garment.

With deliberate care Narsimha removed his clothing and jewels, laying them over a pile of grain sacks until he wore nothing but a loincloth. His excitement was prominent through the thin material. He motioned to one of the men, who pulled a small knife from the folds of his clothing. The man bent over my body, ripping my new dress until I lay naked on the dirt floor. He'd cut me in his hurry to please the king, and the wounds stung and burned. I tried to cover myself, but there were hands at my wrists and ankles, holding me down.

I screamed and spat, and as Narsimha's face closed in on mine, I jerked my head forward and bit his bottom lip. He shrieked and pulled back. One of the guards smashed my head back down with enough force my consciousness dimmed, and a pale whining started in one ear. The back of my head was wet and throbbed. Before I could clear my thoughts, Narsimha's hand smashed into my face. My nose cracked and my lip split open in a sudden gush of blood. My mouth filled with warm liquid, and I coughed as it spilled down my airway.

The room swam in and out of focus. The men laughed and called me disgusting names, egging the king's anger to vicious levels. As shock claimed me, the assault dimmed, but did not entirely disappear. I felt his teeth on my breasts and his nails raking across my face. I hovered there, powerless to stop the physical trauma, and yet as mentally aware as I have ever been. Hatred and wrath oozed from my pores, and promises of retribution escaped with each tear.

When Narsimha finished with me, he ordered the men to have their own turns. They kicked, punched, cut, even burned me with their torches, and as my body succumbed to injury after unspeakable injury, my spirit raged. Each strike against my body seared my fury deeper into my heart and imprinted the image of my attackers on my soul. When the violation stopped, I lay broken and bleeding on the floor. Narsimha's sneering face loomed large in the ocean of my pain. He was the cause of all of it, and my vengeance focused on him.

There was a sudden flurry of activity, above and away from where I lay, but I was too far gone to make sense of it. Men yelled, nonsensical, angry words, and the pain became unbearable.

I succumbed to the blackness.

CHAPTER 20

Eli. Peru. Fifteen Days in.

The four of us charged Achyut without a moment's hesitation. Zhongxing had his hands around the smaller man's neck before an upsurge of power slammed us back into the cell. My shoulder smashed into the stone and a loud snap told me something had broken. I didn't have time to think about the pain and I was on my feet again in a split second. No matter the severity of injury, I wouldn't have given up.

This time the connection felt like running into a slab of concrete. The cold power prevented us from reaching Achyut and vibrated with a gentle hum. Achyut stood still, hand raised with palm forward. Eyes as black and hard as death regarded us from his position of authority, but he did not seem pleased about his ability to control, unlike his mistress. This was an act of self-preservation, not malice.

"Wait," he began. "I am not here to hurt you. I only wish the chance to speak with you." His whispery voice crawled along the room, drawing an itchy shudder of revulsion from me.

"About what?" asked Saskia.

"Harshika. And your freedom."

As I watched, his stance softened. Slowly he lowered his hand and, with it, the force blocking our way vanished. He stood before us unprotected, and this action caused us all to pause. *Is this a trick?*

"I assure you it is not, Eli," he answered my unspoken question. "I, too, have reservations about Harshika becoming the dictator to all of our kind. She is twisted and hateful, and powerful beyond your imagination. If anyone can help you stop her, it's me."

I couldn't have been more surprised if he'd announced he was there selling Avon. He seemed the perfect lackey to Harshika's plans—quiet, cold, obedient. I tried to imagine passing night after night as someone's punching bag and servant. The rage and animosity he would have developed drew another shudder from me. He acknowledged my reaction with a slow, deliberate nod.

"Why should we believe you? After what happened at the meeting. You stood by and did nothing. You let her kill and hurt your own kind. You did nothing to stop her tearing our loved ones away from us. You yourself locked us away in this filthy hole!" Zhongxing bellowed, and I couldn't help but wince at the force of his outburst. His wrath swooped forward, sizzling along my arm. A bright light from the power he exerted flashed in the small space, impressing and humbling me.

Achyut did not attempt to retaliate, though the power must have snapped at him like a strike of lightning. Aldous was at my back, tense and uncertain. Saskia's eyes were bright and moving furiously about the space. Our captor stepped farther into the room as though we had welcomed him with open arms instead of an attempted ambush. Up close I saw how delicate he was and, for the first time, noticed a thin band of scarring about the base of his throat where the neck of his garment gaped. He caught me staring and touched the band of raised flesh with a sad smile.

"I come to you as an ally. Harshika has ruled over me and over all of us in one capacity or another for more than four thousand years and I, for one, have had enough of her cruelty and madness. She has gained her retribution many times over, long past the point that anyone but she and I know the origin of her vendetta. Oceans of blood have been spilt for the crimes against her. There is no need for any more of this."

"You would betray her?" I asked.

"Yes," he answered. "Gladly."

Then he opened his mind and shared the terrible events that had turned a humble servant girl into the vicious, heartless,

undead creature she was today. What had been done to her was
unbelievably cruel and depraved, as low an atrocity as any man
had brought against his own kind.

Achyut's role in all of this became clear. His only crimes
were those all humans are guilty of at one time or another—
love and fear.

Giovanni. San Francisco. Twenty Days in.

"Rachel!" Her name tore its way out of my throat as I crashed
into wakefulness. I'd dreamt of finding her in a strange geo-
metric stone city. Her screaming became a siren, begging for
me to save her, and I'd raced after the sound of her voice with
all the speed I could muster. At last I'd seen the fire of her hair
disappearing around the corner of a crumbling building. I followed and, as my finger brushed the ends of her flowing tresses,
Harshika appeared. She dropped from above, swooping in like
an angel of death.

She grabbed my love about the throat with one tiny hand
and, with the other, emitted a burst of power that stopped my
advances dead. I could do nothing but watch as Rachel struggled and writhed, unable to offer the smallest defense against
the mistress' power. Grinning madly, Harshika squeezed until
there was nothing left of her neck, and Rachel's head fell with a
splash of crimson from her body. It rolled toward me, sightless
eyes fixed and dull. *You said you'd always protect me,* her ghost
accused me.

Harshika's maniacal laughter roared in the background.

It took several minutes to shake off the horrible feeling
invoked by Rachel's imaginary decapitation. The possibility of
her destruction lurked long after the dream ended, blackening
my heart and inciting a reckless need for revenge. *Calm down,
it's only a dream.*

I closed my eyes and reached out. At first, I touched only
blackness, then a jumble of immortal musings from the inhabitants of the San Francisco house swam by. I used my mind's eye
to push them aside, surging past the chaos of human thoughts
and desires, focusing on finding the one mind to which I was
eternally bound. A murmur of familiarity rose above the other

voices then a surge of recognition. For a few brief seconds we met in that psychic wasteland where nothing and everything is real. Our consciousnesses touched and melded, her presence drawing warmth into the hardness of my overburdened heart. Then she was gone. Harshika's cold madness sent me reeling. I was alone.

I dressed and left my room. Alessandra, Mengmei, and Charles waited for me in the hallway and, for a moment, the sight of them together filled me with dread. I stepped in beside them and Charles indicated we should head to Genevieve's makeshift laboratory. For the first time in many nights she was nowhere to be seen.

"She's sleeping," Charles answered my enquiry with regard to Genevieve's whereabouts. "She's been working 'round the clock the past few weeks, trying to find a way to help us. She finally had a breakthrough."

"What is it?" I asked.

"Remember she worked for many years for the Desmarais, studying the unique qualities of vampiric blood?" I nodded. "That's why she sent for her files from England. That effect of the dart on Kieran sparked something, and she wondered if there was some way to combine the make-up of the dart's poison with her research."

"And she's found a way?" I asked.

"Yes. After identifying all the components of the poison, and working through several attempts to recreate the formula, she applied this to the chemical make-up of immortal blood. She's tested various strengths and processes for administration on Mengmei and Alessandra, as they are the oldest here, and thus have the strongest blood. After finding a formula that was able to incapacitate these two for several minutes, she increased the potency by ten. We hope if we can get Harshika down for even a few seconds then we might have a chance to destroy her."

I studied Charles's face, but he gave nothing away. Though his words were positive, I knew there was more to the scenario. "What aren't you telling me?" I asked.

"Well, in addition to the whole problem with Harshika possibly being able to read any of our minds, which could end the element of surprise, the poison needs to be administered close to the heart," he said.

"Why? Our hearts don't beat."

"Well, it's true they don't perform like a human's does, but there is some activity still. Genevieve discovered that even as vampires the heart is still responsible for circulating the blood we consume. Its activity is almost undetectable, but there nonetheless. After we ingest it, the blood is absorbed into our blood vessels and our hearts force it throughout the rest of the body. Unfortunately, the blood always dies, which is why we need to continue feeding. The older we are the longer it survives in our bodies, and the less often we need to replenish it."

"So, we need to be right beside her for this to work."

"Yes, and therein lies the problem. We know we have strong numbers on our side, but we cannot be certain how many are with Harshika, and how many are simply not aligning themselves either way. We go into this with many unknowns. There is going to be a fight, and some of us will surely die, but if we can take her down in the midst of it, then any sacrifice is worth it."

"Any sacrifice?" I asked, remembering my dream with panic-inducing clarity.

"Yes," Charles answered. His voice held conviction, yet it didn't completely mask the hint of worry.

Hadn't we sacrificed enough already? Several comrades were already destroyed, including our ally and friend, Donovan. Several more of our friends were being held captive, subjected to who knew what, and Rachel was in the clutches of the most vicious and remorseless creatures to have ever existed.

On the positive side, our numbers had risen dramatically. We had nineteen immortals in the house with us, eight at Micah's house, and twenty-five more in nearby hotels. Each day more turned up to join us. A few I had met in other circumstances in my wanderings before Rachel. With some I had even spent brief periods of time. Others I had never seen before they arrived on my doorstep. Of course, they had been in the crowd at the meeting in Peru, but in the ensuing commotion it had been next to impossible to take stock of any particular immortals.

Santana had shown up with a group of seven others, ones she had personally persuaded to take a stance against Harshika's drive for control. She and I had crossed paths a few times before. Her maker had been much like Charles and she also entered the immortal realm ill-prepared. Much like me, she learned her own way, and had grown strong and cunning for it. Once upon a time she had come from a wealthy Mexican family, and had survived as a vampire for almost two hundred years.

She brought with her a motley crew of immortals, including one from biblical times and another who had not yet been undead a year. The elder was a strange-looking creature, and I had to wonder if his change had been accidental. He had a pronounced hump to his back and a twist to his jaw that was disconcerting to look at. With his long and meaty arms he would have been intimidating, even as a human, but as a vampire he was terrifying. Yet even in his misshapen form, there was a glimmer of beauty. His eyes were the loveliest colour I'd ever seen, a subtle lavender-blue, and fringed with long, dark lashes. Santana introduced him as Ezekial.

The newly turned was Aaron. Until last year he'd been a regular college kid, into partying and video games and pretty girls. His maker, Clarissa, was among the group. Looking at her, I understood why he'd left it all behind in an instant. She reminded me of a young Jayne Mansfield, all platinum hair, endless curves, and bedroom eyes. The remaining five were Paolo, Jake, Vladimir, Rose, and Inga.

Each night for the past week we'd taken to trying to produce a collective use of our power. We reached out for one another, blending our distinct auras into one combined force, which we might be able to use against the mistress. Several times we'd been successful, and it had radiated over us like a protective shield, but it was difficult to control, and sapped great stores of energy. Yet each attempt came a little quicker and held a little longer. It might be a way to get close enough to Harshika to make our move. Then again, when faced with multiple attackers and the confusion of battle, we might not be able to focus strongly enough for it to be of any benefit.

The group broke up, various members heading out to feed, socialise, or attempt to pull in more allies. I noticed Clellia at the back of the room near the patio doors with a young male immortal who had shown up three nights before. His name was Billy-Joe. Clellia had seemed enamored of the former ranch hand from the first moment she'd laid eyes on him. From a touch of his mind I knew he'd been just shy of his nineteenth birthday when he turned about thirty-five years ago. His maker was here also, a male named Christian. They seemed amicable, but had not been companions for at least a decade. Daniel was resigned to the pairing with wistful approval.

Kieran led Micah out to feed as he had most nights since we'd been back in San Francisco, giving me a small clap on the back as he passed. His taking Micah under his wing couldn't have been more welcome. It was one less issue I had to worry about. Our allotted time was quickly coming to an end, and I feared that despite our best efforts we weren't sufficiently prepared.

"This will work." Charles slid in next to me.

"You sound confident, but I know the odds."

"I firmly believe things will end in our favour. Genevieve needs me."

"And you need her," I said. "But you know she is utterly defenceless as a human?"

"Yes, I do. We've discussed my sharing the Dark Kiss with her many times, but she's not yet ready. Too many years at the hands of the Desmarais conditioning, I suspect. Though she does care for me, she still has much conflict. I've tried to assure her I would not desert her, and I would help her control her urges, keeping her kills to a minimum. I fear if I press too hard, she will leave." Charles didn't look at me as he spoke, and I knew how hard it had been for him to bare his soul like that.

I considered a few responses before speaking. "Unless she is changed, death will find her eventually." I said the words as gently as I could. I'm sure he'd had the same thought many times himself.

"I never understood you until I met Genevieve, and I know we have made our peace, Giovanni, but I think I need to say something to you before we go into this situation with Harshika."

"Charles, it's all right..."

"No, it isn't. I should have said this to you when we first found you at the Desmarais compound, or afterward while you recuperated. I'm sorry, Giovanni. I was cruel and thoughtless, and I'm very sorry for all of it."

If he hugs me, I'm going to lose it, I thought before I could stop myself.

"Don't worry." He chuckled. "I'm not that far gone."

A commotion from the front of the house broke up any lingering sentimentality. Charles and I raced to the foyer where an excited group milled about. A strange mixture of relief and fear soaked the air. I caught a glimpse of Danica and Mary-Jane, both with tears streaming down their faces. Then strong hands grabbed at my arm.

I turned and, to my complete shock, found Eli at my side. I threw my arms around him, and was met with his own bone-crushing embrace. He smelled of damp earth and blood. I kissed his cheeks, and he hugged me tightly again. The sight of him brought a gentle warmth in my chest and I feared letting go in case he might disappear again.

"Where's Micah?" he asked.

"He left with Kieran to feed. They'll be back soon."

"He's okay?" he demanded.

I regarded his concerned expression and the wild brightness in his eyes. "Physically, yes. Emotionally, he's still working through what happened with him and Emmaline. And of course, he's missed you like crazy."

"I've missed him, too." Some warm, anxious energy escaped with his thoughts. I shivered as it washed through me.

The crowed shifted and Aldous appeared, arms wrapped around Emmaline. She laughed, though tears poured down her cheeks, and the ones closest to them were deeply affected by their reunion. Then I saw Saskia and Zhongxing also, and experienced a moment of silent thankfulness.

But none of that prepared me for the cold dread I felt when Achyut walked into the room.

CHAPTER 21

Rachel. France. Twenty-five days in.

A special showing of goddess worship art and artifacts had opened at one of the larger museums in Paris. It would be available for a limited time and by invitation only. Of course, Harshika had secured passes for the two of us, so now we mingled among the rich and elite of French society. Many of the items on display were inspired by Harshika herself, and she found the inside knowledge incredibly entertaining. One small figurine bore such a close resemblance to her physical attributes I was surprised it didn't elicit more curious glances our way.

This had been my existence the past few weeks, alternating between the mistress' anger and her childish and sadistic sense of humour. I could just as easily be treated to a night full of mental and physical punishments. Her mood changes never came with a warning or consistent indicator as to what might ignite her fury and indignation. For sure defiance, or a direct challenge to her authority, would without fail result in some type of punishment, but any slight, imagined or real, could just as easily set her off.

Yet despite her irritation and frustration with me, we seemed to be developing a strange bond. There were brief moments where she was kind, almost tender with me, and I found myself responding. Sometimes I felt comfortable with her, even happy, able to let my guard down. She could be surprisingly funny and thoughtful, allowing me access to information and places I had not even known to exist. And she continued to share her blood with me, increasing not only my strength, but my connection to her.

When caught up in those moments, my memory would often give me a jolting reminder of exactly what she was, her depravity and cruelty. I would remember Donovan's death, or Micah and Emmaline's torture, and any good feelings I'd been experiencing toward her would vanish. Yet as time passed, the intensity of my disgust with her dimmed as though I absorbed some of her callousness and cold indifference. I didn't know which was worse—liking her or becoming like her.

A shrill ring from her cellphone sounded and she snatched it from her pocket. I could tell by the tone and language that Achyut spoke on the other end of the line, and not the first time I wondered why she didn't rely on psychic communication. The conversation was brief, as usual, and I took these calls to be status updates. Her expression never belied her true feelings, so whether things were going as she planned, I could not ascertain.

The phone slipped back into her pocket, and I seized the opportunity. "Why does he call? Can't you read his mind whenever you want?"

Her dark eyes narrowed, and a hot wave of anger lashed out at me, scalding me like a blast of steam, but she pulled it back almost as soon as it escaped her. I tried to hold my reaction in check and a small grimace was all I let out. The effects of her blood had been swift and irreversible, providing me with abilities it would have taken decades to develop, if at all. Being in public saved me from the severity of a usual reprimand.

I couldn't have been more surprised when she chose to answer. "Achyut is strong," she said. "I can always force my way in with close proximity and without distraction, but with the great distance we're apart at the moment our mental communication is tenuous at best. Some things cannot be left open to misunderstanding."

That nugget of information intrigued me. *A weakness?* "But your children? Is your ability to reach them dampened by distance also?"

A strange expression pulled at her mask of confidence. "Are you looking for a way to get the upper hand, my dear? No matter what I can or cannot do, I will always be stronger than you. Remember that."

Just as I was about to answer her, a female called out my name from the swirling masses. An older, heavyset woman approached us, waving with enthusiasm. It took me a moment to recognise her as someone who had moved in the same social circles as my late friend, Charlotte, from our days in England. When she reached me, she pressed a quick peck to my cheek and expensive perfume tickled my nostrils. Harshika couldn't have been more displeased by this unexpected turn of events. Her expression mimicked someone discovering they'd stepped in dog poo.

"Rachel, so lovely to see you. It's been a long time."

I faltered for a moment until the name came to me. "Chantal, this is a surprise. Very nice to see you again also. May I introduce my friend, Harshika."

Chantal extended her hand, which Harshika took in her firm grip. "Hello," Harshika said.

"What brings you to Paris, Rachel? And where is that handsome husband of yours?" An erotic thought about Giovanni passed through her mind, bringing a flush to her ample cheeks.

His face flashed before my eyes and a lump of remorse choked me. Harshika pinched the back of my arm, but kept a neutral expression on her face. "He's away on business. This is a ladies-only trip." I tried to put forth lightheartedness, but my voice sounded strained, even to my own ears.

"I'll be right back," Harshika cut in. Before I could respond, she wandered a few feet away and once again pulled her cellphone from her pocket. The possibility of getting away was nil, but the urge to bolt from the room taunted me.

"Is everything all right? You seem a bit stressed." Chantal's professionally plucked brows knitted in concern.

That had to be the understatement of the century. "I am. Can I ask a favour of you?"

"Of course," she answered. I looped my arm through hers and led us toward the heart of the display. The intensity of Harshika's stare burned holes in my back.

Can you contact Giovanni for me? Pass this information along. She can't always read Achyut. Distance and distraction make it difficult for her. Do you have a pen?

She dug a pen and a small notebook from her Chanel purse, answering me as though my words had been spoken out loud. "What is that supposed to mean? Who's she? Are you in some kind of trouble?"

I pressed the paper with Giovanni's number into her palm and looked her straight in the eye. I concentrated as hard as I could on catching her mind, and to my surprise, I was able to take her with ease. *Just pass this message along. Then lose the number and forget you ever saw me. Understand?*

Her eyes were glazed, but she nodded. "Yes."

"Good. Now walk away and don't look back."

She did as I instructed, and with not a moment to spare. Harshika's presence breathed fire down my back, and she thrust herself into my mind. She rampaged through my thoughts, gouging and prying her way into every crevice of my subconscious, but I held tight to the knowledge I didn't want to share. Then the pressure eased off. She snatched my hand and forced me outside.

"Did you enjoy the exhibit?" she asked as though nothing suspicious had occurred. She led us in the direction of our hotel.

I played along. "Yes, very much. You know how much this type of thing intrigues me."

She smiled, but it was an expression utterly devoid of joy. Her power charged up around her small frame, invoking a cold dread in the pit of my stomach. I would swear this phenomenon had a physical manifestation, swarming like a shadowy mass of mayflies about her small frame. I blinked several times, but the visual did not disappear. The presence pulled in tightly about her body then flared out with a rush of cool wind, mimicking respiration. Her strength hummed, prickling along my body. It was a terrifying and disorienting display, and she was aware of the effect it had. She revelled in the fear she invoked, substantiated by it as much as the blood she took from the lives around her.

Her power seemed to draw in the air, sound, and life from the space around us, sucking us into this vacuum where nothing existed except Harshika's dominance. She glowed a silky, unblemished alabaster, her eyes bright onyx pools in the irresistible perfection of her face. Her lips were slightly less pale than her complexion and the tips of her fangs appeared in her cruel smile.

Somehow, we had travelled from the busy streets to the anonymity of our hotel room without notice of movement or passing time. Behind locked doors I knew there was no escape from her fury. She would hurt me, break me, and take whatever secrets she pleased. She came to me with madness burning in her eyes and her arms wide.

With a Judas kiss still damp on my cheek, my punishment began.

Giovanni. San Francisco.

"What the hell is he doing here?" I asked much louder than I intended to. The room had become quiet as a tomb and my voice reverberated in the cavernous space.

"I come as an ally." Achyut made his smooth, gliding approach in my direction.

"Eli, what's going on here?" Charles asked, appearing at my side.

Eli looked at us both. "I'm sorry. I didn't know how to explain this over the phone. I thought it would be best in person."

Eli's mind read as a scurrying mess while from Achyut there was nothing. When I reached out to him, I touched only blankness, his mind appearing as devoid of activity as a flat line on a hospital monitor. Yet a soft, prickly impression accompanied his presence. It reminded me of the tickle of long grass in the summer, a feeling both gentle and irritating. His approach mesmerised, but I did not feel the threat in his movements as I had in Spain.

Aldous came to our group, holding tightly to Emmaline's hand. The rest of the remaining immortals, those who had not already left to feed, circled around us, anxious and hungry for an explanation. "He let us go."

"Perhaps this is a tactic on his part? A trick to have you lead him right to us. Did you ever think of that?" Charles's voice was quiet and hostile.

The occupants of the room gave a collective bristle and tensed at the suggestion, to which Achyut only offered a look of sadness. Saskia and Zhongxing pushed through the group to join the inner circle of those who had proven their allegiance during the Desmarais attack.

Zhongxing shook his head with vehemence. "This is no trick. I am sure of it."

"He has been most forthcoming with us, allowing us access to his memories and his feelings toward Harshika. He wants to be rid of her as much as we do," Saskia agreed.

"Make me believe," Charles demanded right before he charged Achyut.

Without a moment to think, I joined him. Eli and Aldous cried out in protest, but we'd already closed in on our target. Charles had a grip on Achyut's throat before he even attempted to defend himself. The cold wall of power that had touched me in Peru erupted again, stopping me dead in my tracks and pulling Charles away from Achyut. The effect was jarring, yet not as painful as I remembered my first taste had been. Charles continued to move backward until he was next to me then the phenomenon vanished.

A rustle of surprise touched me and murmured responses circulated through the room. Achyut stepped forward until he was less than an arm's length from Charles, who didn't so much a bat an eye. *Tough bugger*, I thought, not feeling quite the same way myself. Then the guard on Achyut's mind lowered and, though I was certain he tried to be gentle, the barrage that escaped him equalled a bursting dam pouring directly into my brain. Memories and the potent emotions associated with them flung from his mind to impale the parties before him. I fought to not stumble under the assault as the mental barbs burrowed in and took hold.

The intensity drew back to a tolerable level, and the swarm of images made sense. I clutched my head as if it might explode and dropped my arms. A horrible, twisted tale unfolded, leading us from an unrequited love to the horrendous events that spawned the monster known as Harshika. From this savage birth to darkness came a vengeance that would never be satisfied.

Thousands of years Achyut had existed under the hateful,

domineering control of this sickness. Trapped forever in hatred and bloodlust, Harshika had directed every moment of his immortal life and he'd finally had enough.

The only blood he wished to see spilled in his future was hers.

Rachel. Paris.

When she broke my other arm, after my legs and most of my ribs, my consciousness fled my body. I floated in the hostile, red sea of agony, gritting my teeth through the throbbing waves until the pain faded to shades of orange and, finally, yellow. I was still aware of the pain, but it paraded in the background, allowing me enough clarity to watch from my astral position above the inflictor of my injuries.

My body contorted on the floor, bent at angles unnatural to any human and vampire alike. Blood poured from numerous wounds, from my mouth, nose, and both ears. A shard of bone protruded from my left side. The whole scene played out devoid of sound. Her blows fell in eerie silence.

With lips pulled back in a savage snarl and hair flying like a wave of black silk, she struck me again and again. Even in her desperate, unrelenting fury she was breathtaking. A fine sheen covered her skin almost like perspiration, but what was in reality a physical manifestation of her power. Her violent state made it seem as though she were being viewed through a soft hazy light like some old Hollywood movie. The strange association struck me as funny and I attempted to laugh, but ended up coughing instead, which brought about a whole new level of agony.

The assault continued with brutal efficiency. Soon the twitching, bloody heap on the floor became unrecognisable as me. Was it all some awful trick of mind, one of Harshika's sadistic games? Then the pain came screaming back to reality. She left me this way for an indeterminate amount of time where I thought of Giovanni and prayed for death.

My eyes sealed shut with blood and swelling, but I knew she hovered mere inches from my face. I felt her presence seething over me, her temper lost to maniacal levels. My only movement was the involuntary spasms of my damaged limbs. I tried to scream and choked on the ocean of blood flowing down my throat.

"If I don't set your bones properly you will begin to heal this way. And then it will be even more painful to have to re-break your bones and place them back in the correct alignment." Her voice was peaches and cream, the words tossed out as casually as if she read a weather report.

"*Peesss*," was all I could utter through the damage to my jaw. As my tongue lolled about in my mouth, I was surprised to realise she hadn't broken off any of my teeth, a trick she must have mastered over the years.

With a loud snap my left femur was forced back into place. My consciousness dulled around the edges, a soft grey filtering in. I would pass out soon and I was glad, because that meant the pain would end. I was completely at her mercy. I could not stop her, and no words would affect her decisions. She was a creature without compassion or empathy, and didn't understand the meaning of leniency

I let my mind drift, only dimly aware of the sound of snapping bones and the jarring pain associated with restoring my body to its correct anatomical position. I pushed aside all the outside sensations, warming with memories of my loved ones. I remembered Eli as a young boy, reading, riding his beloved horses and talking to me with the keen, mature way of thinking he had possessed even as a child. And now he was a handsome, articulate man—loyal, kind, and finally in love. I thought of Charles and how much I had feared him at first, how he could unnerve me still, even though I knew he was a true friend. I loved the way Genevieve had softened him, had given him a happiness he'd never experienced before, not even in his human life.

Memories of the long talks I shared with Emmaline weaved through, intermingling and overlapping with images of Danica, both as a child and now as a grown woman. I heard Mary-Jane singing, Kieran's good-natured ribbing, and Aldous speaking in his native tongue. I thought of Alessandra, Saskia, and many others who had become a part of my life.

And Giovanni. His angelic face beckoned, the silky caress of his voice overrode everything else spiralling about in my brain. His smile lured me away from the lingering pain. His eyes, bright and bluer than the clearest skies soothed and reassured me everything would be all right. In that moment I would have gladly drowned in those eyes, surrendering all I was, to have them be the last thing I would ever see.

A presence intruded on my reverie. It wormed its way through the happiness I clung to, erasing my loved ones with its blackness and billowing stench. One by one they slipped away until only those blue eyes remained. I clung to the image, desperate and afraid I would never again see them in real life.

"Hasn't he caused you enough trouble, my child?" Harshika's voice came through, even and cool, her fury and vindictiveness having been momentarily satiated. Her moods could come and go in the blink of an eye and, like a child, once the tantrum was over it was soon forgotten.

I lay on top of one of the beds and, though a whisper of pain lingered, my body now felt predominately stiff and heavy. I tried to raise my arm and struggled. I tried to talk, but my jaw was held in place, unmovable.

"I have wrapped you up to hold your body in place as it mends. Even with our accelerated healing abilities and the infusion of my blood, it will take several days to reverse all of the damage." Her face swam into focus, so close I squinted to see her clearly. "I suggest you don't attempt something like that again. Not that it would matter, because by the time you've healed from this, the time I've so graciously given your friends will be up."

I heard her rise from the bed and, though I could not turn my head to follow her movements, I was aware she was still close by. "And then they will follow my word or they will be crushed."

Her words brought a jolt of anger so sharp it competed with the pain of the earlier assault. I lay there with fiery tears brimming in my eyes and vengeance surging through my veins. *She can't win!* There had to be a way to stop her.

I pray you've found the answer, Giovanni.

CHAPTER 22

Giovanni. San Francisco.

A small assembly comprising what I had come to categorise as our core group settled in the back room with me to listen to what Achyut had to say. There were eleven of us—Aldous and Emmaline, Zhongxing and Mengmei, Eli and Micah, Charles, Kieran, Alessandra, Saskia, and myself. We were all tense, suspicious, and afraid. We had willingly let the lion into our home and knew there was no way we would all make it out alive if he chose to attack.

Achyut's soft presence murmured to me, a lulling feeling begging for defenses to be dropped. It was a strange sensation, not intrusive, but persistent. Had my anxiety not been running on high it would have been easy to slip into complacency and been vulnerable to his whims. He didn't push or seem to make any attempt to force thoughts upon us or manipulate our feelings or actions in any way. If anything, he seemed sad.

"Thank you for your agreement to hear me out," he said in his quiet, raspy voice.

"I trust Eli, not you. What do you want?" I asked, not feeling quite as certain as the words I spoke.

A thin smile crossed his face as though he understood my reticence. "I know this is hard. You are all angry and frightened. And you especially, Giovanni, must be worried for your partner, Rachel."

He looked at me then and I couldn't help but grimace at the sound of his voice uttering Rachel's name. "Do you know how she is?" I asked.

"She's alive. Harshika hasn't let her out of her sight. She's become somewhat attached to her. I can't fully explain her actions on this."

"Has she hurt her?"

"Yes," he answered. "She has. She always hurts those close to her. That is her way and this has gone on for far too long for her to be any different now, no matter what the circumstance."

Charles must have understood the effect his words had on me, for he jumped into the conversation and steered it back to the matter at hand. I shook as I thought about what might be happening to Rachel. I remembered the scene in the temple chamber and felt my nails biting into my palms. "What is it you think you can help us with?" he asked with enough bluntness to sting.

"I like to think of this as a way we can help each other."

"Why would we want to help you?" Alessandra asked.

"A good question and not one with an easy answer. Perhaps if I share with you my story and the truth of Harshika's transformation you might better understand."

"How can we believe you?" I asked.

"I offer to lower all my defenses and allow you access to my memories, so you may feel and see and hear all the things I experienced. I have never done that before. The only one who has ever touched my mind or known me intimately is Harshika, and it was never an occurrence of my choosing."

He delivered his words with such solemn conviction it was impossible to ignore the sentiment. This was a tale long hidden, one that needed to be released and understood. His hand had travelled to his throat as he spoke and one finger gently stroked the ring of scarring. He caught me watching his movement and quickly adjusted the neck of his garment so the scar vanished from view.

"Do you wish your mistress destroyed?" Charles said.

"Oh yes," he answered. "There is no other way. She is mad and she cannot be reasoned or bargained with. For her there are only two ways—complete obedience or destruction."

"You would assist us with *her* destruction?"

"And return Rachel to us safely?" I interjected before he could answer.

"Yes, to both counts. There is no way to get close enough to inflict damage to Harshika without my help. And by extension, no way to get close enough to facilitate Rachel's release. But remember it is not only Harshika to contend with. She has amassed a large following of some of the oldest and strongest of our kind, many as cruel and violent as herself."

"We have many allies also," Alessandra said, eyes narrowing as though his words were meant to insult.

"Yes, a very impressive number, too. You are well prepared, but the mistress is a formidable creature." He paused with eyes closed and a strange expression pinched his features. "And some humans, too?"

"Yes, Rachel's niece is here and Charles's partner, Genevieve," I answered, momentarily panicked at the thought of harm coming to either one of them.

Achyut looked from face to face and I made every effort to keep the details of Genevieve's work and our plans concealed. Of the others who were privy, all had hard expressions and steel cages locked around their thoughts. If looks could kill, then Charles would have Achyut's lifeless form at his feet. As reserved and cold as he generally was, I knew his love for Genevieve was fierce and he would do anything to protect her. I touched his arm as a warning to tone it down. His shoulders relaxed.

"I didn't mean to imply disapproval, merely surprise. I understand the appeal, and have enjoyed the brief chances I get to mingle with humans. It's helped to keep me from turning into a thing as vile and unfeeling as Harshika. I've never considered one as a companion, though...and I guess you can understand why."

"Because she'd never let you," Saskia offered.

"Exactly. So, shall we continue? There are but a handful of days left and the ultimate consequences at stake."

"Wait a moment. Doesn't Harshika know you're here?" I asked.

"Yes and no. She knows I'm here, but she thinks at her bidding. She doesn't know my true motivations. She thinks I am here to offer you one last chance to come to her willingly. She has no idea I have released your friends. The distance between us puts a strain on her mind's eye. I may have been her lackey, but I am also the only one who truly knows her. And that means being aware of her weaknesses."

"She wishes us to believe she has no weaknesses." Charles nodded at my statement.

"And that in essence is her biggest fault—her arrogance. Her arrogance makes her blind to her illogical thinking and over-sights. She is childish and impulsive, quick to anger, quick to change her mind. Her madness reassures her that she is omnip-otent, without mistake. This we can use to her detriment."

"You really despise her, don't you?" Eli asked.

"I loved her once," he answered with an aching wistfulness. A warm but distant sentiment accompanied his words, wind-ing around my heart. For a fleeting moment it reminded me of my love for Rachel. "More than my own life. But any love I had for her died with my mortality and, though I struggled for centuries to reconcile those feelings with the monster she has become, there was no use. There is nothing left in her to love. She is simply a walking embodiment of hatred and vengeance, and even her physical beauty is something that fills me with disgust now." There was nothing but truth in his words and, surprisingly, it touched me.

"Let's sit down everyone and listen to Achyut's story, and from there we will make our decision," Charles instructed, and all complied with obvious unease.

"Well, I suppose the only place to start is the very begin-ning, the very first time I ever laid eyes on Harshika."

His words were so gentle, hypnotic, invoking feelings of relief and contentment. It was easy to relax and be pulled along the melancholy passageway of his memories. I sensed the space about me changing, softening, but not in any definable way. It was like being on the verge of sleep, the gentle call of nothing so warm and inviting.

"She was just a girl then, about twelve years old. She had been picked up by the area's holy men, given to them in exchange for protection and support to her family. Be assured this was a common enough practice, and was considered a great honour to have a family member in service to the religious community or the royal family. It exalted one in status, and meant none would ever want for food or shelter or spiritual protection." His words became like a running commentary on memories I could now see, hear and taste. It was so real I almost believed I could reach out and touch Harshika's mane of silky hair.

"She'd been trained for about one year's time in music, religion, and domestic service. When she came to the palace she was on the cusp of womanhood and as beautiful a girl as I had ever seen. She caught the eye of many an admirer, my brother, Narsimha, included. He was nineteen years old then and I three years younger. Where he was bold and forceful, I was timid and withdrawn. I had been sick as a child and retained a slight stature as I grew into manhood, but Narsimha was tall and muscular, handsome, but he was also cruel and selfish. Everything had been handed to him, and he had no thought to other people's feelings or needs. Others were there to serve him.

"For many years we both watched her and, as each year passed, she became more and more beautiful. Of course, there was no way that either Narsimha or I could have any kind of relationship with a servant girl, but it didn't stop us from lusting after her. I often watched her from afar, doing her chores, going through her daily duties, but her activities outside her service intrigued me even more. She often went out to river's edge or the jungle and danced and sang. She had the most wonderful voice and her body moved like magic. I was completely smitten.

"Narsimha also paid more and more attention to her, often cornering her alone, but where she could not refuse his attention because of his authority over her. It didn't take long before he touched her and forced her to pleasure him. I often watched these encounters from the shadows, cursing my own weakness and cowardice. Her tears burned my soul and her cries for him to stop were daggers in my heart, but he was the first born, the one who would be king, and there was nothing I could do.

"One evening after a particularly vicious assault, one that left her bloody and bruised, I followed her. After these incidents she would flee to where it was dark and deserted to cry and clean herself. And pray. Pray to have the incidents stop, pray to die. I noticed when calling on the spirits, she herself seemed magical, as though her devotion and convictions filled her with light. She was too lovely to be real, too lovely to ever want something to do with a sickly, weak boy like myself.

"This time, this evening, she did not pray. She simply lay on the grass at the edge of the dark jungle, motionless and silent. She didn't cry. She didn't wipe away the blood. I worried she had been hurt so badly she had collapsed, or was in shock. I came to her side and shook her gently. She didn't respond, so I shook her again, this time with more force. She murmured something I couldn't understand and then her eyes, which had been closed, fluttered and finally opened wide. She turned to me, clearly surprised to find me, of all people, there in the darkness with her.

"'Achyut?' she asked, reaching up a hand coated with dried blood to touch my cheek. When she connected with my flesh, she seemed shocked, as though she expected my presence to be a figment of her imagination.

"'Yes, Harshika, it's me, Achyut. Are you all right?' Of course, she wasn't, but I didn't know what else to say.

"She struggled to sit up. Her dress had been torn and, as she shifted position, the top portion of it slipped, exposing one small, perfect breast. I turned away quickly, my face burning, and when I looked back, she had adjusted her shift to cover her nakedness. She was so weak she needed to rest, so I held her against my chest and waited. After a long time, she asked me to assist her to the nearby river where she could wash, and help her back to her sleeping quarters. I was more than happy to oblige.

"The moon was bright and silvery, dancing off her long ebony hair. She was as beautiful as any goddess could ever dream to be, and I knew as I sat watching her, I would love her until my last breath. I may not be able to stop Narsimha's advances, but I would do what I could. After I got her back to her bed, I found fresh clothing and laid it outside her door to find the next morning. After that night, I couldn't stay away.

"We met most evenings, long after her duties were completed

and I was thought to have retired to bed. The night was our guardian, assisting in keeping our friendship hidden from those who would not understand or approve. And despite my feelings for her, we remained only friends. I never attempted to touch her inappropriately or do anything to make her uncomfortable. Just being with her was enough, for she was sweet and kind then, so thoughtful and inquisitive. I taught her to read our burgeoning writing system, and showed her delights from the many traders and sailors who came to our shores. I relayed the stories I'd heard of distant lands and cultures very different from our own. We sang together and danced, and she never once laughed at my clumsiness.

"I gave her a small wooden tiger amulet, which I'd had carved by the best artisan I could find. I'd paid handsomely for it, too, but I knew Harshika had a strong affinity for the tiger goddess who was worshipped in our culture. She was supposed to be a protector, a guide, and Harshika with her broken spirit needed to believe there was someone who would protect her. Unfortunately, it couldn't be me. She was so touched she actually kissed me, and once the amulet was tied about her neck, she never took it off.

"This went on for many years. Narsimha's interest waned, but his assaults did not stop altogether. He was often away on family business, or in training to take over from our father, and I assume during these times he turned his lust and cruelty elsewhere. For certainly it was not Harshika herself he coveted, it was simply the power he had over her, and it was an easy way to get sexual and sadistic gratification. She could have been anyone. He just happened to find her physical form appealing. I, on the other hand, loved her for everything that lay beneath her outward beauty. I loved the true Harshika, the one no one knew existed except me.

"The year Narsimha turned twenty-five our father passed away. After a sufficient period of mourning, the preparations began for my brother to take his place. He would be responsible for the financial, social, and spiritual well-being of all the residents of Mohenjo-daro, and he would be expected to take an appropriate wife. It was encouraged to join with other powerful families of nearby regions to ensure good trading practices and periods of peace. My mother reviewed many perspective candidates before giving her approval. She was a lovely girl, but nowhere near the flawless beauty Harshika possessed. I think that pleased Harshika immensely, though she never said as much.

"Preparations were underway for many months. Repairs and additions to the city were made, oils and materials brought in from distant lands. It was to be an occasion the likes of which had never been seen before. It would be a celebration to last several weeks, with events for all the citizens to participate in and special proceedings only for the elite of our society. There were many layers to these celebrations—spiritual, social, and simply for pleasure. Despite my utter hatred for Narsimha, I found myself swept up in the excitement.

"Each night I would rush to meet Harshika to tell her about all the happenings, the people I'd met. I snuck out food to her, and other small trinkets, for which she was always delighted. I sometimes let myself fantasise it was Harshika and I getting married, and that we would soon be rulers of our majestic community. I imagined how beautiful she would be in the traditional wedding attire and makeup. I dreamt of lavishing her with spectacular jewels and gold. Nothing was too good for her, not in my mind, anyway.

"The night before the wedding, there was a grand feast with invitees from as far away as Egypt and Mesopotamia. It was a full-day event with food and wine, dancing, singing, and spiritual ceremonies. By the early evening most participants were drunk and heavy with more food than one would normally consume in several days. Narsimha had been drinking copious amounts of alcohol. I don't think I saw him once in the entire day where he didn't have a glass clutched in his hand. The more he drank, the darker his mood. He was short and crude, dispersing insults to anyone within hearing range.

"Harshika, of course, was busy attending to the guests, as were all the servants. Many had been brought in from the fields and other capacities to keep up with the demand. All had been dressed in the finest clothes, bathed with expensive oils to show our guests how rich and elegant we were. Of course, this was probably the only time many of our servants would ever be treated in such a manner, but the lie had to be perfect for our appearance to our guests. Under other circumstances, most of those gathered would be considered rivals if not outright enemies, but this was a time for status, not war.

"Harshika was glorious as she whirled about filling glasses and replacing empty platters with full ones. She smiled and offered the appropriate respect to all the guests, even the lecherous or rude ones. I saw her eyeing the dancing girls and the musicians with envy, and maybe a touch of sadness. Had her birth been of higher class, these positions would have been options. As it was, she had done well. She was well-fed and clothed, and was given certain freedoms. Several times we made eye contact, and she gave me a small smile or nod.

"Some time after the last round of food had been served, and the musicians and dancers were still entertaining the crowds, I saw an exchange between Harshika and Narsimha. She pulled away from him and fled the room, and I followed closely after. I felt Narsimha's gaze like burning coals on my flesh as I left, and I knew there would be consequences to my actions. At that point I didn't care any longer. The only thing that mattered to me was Harshika and the chance to have a life with her. If that chance meant we would have to move far away from my family and the comfort of their wealth, then so be it. Anything would be better than how things were.

"I caught up with her outside and pledged my love for her. I told her I wanted to marry her, and to my surprise and delight, she agreed. We wandered to one of our favourite spots in the jungle and waited out the hours until we thought it would be safe to return without the chance of crossing paths with my brother.

"When we returned to the palace grounds, it was deserted and still as a tomb. I dared to give Harshika a parting kiss, a moment so wonderful and pure I will never forget it. It would be the last one between us, the last time my sweet, beautiful Harshika would ever exist. My brother appeared then, angry and emboldened by the liquor he'd consumed. His guards were equally drunk and their moral compasses set by his direction. What he ordered, they did. We were ripped apart and, though I managed to connect one solid punch, the guards were quickly on me and dragged me away. I heard Harshika screaming and begging, the sound growing fainter until I could only imagine her anguish. I sat for what seemed like days in a dark cellar room until the guards returned for me. Now I wish they'd left me there to rot.

"I was taken to where Harshika was, where…she…" Achyut struggled for a moment before regaining his composure and continuing with his story. "They had assaulted her, brutally, and beat her so badly I feared they'd killed her. The only thing recognisable about her was her long dark hair and the new pendant she wore. As I looked closer, I realised the tiger amulet was still clutched in one battered hand. Something about the sight of that unleashed a torrent of fury I didn't know I was capable of feeling. I broke away from the guards and charged my brother, who still stood unclothed as though what he had done was nothing to be ashamed of. I knocked him to the ground and we fought before the guards pulled us apart.

"Narsimha ordered his men to hold me while he beat me. While this happened, I noticed the shaky rise and fall of Harshika's chest, and understood she wasn't yet dead. I racked my brain, trying to figure out a way to help us, when my brother grabbed a small dagger from the floor and came at me with vengeance burning in his eyes. He sliced the blade across my throat, smiling as he did so.

"There was no pain at first, but then a tight, angry burning emerged, searing along the line of the wound. My hot blood spilled out then a throbbing urgent pain took hold, surging in tempo with my heartbeat. Weakness started in my arms, then my legs, and the world went dark.

"When I came to, I'd been taken to my own room and a fever burned through my body. Miraculously I'd survived, discovered by a young servant boy cleaning up from the evening's festivities. My brother had left me on the floor of the storage room to bleed to death while he and his men returned to their rooms to sleep off their intoxication as though nothing out of the ordinary had occurred.

"The boy roused the house and one of the city's healers was brought to attend to me. The cut had damaged my vocal cords and I was not able to speak at all for many days, too weak to attempt to draw or write down what had happened. The wound was stitched closed and the pain was treated but, even with the care, infection set in. I went in and out of consciousness for many days before the fever broke. By that time my brother had passed around a story about would-be thieves and two unfortunate servants had been killed to cover his actions. All I could think about was Harshika.

"Narsimha eventually came to me five days after he had attempted to take my life. He had the gall to say he would forgive my actions if I kept my mouth shut. *He* would forgive *me*? The nerve of the bastard! I opened my mouth to yell at him, and only this horrible whispery voice came out. This would be my mark to carry forward into my immortal life as the damage had already begun to heal by the time Harshika's undead blood touched my body. He laughed at me and called Harshika a whore. I begged him to tell me what he had done with her, and he told me she rotted somewhere on the jungle floor, if the wild animals hadn't gotten to her first. That image seared into my brain and I wanted to die along with her.

"Later that night I would learn she wasn't really gone, at least not physically, but she was not the same and never could be again. Emotionally she was as different from the girl I loved as could possibly be. The night she returned would change all of our lives forever.

"It was very late and I'd fallen asleep. I'd tossed and turned. Each time I closed my eyes I'd see Harshika's battered body, and my shame and anger were so great I couldn't get my mind to settle down. I'd been brought a wonderful meal, but I hadn't touched a bite. I felt as if I'd never eat again. I felt as if there was nothing left if Harshika was gone.

"A sound woke me and I sat up, heart hammering. I held my breath and listened, but there was only silence. I lay back down and, as my eyes grew heavy again, there was another sound. I heard voices and a loud crash.

"I jumped from my bed and followed the sound down the dark hallway to Narsimha's room. Behind the doors a violent argument brewed. I was afraid, but I had to know what was happening. I opened the door to his room and slipped inside. A small group of Narsimha's men and his young wife cowered on the ground. The men were yelling, his wife crying. Then a sudden movement caught my eye and, as several of the guards fell backward, the most surprising sight appeared before my eyes.

"Harshika stood in the middle of the room. Under the layers of dirt and blood her skin gleamed white, her eyes wide and wild. Tattered clothing wrapped about her lithe frame and her feet were bare. She had Narsimha by the throat and, with her delicate arm, she held him several feet above the floor. The scene made no sense at all. Harshika was not strong enough to attack a full-grown man, especially not one with several guards present for his protection.

"I stepped farther into the room and, as I did, I saw there were several more guards lying in bloody, broken heaps on the floor. The head of one had been turned completely around, now staring back at me over his wreck of a body. Harshika saw me then and, for a few brief seconds, joy overtook her wrath and she smiled. Then my brother cried out, begging for her to stop, and the hint of the old Harshika vanished forever.

"With her free arm, she slammed her fist into Narsimha's abdomen, yanking it back out a few seconds later with a handful of slippery, throbbing intestines. A nauseating stench filled the room. Next she reached down between his legs and grabbed his manhood with an expression of mad glee. She squeezed until a soft, popping sound filled the room and bloody ooze slipped from her fingers. Narsimha's body dropped from her grasp and she swooped down on him, tearing and biting, ripping his body limb from limb with a mesmerising psychotic frenzy that none dared to try to stop.

"When she was finished, her face was a mask of blood, her hair a wild, damp mess. The remaining guards had frozen in place, utterly terrified by the spectacle. One by one she killed them, lapping at their spilt blood like a lion at a watering hole. Within minutes everyone was dead save for me and Narsimha's wife, and the room was drenched with crimson.

"She looked to the wife and said, 'I have done you a great favour.'

"As she approached me, many things raced through my mind. I was certain I was dreaming and, at the same time, knew it must be real. She stepped closer and I raised a shaky hand. I brushed my fingers over her sticky cheek, my tears of shame and love burning my skin. Her eyes, dull and lifeless shadows of their former beauty, paralysed me. Her features had become thinner, more pronounced. Up close her skin was even paler than I'd first noticed, so white and papery thin, but displaying a strange, beguiling radiance. As her lips pulled back, she revealed sharp white fangs.

"'I thought you were dead,' she said.

"'It's a miracle I'm alive. Just like it's a miracle you're standing here before me,' I answered, truly meaning the words I spoke.

"She laughed, a hard, bitter sound that caused me to tremble. 'A miracle? You call this a miracle?' She waved her arm to indicate the gore-spattered room.

"'But you're alive. Narsimha didn't win. Now we can be together.'

"Her eyes narrowed at the sound of my brother's name. The wife, still on the floor, slumped over in a dead faint. 'I don't know what you call this, but I'm certainly not alive.'

"I took a step backward. 'But you're not dead. You're standing here before me, moving and talking.'

"'Yes. But I no longer breathe, I don't eat, the sun burns me. As you can see, I am stronger than any man, faster, too.' With a blur of movement, she was gone. I scanned the room, looking for any trace of her, when she tapped me on the shoulder. I whirled about in surprise. I should have been able to feel her warmth she stood so close, but there was none. As the blood dried on her skin, I saw not all of it was from her victims, but that a series of wounds, both deep and superficial, patterned her exposed arms, neck, and face. There must have been a struggle with the guards before I arrived. The deepest of the cuts wept a thick dark blood.

"She ran a hand up my arm, it felt like a block of ice. The fingers found the scar at my throat, tracing along the line of raised flesh. Sweat dripped down my back and my legs threatened to buckle underneath me. A soulless, evil creature stared back at me from Harshika's body, the light and joy she once possessed extinguished forever.

"'We can still be together, Harshika,' I said, my bowels hot and loose.

"She ignored me. 'Where have you been, Achyut? Why didn't you look for me?'

"'I was sick with fever. When I came to, I was only told you were dead, not where they'd taken you. If I'd known or suspected, I would have come! You have to know that.'

"'You failed me. These are excuses! But it doesn't matter, for I don't need anyone's love or protection now. All I need is blood.'

"I tried to run, but she was on me. And, with that, she ripped the scar at my throat wide open and blood gushed forward. I slumped to my knees and her greedy mouth was on me, sucking and drinking my life into her body. We fell to the floor, her hard but light body on top of me.

"She stayed there, lying on top of me like a lover as the cold hand of death crept through my body. My mouth pressed to her throat, and a thick liquid spilled over my lips from one of her deeper wounds. Its voyage over my tongue and down my throat brought a dim, hostile sensation as greyness filtered in. The last thing I heard was Harshika wailing, over and over again, 'Why didn't you come, Achyut? Why did you let this happen to me?'"

The room had been stunned into silence. I ached and throbbed, and felt chilled to the core. Achyut's anguish ate at me, his grief and shame my own. As I looked at each face in the room, I knew the others were similarly affected. Achyut's cheeks were stained with crimson streaks and the pain he'd unleashed made him age before my eyes. This indignity and sadness had been an enormous burden to carry for as long as he had.

"Were you changed by this accidental exchange of blood?" I asked.

"Yes. Harshika did not know then how to create another, but

it was plain to see after the fact that the infusion of her blood changed me. I awoke the next night in one of the underground chambers of the palace where all the bodies had been taken. I'd been assumed dead, so I lay on the floor, wrapped and waiting for a proper goodbye.

"I opened my eyes, able to see perfectly in the darkness. I tore the wraps from my body, amazed to find I was unharmed. The wound at my throat had once again healed, and I no longer felt the infection and fever. I felt wonderful, strong. I heard sounds from all over the city, had the strength to tear the locked door from its frame to escape. Once outside I found I could run as fast as any wild creature, and I used this speed to move deep into the jungle. Once far from the palace I stopped, seeing like I never had before, smelling and tasting the very air around me.

"Once alone, and somewhat calmer, I also discovered a terrible hunger, but it was a craving and a compulsion like I'd never known before. My mouth was bitter and dry. My stomach clenched and my brain screamed with a need I could not comprehend.

"And then Harshika appeared. She took my hand, understanding I had become like her, and she led me to the small cave she used as her hiding place from the sun. Inside she had three wasted corpses and one body still warm and alive. She brought me to the man, opened a vein, and pushed my mouth to his body. I drank his blood, drank every last drop. I found it just as she had described. I was something not alive and also not dead. But I did not have the strength or speed of Harshika, which she used to her advantage. I have been with her every night since. Always in her shadow and under her thumb and, for the longest time, that's exactly where I felt I belonged.

"I want this to end. I never want to see her face again. I never want to hear her voice or do her bidding. I want peace with the past and what I am."

My phone rang, startling all in the room. I pulled it from my pocket, not recognising the number on the call display. It could be someone wishing to join our ranks, so I answered. "Hello."

"Giovanni?" an older female with a British accent asked.

"Yes."

"Oh, thank goodness. You may not remember me, but my name is Chantal Midling-Carter. My son, Simon, attended the same school as Eli, and we met at a number of social functions. Anyway, I know this sounds strange, but I ran into your wife tonight. She asked me to get in touch and a pass along a message."

Hot surprise streamed through my blood. Her words had caught me off guard and I had to force myself to focus. "Yes, I remember you. What was the message?"

"She said, 'She can't always read Achyut. Distance and distraction make it difficult for her.' Does that make any sense?"

"Completely. Thank you so much, Chantal. It was lovely to hear from you. I don't mean to be rude, but I must go now."

"Of course. I hope everything is all right."

"It will be. Goodbye."

"Au revoir."

Everyone watched me, scrutinising my words and reaction. Something clicked in my brain and everything we needed to do seemed to fall into place.

"I guess I don't need to ask if everyone heard that? This seems to confirm what Achyut told us. Harshika is not as untouchable as she would lead us to believe."

"She is still stronger than all of you," Achyut said. "But I may be able to help with that also. We have a few days left, so it might be possible."

"What do you have in mind?" I asked.

"We need to work together. Only then will we find a way to destroy her."

CHAPTER 23

Rachel. On the Move.

Harshika left me to rest for two days before moving us toward our destination in Peru. We flew from Paris to London, then to New York. From there we jumped to Los Angeles, which made me ache with need, being so close to San Francisco. I suspected Giovanni and the others would have gone there, at least initially, but whether they had stayed or moved on to other locations I couldn't be sure. Harshika blocked me, making sure nothing slipped from or to me, though there was a recognisable feeling that stroked me intermittently during the night we spent in Los Angeles.

The sensation sparked urgent memories, familiar and comforting, its existence soothed me. Harshika was aware of the presence also, as each time I picked up on it her expression hardened and the void she kept me in solidified tighter about me. She wasn't taking any chances and, to be truthful, I don't think I could have survived another punishment had the opportunity for contact presented itself.

At each stop we acquired several more followers, so by the time we'd made it to South America we had a large assembly with us. Some of the faces were familiar from the Desmarais attack or successive meetings, but most I did not know at all. That many were very old and consequently much more powerful than me was undisputable. The older ones had the clearest skin and the hardest eyes, as though time could only be kind to them physically or mentally, but not both. I also noted that of the older immortals, being without companions was the norm.

Of course, there were a few exceptions, but for the most part only the immortals less than a thousand years old had partners, or companions of any permanence.

Sorcha and Samaria appeared together in Mexico City in a small group of immortals. They seemed quite chummy, but I didn't sense any heart-to-hearts going on there like I might have had with Emmaline. This was simply a partnership for gain with some common ties of their past to make their union more understandable. These two had played about the periphery of the group of immortals Giovanni and I had come to trust and call friends. I was disappointed, though not entirely surprised to see Sorcha had abandoned her connection to Charles so easily. Then again, the chance to destroy was something she enjoyed, and I don't think the reason for the dispute ever mattered. She was quite like Harshika in that regard.

Samaria, I knew little about, except that she was Emmaline's maker and a bit younger than Sorcha and Alessandra. It was quite obvious how she felt about me. Her eyes were black holes of contempt every time she caught my glance. A fierce hatred radiated from her whenever I was in her presence, though I could not pinpoint anything I might have done to enrage her so. Harshika picked up on this also, but was more amused than bothered. One look from her and the flare of Samaria's hatred extinguished. It was blatant enough to be worrisome, though, so that meant, to my horror, I needed to stick even tighter to Harshika's side lest she find a way to have me meet with some kind of accident.

We ended up back where we started in the ruins in Peru. We settled within a series of winding caverns in the mountainside that backed the large temple structure. There was space enough for all to rest for the last two days and, in the evenings, most went to feed in the nearby towns and villages. Harshika had a private chamber, which I shared with her, with a raised stone platform covered in musty blankets and pillows. Each day I lay at her side, angry and afraid, knowing the slightest movement on my part would trigger a harsh and immediate reaction. In the evenings I followed her to the city, feeding only on whom she allowed.

The damage to my body had more or less healed, but I still ached from too much exertion and sometimes became dizzy from the new speed at which I could travel. But my strength did not waver. It only increased, steadily so, with each infusion of the mistress' ancient blood. Every mouthful was a shot of vampire steroids. Her blood blended with mine, bringing me to new heights of power, but also powerful moments of madness and hatred so consuming it proved difficult to shake. A transformation had begun, but I couldn't be certain about what I might come out as on the other side. My only redeeming qualities, my capacity for love and compassion, dimmed. Even if we were to be the victors in this conflict, I may never be the same person I once was.

Achyut appeared on the last night before the final event. *The Final Event* was how I'd come to view what was about to happen. Everything came down to this one night, one moment that would change everything. The end would be quick and brutal, I was sure. Without a miracle or a monumental mistake, I didn't see how Harshika could be conquered. I accepted my place at her side and what her influence would turn me into. A terrible pressure squeezed my heart.

I picked up on the difference in Achyut's presence within minutes, inspired by Harshika's reaction to his arrival. Her face pinched with displeasure and a soft growl she may not even have been aware of escaped her slender throat. The tension between them became apparent immediately. Harshika circled him like a lion stalking its prey, looking for a vulnerability. Achyut's expression remained neutral and he waited out her perusal. I saw a flash of fang from Harshika and knew she was upset. I hoped I wouldn't be in the line of fire if she erupted.

She surprised me by remaining calm, a deliberate calculation on her part, I assumed, for she never held back. When she spoke, her fangs had retracted and her false innocence was in place. "You've accomplished your task?"

"Of course, mistress. Was there ever any doubt?" he answered without missing a beat.

Harshika suspected something amiss. The thought slid to me, surprising me, as she had been so controlled around me during the past few days. Her worry had caused her to slip, bringing a small sliver of hope that she might be vulnerable when challenged or distracted. She passed a poisonous glance between the two of us then dismissed Achyut with an impatient flick of her hand. She was rattled. Good.

As he retreated, unmistakable triumph flashed across his face. Harshika had turned her attention away as a child might when irritated or flustered. Our gazes met and something passed between us, a spark of insight, so swift it could have been my imagination or my frayed nerves, but it was real, I was certain. What it meant I couldn't explain with any clarity, but my hope burned brighter because of it. A smile pulled at my lips and I turned away from Achyut to keep it to myself.

Maybe there is a way for me to get out of this alive? As soon as the thought came, I deliberately abandoned it lest Harshika pick up on anything suspect. When I looked up again, she stared at me. Her jaw clenched and she tapped her fingers together, a habit she had when irritated. Since this was her most constant mood, I'd seen the finger tapping a lot. I looked into her eyes, shining onyx pools, and she had me. I tried to resist, fought with my newly acquired power, but it felt as if she'd reached in and yanked my brain by its stem. The pain was horrendous. I fell forward, but she caught me with delicate hands so in contrast with the formidable strength I knew they possessed.

"Rachel," she whispered, so seductive and sweet. "What's going on with you? You are thinking strange things and I don't like it."

There was no trying to reason with her, so I played dumb. "I can't help the thoughts that go through my mind sometimes, especially when I'm so scared and upset." My voice hinted at defiance, fed by the simmering rage I'd absorbed with Harshika's blood, but she seemed to let it slide.

"I forget sometimes how young and inexperienced you are."

"Easy to do, considering what's going on right now." My lips quivered as the words left my mouth. She worked at me, chipping away at my defenses while she acted as though she wasn't. My anger flared, fighting against my conscious decision to hold it in check. I wondered if I might reach the point where

I would no longer be able to contain it, or where I may not even care.

"Don't placate me, Rachel. It makes me angry." As a reminder a wave of her power struck me across the face. My cheek split open with a wet gush of blood.

I refused to cower and fought against raising a hand to my now stinging cheek. "I'm sorry, mistress."

"Of course you are," she said.

It seemed as though she would continue the conversation when something caught her attention. She called Samaria over to where we stood and ordered her to keep an eye on me while she left to speak with a male vampire, one I had not seen before the last few days. He had joined us in Los Angeles before disappearing again after a brief consultation with Harshika.

With short brown hair, brown eyes, and average height, he was rather plain, but lovely as all immortals are. His power was ice and rock, indicative of his long existence. He did not speak to me, though gave me several slow perusals. His psychic presence attempted to probe my mind on several occasions, but Harshika stopped his intrusions. After that he was nothing more than a foggy presence on the perimeter of my awareness.

He and Harshika engaged in a very animated conversation with hot and cold tendrils flaring out from her in reaction to whatever he relayed to her. I flushed and shivered in accordance, too closely tied to her now not to taste her feelings. She painted her emotions over mine, often smothering my true reactions and muddling the line between what was real or forced upon me. My brain tired from fighting and faltered against resisting the absorption of her into me. I had become her shadow and a pale reflection of her inner demons.

That last night I dreamt of Harshika's change in haunting detail. I relived her attack by the king and his men as my own past. It ran in a painfully slow loop where I was forced to experience every injury, every insult firsthand. The faces of her attackers loomed larger than life, demonic and taunting, their drunken laughter acid in my slumbering brain. The contact with the ground through my bones as they callously dropped her on the jungle floor jarred me awake on several occasions.

There was a long period of suffering in the darkness, its injury my own agony. The eerie cry of the dying tigress slithered over and through me, beckoning me to heed its call. The rough ground tore at me as I crawled toward the source of the sound. Death pulled at me.

The animal's fur was soft, but littered with grit, the coat about its neck damp with saliva. A pungent and nauseating stench assaulted me, yet the smell didn't deter me. In fact, it seemed to incite my hunger even more. A startling fury and urgency exploded within me and I attacked the defenceless creature with hands and teeth, my spirit knowing before my brain that the blood coursing through the animal's veins was what my battered body needed to heal.

But the healing was the tip of the iceberg; this blood, this moment, incited by rage and vengeance, was the beginning of an unnatural transformation. This was the birth of a creature never to have walked the face of the earth before, a creature who, from that moment on, would hold humanity at its mercy.

CHAPTER 24

Rachel. Peru. Time's Up. The Final Event.

I sat at Harshika's side, held in place in my wooden chair with invisible restraints. The bands of her power were stronger than any rope or metal, so tightly wrapped about my body I could do nothing but move my head. My body remained stiff from my punishment a few days earlier, and the pressure was excruciating in places where the worst damage had been inflicted. Even if I were freed, I didn't know how much help I'd be in my current state. The only reason I could function at all was from the infusion of the mistress' potent blood.

Achyut stood as a silent sentinel on the opposite side of Harshika's throne. Those who had joined her ranks gathered behind us, tense and restless for violence. A soft rustling of movement and a flurry of nerves and self-righteousness permeated the atmosphere. I noted an undertone of doubt, vague but present nonetheless. Everyone was well aware of what was at stake, and that not all would make it out in one piece, if at all. A definite winner would be crowned today, and a status quo changed forever.

Sorcha and Samaria both watched me with malice in their eyes, making no bones about how much they didn't like that I had become Harshika's pet. They both imagined ways to eliminate me, each one more violent and degrading than the last, until Harshika knocked them both on their asses with an impatient sweep of her arm. Sharp words of warning about questioning her decisions came with the physical punishment, and both were cowed before her rage. After that they looked anywhere but in my direction, and kept their thoughts to themselves. I had to admit the sight of them sprawled in the dirt with indignant expressions on their lovely faces made me chuckle. It was now so easy to slip into Harshika's childish anger and gain satisfaction from her petty torments.

"They're here," Harshika whispered and, as soon as the words left her lips, I felt the approaching presence.

This time we'd gathered at the top of the monument, which several of Harshika's minions had cleared completely since the first time we had gathered. From our vantage point we had an unobstructed line of sight to the entrance from the jungle. Even from such a distance I discerned a long line of immortals with Charles leading the way. His familiar presence was strong and bold. I searched the faces I saw clearly, looking for the one that mattered most.

Giovanni's energy touched me and something hot and urgent flared to life inside me.

"*I'm coming*," he thought, and his voice in my head was confident. For the first time in many weeks I dared to hope. The pure joy I experienced at being close enough to Giovanni to know his psychic touch seemed to lessen the intensity of Harshika's dominance over me. Her influence wavered, then shot back up to full capacity, effectively severing my connection with Giovanni.

He shot a look in my direction. He'd felt the same thing I had. Menace, dark and hungry, lurked in his sapphire eyes. There was something different about him, but I couldn't quite put my finger on it. Charles made eye contact with me, his infuriating and unreadable blank mask in place. Behind him I saw a few faces I recognised, and many I didn't.

Alessandra, Eli, Saskia, Mengmei and Zhongxing, as well as Aldous and Emmaline flanked Charles and Giovanni. The rest filed behind like dutiful and focused soldiers, which in a twisted way, they were. Faces grim, minds hard. What little escaped from their mental shields was angry and bitter. Unlike some of the mistress' followers, I didn't detect even a whisper of reservation from my friends and allies. They were there to make a stand, perhaps their final one.

The group stopped at the base of the temple. Harshika rose

and her legions tensed behind her, ready to move at the slightest provocation. Charles took a few steps ahead of the group he led and met Harshika's gaze. The Charles I loved and feared so greatly stood before us, composed, haughty, and ruthless. The perfect posture and arrogant way he held his jaw clearly pissed Harshika off. Her irritation was a warm caress and I couldn't help but smile. Out of the corner of my eye I caught a slight movement and, as I turned my head, Achyut covered the lower half of his face with one slender hand. I'm sure he camouflaged a smirk.

"You have come to surrender yourselves then? To ask for my forgiveness?" Harshika asked with not a hint of uncertainty. She was solid in her belief that none would dare challenge her, or be stupid enough to doubt her dominance.

"Not quite, mistress, we do not wish to be under anyone's authority. We wish to govern and, at times, police ourselves. We have done well enough on our own thus far," Charles answered in his most refined manner. He kept his hands clasped behind his back as though addressing an equal, unworried about a possible attack.

Harshika was a blur as she raced down the steeply inclined staircase and met Charles face to face. This night she had chosen a pale-yellow sleeveless shift that billowed about her like mist, exposing her deceivingly slight frame. Power enveloped her as a hazy, shifting shadow. Her indignation at Charles's challenge charged the atmosphere. The air became denser, pressing outward with rolling waves of fury, crashing against and through those in attendance. It was a surge of heat and a snap of frost, bursting, writhing power that swelled with every passing second. Her reach seemed to know no bounds, her influence unstoppable.

"You dare to challenge my authority?" She sneered.

"I do," Charles answered without hesitation.

"As do I." Giovanni stepped to Charles's side.

Harshika's eyes became slits and, if I didn't know any better, I would say I witnessed a slight tremble in her hands before they clenched into fists. Then she was gone.

I scanned the crowds and the encroaching darkness, but

saw nothing amiss. A small cry sounded and, before I could track the origins, Harshika was back. In her small hand she held a male vampire I did not know. Charles flinched, but before he could even take a step toward her, Harshika had reached over and crushed the vampire's head with the ease one would squeeze a ripe tomato. The body dropped to the ground and, with exaggerated motions, Harshika licked the thick coating of blood from her fingers.

Aldous appeared at Charles's other side, and he stopped our friend from going farther with a lightning fast sweep of his arm. Both their movements were much faster than I had ever seen from either of them before. The men's gazes met and an unspoken understanding passed between them. The crowd behind Charles rustled with anger.

Harshika made her way back up the nearly four-story high staircase to her throne and waiting followers. "You dare to defy me when I am capable of destroying any one of you I choose?" What Charles and Giovanni might not have been aware of was how desperately she wanted the two of them at her side.

"You can't destroy all of us," Giovanni answered.

She had reached the top, the moon full and bright behind her. In that moment, she was every bit the goddess she believed herself to be, with the silvery, otherworldly light shimmering in the background. It reflected off her ebony hair and illuminated her skin like bleached bone. I felt something for her then, an intimate connection that both pleased and repulsed me. If her destruction was meant to be, some part of me would be sad to see her go.

"That may be true, but my followers are strong and fast."

"As are ours," Charles said.

Harshika let out a peal of laughter, the sound shivering along my arm. "This rag-tag bunch of vampires? You really think you stand a chance?" Then she made a *tsk-tsk* sound and shook her head. Her inner confidence did not quite match her outward bravado, but none except for Achyut and I would have known that.

She snapped her fingers and two vampires disappeared inside the opening at the rear of the temple's platform behind the crumbling sacrificial stone. She turned back to Charles, eyes shining and a tight smile on her lips. "Perhaps you might be persuaded another way?" Now she had lost her patience and her anger smothered any lingering desire to acquire Charles. She wanted his pain.

The crowds about her stirred and murmurs and barks of laughter rang out. The two emerged, pulling a struggling female form between them. I knew in an instant from the scent this was a human. Her heart pounded, her rushing blood a scintillating aphrodisiac. Strangely one name sounded over and over again in her mind—*Charles.*

The woman was brought to Harshika, and with a toss of long, pale hair, the woman's face was exposed. *Genevieve!* I struggled against the power holding me to the chair, my anger catapulting me to new levels of strength and breaking Harshika's hold over me. Too late I leapt from my chair, but Harshika had already tossed Genevieve over the edge. Her screams assaulted my ears. The terrible juicy thuds she made smashing against the stone as she plummeted sickened me to the core. My knees buckled but I forced myself forward. Just as I started my descent, a strong hand caught hold of my hair and pulled me back.

I tumbled to my knees, but I could still see over the edge. Charles shot forward, catching Genevieve about three-quarters of the way down the temple staircase. A trail of splattered crimson followed to the spot where Charles caught her. He disappeared from my view with Genevieve's broken body cradled in his arms. The sight of them was swallowed by the surging mass of vampires. I looked up and realised it was Achyut and not Harshika who had held me back and, as our gazes met, an urgent message was transferred from him to me. *"Trust me."*

By now both sides had charged and battle waged. The temple became a river of blood, the night overburdened with grunts of exertion and cries of pain. Achyut released his hold and I grabbed the vampire closest to me. It was one of the two who had brought Genevieve, a short heavy male with almond-shaped eyes. He seemed surprised I'd turned on him and I took the moment for all it was worth. I'd ripped both his arms from his body before he was able to react and, even then, he could only kick out at me ineffectually, and with the effort slipped in his own blood. He tumbled to the ground and I was on him, ripping out the flesh from his throat all the way down to his glistening spine. I surprised myself, fighting with such efficiency despite my injuries. I'd never moved so quickly, the motion happening almost before my thoughts had completed.

A hand touched my shoulder and I sprang to my feet without missing a beat. I swivelled about, lunged into the person, and fell with them to the ground. We rolled, and as I was about to attack, I realised someone said my name. The face above me became clear, blue eyes shining.

"Rachel," Giovanni cried before crushing his lips against mine.

"Giovanni. I never thought I'd see—" I started to say before he yanked me to my feet.

"Not enough time. We need to get Harshika."

As I was about to ask what he meant, Achyut appeared beside us. "We need to go now," Achyut said and, to my amazement, Giovanni nodded. "She's gone down the side. Find as many who know as you can."

Achyut vanished over the side and we were not too far behind him. The scene below was chaos, bodies flying and violent thoughts bombarding from all directions. Expletives were tossed about in every conceivable language and the intensity of the anger and fear churned through the air like a whirlwind of fire. A large hand clamped around my arm and I spun around until I was face to chest with an enormous bald-headed male vampire. He peered at me with black eyes from under a hawkish nose.

"Duck," he said and, in the same instant, a fist the size of a Christmas ham flew in my direction. I did as he said and the punch connected with a smaller male behind me, knocking him right off the side of the temple. A shriek of rage followed then a meaty, wet sound as he hit the platform below.

"Thanks," I said, but my saviour had already moved on to his next victim.

Several bodies and sometimes just pieces flew past, showering us with cool blood. The stairs had become slick with it, to the detriment of even the most-nimble immortal. Vampires slipped, rolling and crashing into one another. Hands as strong as twenty humans ripped at throats, limbs, or hair—whatever they could get a hold of. Bodies were torn apart and drained of their ancient blood. I searched the blur of faces with tremulous worry, praying none of the husks or twitching parts belonged to any of my loved ones.

Giovanni pulled me along behind him, making swift business down the side of the temple. We bypassed much of the battle, offering a united front when forced to engage. A chunk of my hair was yanked from my scalp and ragged claws left their mark on my throat as a bushy-haired female tried to throttle the life out of me. Giovanni came at her from behind and forced her head around until it faced in the opposite direction before draining her blood. His strength was more than I remembered, more intense than before the damage from the Desmarais. Over his shoulder I saw Kieran fighting off a male with hair so white it looked like raw silk. He also seemed amplified in his strength and speed, able to continue fighting despite an obviously broken arm held close to his torso.

Within the last few feet from the bottom, I spotted several other familiar faces. Emmaline and Aldous battled a small group with Eli and Zhongxing close by. Eli had lost his shirt in the ensuing battle, exposing his back now lined with deep, bright furrows and pouring an alarming amount of blood. The crowds shifted and Alessandra and Saskia could be seen, both hurt and saturated with blood. Alessandra screamed something in her native language, a sound full of anguish and rage. I didn't understand the details of her outburst, because I had spotted Charles and Genevieve.

I ripped my hand from Giovanni's and pushed aside everything in my way to get to them. In that moment I didn't care about Harshika, or who we might have lost. Saving Genevieve was the only issue on which I could focus. Convulsions wracked her body and it was obvious her back was broken from the unnatural way she was sprawled on the ground. Charles alternated between screaming and sobbing as I knelt down beside him.

"Do it, turn her," I ordered.

"She doesn't want to be like us!" Charles wailed. Tears streamed down his face.

"Then your only choice is to let her die."

"I can't. She doesn't want our life," he said.

Genevieve made loud, whooping gasps for air and I knew no time remained. I lowered my mouth to a gaping wound on her chest and drank what little blood remained in her body. I ripped open a vein at my wrist with my teeth and was about to put it to Genevieve's mouth when Charles thrust me aside.

"I'll do it." He was back in control and sounding like his usual hard self.

Drops of blood splashed onto Genevieve's white lips as Charles lowered his wrist to her mouth. He squeezed his hand, pumping the immortal blood into her as quickly as he could. Thirty agonising seconds passed before she responded. Genevieve suddenly coughed, choking on the flow of blood before she drank in earnest.

"Let me help," I said. "You need your strength."

I replaced his wrist with my own and let her drink. The strength of Harshika's blood would help heal the damage to Genevieve's body. I prayed it was enough to repair her injuries before the change was complete, or she would be trapped in her broken body forever.

When Charles deemed she'd had enough, he dragged her away from the site, into the long grass. He returned to me and together we searched for our friends. Giovanni found us and with him were Saskia, Alessandra, Eli, Micah, Mengmei, Kieran, and a handful of immortals I didn't recognise. Eli drank from the wrist of a large, hump-backed male who nodded in our direction as we closed the space between us and the group.

"No time for introductions," Giovanni said by way of greeting.

"She's back here!" a male screamed, and we all looked toward the sound. Zhongxing waved frantically, and when he was sure he had our attention, he disappeared around the far end of the temple's base. We all raced after him and, rounding the corner, found ourselves in a small clearing sided by several smaller buildings, the temple, and a section of jungle.

At the mouth of the narrow space lay a female vampire of Hispanic origin with a sturdy male and a delicate blond in attendance. As we closed in, I saw the head of the woman on the ground had been ripped from her body, attached now only by a strip of tendon. Her mouth moved, but no sound came. The two at her side looked at us with pain and anger bright in their eyes.

"Solange!" Giovanni rushed ahead of the rest of us.

He knelt beside the body. With the realization that nothing could be done to save her, he lowered his head. The ground beneath his knee was saturated with the vampire's blood.

"I couldn't get to her quickly enough," the male vampire said to Giovanni.

"David, we all knew the risks. Don't blame yourself."

"Let's get this over with," David answered.

He and the blond joined our group and raced forward with us into the clearing. Anxiety fouled the atmosphere, amplified by the distress Giovanni felt over the loss of Solange.

Harshika waited, confident, with a small group flanking her. I took a frantic inventory of our numbers, pleased to see we were about evenly matched. Aldous and Emmaline, and Jeremiah pulled up the rear.

Where was Achyut?

"Rachel, pet. So good of you to return," she said, so lovely and awful. She crooked a finger in my direction and I jerked forward.

Charles grabbed one arm, Giovanni the other, fighting with all their strength to stop me.

"The only thing you're going to accomplish with that is pulling her arms off her body." Her laughter smothered me and cast aside all other sensations.

"Let her go, Harshika." Achyut dropped from overhead a fraction of a second behind his whispery command. He landed between Harshika and myself with his feline-like grace and her connection to me dissipated. I staggered, returning to Giovanni's side.

"I knew you were up to something." Harshika shook with anger. Her finger was a dagger of accusation as she pointed at her offspring. "You thought I didn't know there was something going on? You have tried too hard to block me these last few days, seeming so smug. After all I've done for you, you're going to turn on me now?"

"On the contrary, mistress. I'm going to repay all you've done for me. In kind."

There wasn't even time to blink before Harshika lunged at Achyut, but instead of attempting to protect himself he met her attack with equal speed and fury. They collided with the force of two transport trucks, and a vicious struggle of movements too quick to track ensued. They crashed into the side of the temple and rock debris showered on the two of them. A shriek rang out as a chunk of stone the size of a small car landed in the clearing, crushing one of Harshika's minions beneath its weight. The two continued fighting as though nothing had happened.

As they tumbled to the ground, a gentle mist splashed across my face and a heady, delicious liquid slipped over my lips. I licked the last drops from my face when a loud slamming startled me, followed by a shriek of indignant surprise. The struggle came to an abrupt end with Harshika immobilised on the jungle floor and a bleeding Achyut next to her. She was on her side, face frozen in mid-scream, but there was no accompanying sound.

Achyut waved us forward with his hand. His other arm was twisted backward at the elbow. A gash deep enough to show bone had been inflicted at the shoulder. Harshika's subordinates remained frozen, unsure of what had happened or how to proceed without her direction. Their hungry, furious gazes watched as uncertainty panted its pungent breath, adding a layer of slickness to the already humid air.

He stepped back to allow us access to Harshika and, as we neared, I saw she wasn't dead but powerless somehow. A small syringe protruded from her thin chest. Her body quivered, lips twitching.

"Quickly," Achyut said. "It won't keep her down for long." He twisted his lower arm back into place with a quick, crunchy thrust then clamped his good hand over the seeping wound at his shoulder.

Giovanni sent me a wordless message and I followed his example. We fell onto her body like a pack of wild dogs, sinking our teeth into wherever we found some exposed flesh. Her blood was pungent, spicy and yet sweet as honey. As I drank, the effects took hold immediately. The blood screamed fire through my veins and I felt as though I could tear the temple to the ground with my bare hands. Images of Harshika's time as an immortal intruded into my reverie, at first bright and painful, then fading with the draining of her blood. When there was nothing left in her body, the images ended with jarring abruptness. I snapped back to reality and the bloody, excited faces of my nearest and dearest loomed large. Somehow, I understood it was not just the mistress' blood we'd absorbed, but also her essence.

Harshika lay in the middle of our group. The wasted, shrunken body was a sick parody of the vibrant, dominant creature she had been for more millennia than any of us could even fathom. Her once-lustrous black hair had become brittle and lifeless. Her smooth, milky skin had shrivelled and yellowed, looking like an old piece of leather left to the elements. Her lips had drawn back in a snarl, fangs exposed to the gum line. Delicate hands were gnarled, drawn up as though to choke the life from any who dared approach her. Even in final death she was defiant. A tear slipped from my eye to land on the arm to which I still clung. Harshika's demise burned inside me, twisted a knife in my gut.

A familiar hand covered my own, gently pulling my grasp away from Harshika's corpse. I turned my attention to Giovanni and collapsed into his arms. My cheek pressed against his chest and the familiar feel of his body comforted me. I knew Harshika had to die, I understood with every fiber of my being what a horrible, vicious monster she'd been, but a terrible anguish ate at me while I looked at what we had done.

"Don't stop now. We must destroy her completely. She is more powerful than you can ever imagine and, if there is a way to come back from this, she will do it," Achyut said.

Until that moment I hadn't realised he was by my side, his damage already healing. I looked back at Harshika's corpse and, to my astonishment, she started to regenerate herself. The change was subtle, but not to be ignored.

Charles, Emmaline, Mengmei, and Kieran seized her corpse and, as they tore it apart, Harshika's followers surged forward, outraged and brazen with the need to avenge their leader. A small number reached our group and Eli was grasped in the powerful hands of Sorcha and a male vampire I did not have a name for. He struggled against their combined attack, forced to his knees.

"Eli!" someone screamed from behind me. Sorcha and her accomplice turned at the sound as did I, and I was astounded to see Micah burst through the crowd. He held something under one arm, which I did not immediately recognise as the head of one of the statues from the base of the temple. With amazing precision, he fired it forward like a giant shot-put, knocking the male vampire's head cleanly off his neck. The body remained standing for half a second as though surprised, then crumpled to the ground in a shower of blood. Charles's hand closed around Sorcha's throat.

"Holy shit!" Eli said, amazed. He looked from the head, to the body, to the mess Charles made of Sorcha's writhing remains before returning to Micah's face. The two regarded each other and Micah's surprise at his actions seemed as genuine as Eli's.

"I'm stronger than I thought I was," Micah said, a bright smile emerging. They both laughed and came together amid the gore and violence, strengthened by how close the call had been, but it wasn't yet time for guards to be let down.

Samaria barrelled into me, lightning fast, knocking me face forward to the ground. She seized a chunk of my hair, twisting my head over my shoulder, straining the tendons and muscles that held it in place. Instead of fighting it, I rolled into the attack, pulling Samaria down to the ground with me. She was far older than I, but I'd become strong after drinking Harshika's blood. My power surprised her. I drove an elbow into her mid-section, receiving a grunt for my effort.

Her hands snaked about me, attempting to get me in a hold, but I was too fast for her. Before she had a chance to retaliate, I was up and on her with a knee on her chest and my hands about her throat. I pulled my arm back, then smashed it down into her face with a satisfying crunch. Over and over I pounded until her head was nothing more than a gooey, lumpy mess at the end of her neck. Blood gushed out, spilling onto the ground. I put my lips to the ragged end of her jugular and let the last remnants leak into my mouth. I swooned from the elixir, and from the satisfaction of taking the bitch out.

Achyut stood and whirled about. A wave of power burst from his body, knocking the group back several feet. Some landed swiftly on their feet, many tumbled to the ground, hurt and bewildered. The strongest charged again.

"Remember what we practiced," Giovanni called out, rising from the pile of body parts at his feet.

All around me were the convulsing, flailing remains of many of Harshika's ardent followers. All of my friends had become very strong in my absence. With Achyut leading the way in our rebellion, I came to understand why. The group moved together, standing so close to one another their shoulders touched. Several clasped hands. A warm, urgent pressure ignited from their closeness, spiralling outward and crashing into me where I sat on the ground. I tumbled over, landing on top of a scratchy chunk of something. It took me a second to realise it was a piece of Harshika's leg. I scrambled to my feet.

In amazement I watched as the group was able to combine their strength and force it outward as a physical presence. It danced forward as a mass of agitated fireflies, sparking and snapping, picking up momentum as it advanced. The wave seemed to combine with Achyut's power then shot forward like a lightning bolt. A child-like female vampire at the back of our group had her eyes tightly closed as though any outward distraction might break her concentration. The sensation chaffed against my skin, prickling and pulling at me.

The power struck the opposing vampires and, as it did, the air crackled, and there came a stench of burning hair. The surrounding trees quivered and the foundation of the temple rattled as if an earthquake had struck. The affected immortals jerked, eyes bulging. Mouths opened, but there were no screams, only haunting, terrible silence. Then the bodies swelled, spun, and jerked, exploding in a shower of blood and bone. In the end, there was nothing left but a slick mass of bubbling, dark liquid on the jungle floor.

A collective sigh of relief flooded through the remaining vampires, many showing obvious signs of distress as a result of the massive exertion of power. Some of the younger vampires sagged, trembled, or fell to their knees. Giovanni turned to me and, as I was about to step forward, something snaked around my ankle. I screamed, shaking my leg furiously. With horror and shock I discovered Harshika's wasted, skeletal hand clasped on my lower leg. My gaze trailed along the sinewy arm to the string of damaged tendons barely attached to the stump of her shoulder.

Her mouth opened and closed, a horrible raspy, mewling sound escaping. "Rachel," she said. "Rachel..."

I screamed again and several of the group shot forward. They tore at her body, reducing it to nothing but chunks of brittle flesh, smaller than the size of my fist. All but the head, which Achyut snatched by the hair and, with a huge smile, smashed against the side of the temple. The skull shattered and brittle, powdery pieces rained to the ground. The group cheered him on.

He raced ahead with astonishing speed, leaping halfway up the temple, returning with a burning torch in one hand. He touched the flame to the remains of his maker's head, delight bright on his face as the fire flared and consumed all that was left. He then came to the pile of her torso, but before he touched the flame to the remains, he lowered to one knee. His expression was pained as he reached down to pluck a small object from the pieces of her body. He slipped the item into his pocket and, without comment, set her remains on fire. Within seconds the only thing left of the great mistress Harshika was a small pile of ash. Achyut scooped up a handful of the residue and a single tear slipped down his cheek.

Charles was at my side. "Genevieve." Then he was gone.

CHAPTER 25

Rachel

Charles was out of my sight before I could respond. Giovanni approached me, and squeezed me so tightly I thought he would break my back. Emotions flooded me at his touch, my love for him soaring above all the rest. His embrace loosened and many arms wrapped about me, my friends expressing their relief at having me returned in one piece. The joy I soaked up from them overshadowed the persistent vileness of the past month under Harshika's control. I took the time to hug them all in turn. I cried with happiness at finding them all alive and accounted for.

Eli was the last one I came to, but the one I clung to the hardest and longest. I crushed him against my body, sobbing and stroking his hair. I hadn't known what happened to him after Harshika took her prisoners and I'd spent so many of my waking hours consumed with fear and worry for his safety. Even after all this time and the way things had turned out, he had never been far from my thoughts. After several minutes, he used his hands to loosen the iron grip I had on him and I saw his cheeks were also crimson with tears. We had a bond, he and I, which no one else could fully understand or touch.

"I'm okay, Rachel. Really." His voice cracked with emotion.

"I was so scared. She was so sick, so twisted. There was no telling what she might have done to you, or any of us."

"She's gone and she can't hurt any of us anymore."

I kissed his cheek, tasting dirt and blood. "I love you, Eli. I don't know what I would have done without you."

"Never gonna happen."

I hugged him again and saw Micah standing behind us. Our gazes met and I waved him forward. He wrapped his arms around Eli, sandwiching him between the two of us. Before moving away, I kissed them both on the mouth, whispering how glad I was they were okay and that they had each other. When I looked back as I made my way to Giovanni, they kissed and hugged each other, oblivious to everything else around them. I understood how they felt, their joy as my own, but something nagged at me.

Giovanni waited patiently throughout the entire exchange, letting me do what I needed to. He took my hand and smiled, eliciting a reaction that rode through my body to the tips of my toes. I looked at his face, amazed at how much I loved him. With my finger I traced the curve of his cheek then brushed his tangled hair back from his eyes. There I found love and appreciation looking back at me, a deep sense of belonging I'd never known anywhere else. Adequate words did not exist to describe the response his presence evoked. He was in my heart, my blood and tears, my every waking thought. It was a blessing we'd found each other at all, a miracle we'd survived everything that had happened since.

Achyut watched without comment as the remaining immortals interacted—hugging, talking, laughing, and crying. Our behaviour must have seemed so strange to him after so many years without intimacy or kindness. From around the front of the temple came more of our kind, bloody and drained from the toughest fight of their existences. They came to make sure what they heard and felt was true—that Harshika had been destroyed. There were cheers and hugs, high-fives and quiet relief. Many clapped Giovanni on the back and shook Achyut's hand. If there were any of Harshika's minions still present, they had either wisely departed or assimilated into those remaining.

Emmaline was at my side, hugging me for about the twentieth time in as many minutes. Her hair was soft and fragrant, her closeness filled with a surprising intensity of happiness. I'd missed her. The relief of seeing my friends again surged through my body, my blood, overwhelming me. It was as if I couldn't quite trust our freedom to be true. A breeze whispered past, sprinkled with the ashy remains of Harshika's body, taking part of me along. Panic clawed inside me and I had to turn away.

I looked up into the sky where the moon dominated the dark with its silvery presence, and for a split second, I saw Harshika's face. Though she may be dead and destroyed beyond a chance of resurrection, for me she would never fully be gone. I had shared too much with her, both her blood and her spirit, to ever return to my former self. My newfound strength and speed were nothing compared to the sharpness of my mental abilities. Save for Achyut, I could read everyone's thoughts to some degree and was aware of chaotic emotions released, flooding me until I couldn't separate my own feelings from the rest. I'd also acquired the capability of shutting off what I wished, like a flick of a switch, and zero in on whom and what I chose. I blocked everyone but Giovanni.

My control was nearly perfect now and I wondered whether anything would change between Giovanni and me because of it. We'd always been close and open to each other, but my role had always been secondary in that regard. I'd been easy for him to read and project his thoughts and emotions onto, but I'd never been able to fully reciprocate. Now I would be the stronger one. Harshika's madness had left its mark on me, and I would not be the same Rachel Giovanni had fallen in love with almost twenty-five years ago. I felt her hatred simmering and I had to be conscious of containing it lest it become unleashed.

Achyut pulled me aside. "I know you're scared of what she's done to you, Rachel. And I won't lie to you and say it won't be difficult, but you can escape her mark on you. It will be a struggle at times, but your love for Giovanni will get you through." He turned me toward him, looking me in the eye. There was a connection so sudden and profound, the space between us crackled like static electricity. "We will both escape her."

I put my arms around his slight frame, his body as solid and strong as stone. He stiffened at first then embraced me in return. As he pulled away, he pressed cold lips to my cheek and whispered, "Just think of me and I will come."

"Thank you. What are you going to do now that she's gone?"

"Be free," he answered.

"Where's Charles?" I heard Kieran ask. I turned my attention to the group standing nearby. Like school children, we had filtered back to our familiar cliques, and only Alessandra, Saskia, Kieran, Mengmei and Zhongxing, Aldous and Emmaline, and Eli and Micah remained close by.

Giovanni stood with a second group, including the young girl I'd seen earlier, his profile to me. A gorgeous, ebony-haired vampire that reminded me of Salma Hayek had an arm draped over his shoulder. *Santana.* He smiled at her, and she had her head tossed back with a flirty laugh. She caught my scrutiny and looked over her shoulder in my direction. A touch of Harshika's anger flared, taunting me to wipe the smile from her gorgeous face. I was already moving forward when Achyut grabbed my arm, holding me back from making a terrible mistake.

"This is not you. Remember that."

As soon as his hand had touched my arm the anger vanished. I felt foolish and frustrated. It was even worse than when I'd first changed, when it was so easy to lose one's self to the hunger and arrogance of power. I closed my eyes and forced the impulse aside. Then I walked to Giovanni with Achyut trailing along behind me. I came to the side that wasn't occupied by his new friend and took his hand. He leaned in and kissed me with unrestrained passion.

"This is Santana," he said after pulling his lips from mine.

Santana reached a hand around Giovanni and I shook it. "Nice to meet you, Rachel. Giovanni had told us much about you. We're all so happy to have you back safe and sound."

The sincerity of her voice put me at ease, coaxing my anger back into its cage. "I'm glad to be back."

"So, these are some new friends, Rachel," Giovanni said before introducing me to the circle of unfamiliar faces—David, Daniel, Ezekial, Lucy, Billy-Joe. There were many others, but the names blurred. The only ones that caught my attention and remained vivid were Clellia and Billy-Joe. Clellia was the young girl I'd seen earlier with eyes clenched tightly to focus her power against our attackers. A series of images from her past shot into me like contact with a red-hot poker when I touched her. The whole incident didn't last more than the few seconds I held her hand, but it was long enough to know the truth. She gave me a shy smile.

Daniel stood beside her, quiet and reserved, a far cry from the monster of her memories. I looked at him and couldn't separate the past from the present. The anger was back, crawling a warm flush over my skin. I imagined I was just about frothing at the mouth from my desire to wrap my hands about his throat. I trembled from head to toe, and Giovanni gave me a hard, worried look. My thoughts were red and black, terrible urges snarling and biting, struggling to be released. I forced myself to remember Greece, the home I'd loved so much, and the rage slowly subsided. My attention turned back to Giovanni.

"Where is Charles? Has he come back yet?" I asked.

Giovanni shook his head. "Not yet."

"We should find him and make sure everything is okay."

I searched with my mind until I found Eli. *"Come with us."* A handful of seconds later, he stepped from the crowd with Micah at his side. The two of them followed us from the clearing, around the base of the temple, and out to the jungle's edge. I led them to the place where Charles had left Genevieve's body and, sure enough, they were there.

Charles sat with Genevieve's upper body cradled on his lap. He stroked her hair, gaze locked on her still form. The damage to her body appeared healed, but it would not be certain until she awoke the next evening whether any ill effects of her fall would be permanent. Her face was so white, her lips slightly parted. When Charles looked up, he was crying, and the sight of him so vulnerable twisted my heart.

I knelt. She looked so fragile and I remembered my own anxiety from when I turned Eli. Those long hours where the body lingered between life and death during the change to immortal was an eternity of desperate hope. I'd hovered over Eli, searching for any indication the Dark Kiss had taken, almost mad with fear that I'd killed him. Charles was in a similar state, but more dignified than I could ever hope to be. For the first time I was able to feel him and it was a strange sensation to connect with him like that.

His love for Genevieve stroked me with petal-soft fingers and his concern was a cold northern rain. The hard-coiled mass of his power lay ready to strike at the slightest provocation. I wondered if he was always so tightly wound and whether his outward cool was a cover for a not quite so confident reality. He must have become aware of my psychic presence then, for his green-eyed gaze flashed to my face, and a wall shot up about his inner turmoil. His expression was stoic, his tightly clenched jaw challenging me to call his bluff.

I leaned in and pressed our foreheads together. "Your secret is safe with me," I whispered, the sound too quiet for any of the others to hear.

He patted me on the back. "I don't know what you're talking about," he whispered back.

I smiled.

"We need to get her inside," Giovanni said and the rest of us murmured our agreement.

"Follow me." I led them through the labyrinth of passage-ways to the chamber that had once been Harshika's.

After helping Charles get Genevieve settled, I closed the door behind me and joined Giovanni, Eli, and Micah in the larger outer chamber. They were close together, conversation quiet and intense. They didn't realise their thoughts leapt into my brain as quickly as the words escaped their lips. They speculated about what would happen to Charles if Genevieve didn't make it through the transformation. They were also worried about what occurred during my imprisonment with Harshika.

I squeezed between Giovanni and Eli, the sense of always being in that position not lost on me. It had been such an ordeal to heal myself from Giovanni's loss and allow myself to be open to a life with Eli, only to have Giovanni returned to me. The shame of my actions after his reappearance almost ate me alive. Truth be told, a part of my heart belonged to Eli still. My feelings for him were not the same as the burning, consuming, undeni-able passion I felt for Giovanni, but were true all the same. As I sat there, and gazed at both their faces as they watched me with concern, it was the first time I'd allowed myself to admit it. Our time together had come to a sudden end, but it didn't mean the feeling had vanished. The abruptness didn't lend itself to a proper time to heal and make peace with what had happened and what would never be.

"Stop worrying about me," I said as I sat.

"You heard us?" Eli asked with surprise.

"I can hear better than all of you. Better than all the immortals, except for Achyut, I suspect. I can also hear your thoughts like a stream directly into my head."

"She shared her blood with you?" Giovanni asked.

"Yes. Several times. It's made me strong and fast, and my mind is so aware."

"I'm surprised," Giovanni said.

"Me, too, but she seemed to...like me. I mean as much as she was capable of liking anyone. I think if things had ended in her favour, she would have had me stay with her as a new pet. Maybe taking Achyut's place."

"You aren't the only one who's had ancient blood."

That surprised me. "Really?"

Giovanni gave Eli a hard look before answering. "Achyut shared his blood with us—me, Charles, Eli and Micah, and the rest of us. It was a small amount, and only for the last few nights, but it made the difference all the same."

"I thought you seemed faster and stronger. I wondered if it was my imagination."

"We are all stronger. Achyut wanted the best chance at succeeding," Eli said.

"And he was obviously right."

Hollow, knocking footsteps announced the arrival of other immortals. The four of us joined them, finding a group of about thirty vampires in the large cavern where we had first met Harshika. Aldous explained that most of the others had already left, some offering to keep in touch, others only promising to stay out of our way. As long as there weren't any further power struggles, I had no opinion on how others chose to continue on. Being a solitary creature can be a hard habit to break. Of those who desired friendship, I would return the feeling with gusto.

I wandered about, made conversation and picked up names for new faces, all the while turning something over in my head.

This was a clean slate and; even though Giovanni's return had been a new start in many regards, I hadn't freed myself fully from the past. Not enough to prevent it from creeping back into my future. If I'd learned nothing else from my time with Harshika, it was to let the past be. Dwelling there, in either the good or bad, only stole from the present.

I came to Giovanni, who spoke with Alessandra and Jeremiah, and told him I would be right back. He didn't question me, but his lips pressed into a thin line as he watched me take Eli's hand and lead him outside.

We walked into the damp jungle, far past the point we could be overheard. Most would not even be able to psychically eavesdrop, though at that point I no longer cared. I needed to be honest and allow that honesty to set us all on the right path once and for all.

"I'm surprised you asked me to come with you, Rachel. I would have thought you'd want to be with Giovanni right now." When he spoke, his words were hesitant and curious.

"I have to clear some things up with you, Eli. There are things I should have talked about with you way before now."

"Okay." He took a seat on a fallen tree trunk and patted the place next to him. I flashed back to the night in England under the falling snow. I'd been so upset and confused then that I hadn't handled things the way I should have.

I sat and took his hand, concentrating on it, because I knew if I looked at his face I'd break down. "After Giovanni came back and you realised we weren't going to be together, I didn't say all the things to you I wanted to. I don't know if I could have then, I was so confused. I was in shock, and I don't think the way I reacted was fair to you."

"Rachel, it's okay. I understand. It was a shock to all of us."

"Yes, but that doesn't make it right. After we talked, I think you left with the impression I never loved you and that certainly wasn't the case." My voice shook, my throat thick.

"I know you loved me, Rachel." His voice was as affected as mine.

"I did love you and we could have been very happy together. I cherish the time we spent together. I loved the nights we talked for hours and the way you used to look at me as if I was the most amazing thing you'd ever seen."

"You were. I haven't forgotten."

"I'm sorry. I've been trying to figure out the best way to say this and, now that I'm here, nothing is coming out the way I want it to."

"What is it you want to say to me?"

I let my gaze trail up his arm and shoulder, over the curve of his lips to his ocean-blue eyes. "I did love you, Eli, still do. You were never second best, or the consolation prize. I was with you because I loved you. I made love with you because I was attracted to you and it felt good to have you in my bed. What I felt or feel for you is separate from anything I feel for Giovanni, and it should never be compared or rated against the other. I fought so hard not to feel for you what I did, because I thought I betrayed Giovanni, and I was cruel to you. I tried to make it seem as though it was all one-sided and you pushed me, but the truth is I could have stopped it at any time and I didn't. I wasn't honest with you, and I was only honest with myself about all of this very recently."

"Rachel, where is this coming from? I think you're still upset from what you went through with Harshika and how you didn't know what happened to me. We're okay, we've made peace, everything."

"Yes, we have, and we're both with people we love very much. I know I belong with Giovanni, and I've been touched by your feelings for Micah, so I know how powerful and real they are. I don't doubt for a minute that you love him very much and that he satisfies you and makes you happy."

"And I don't doubt your love for Giovanni. I was there every day when you suffered with grief over his death. I felt you mourn him."

"I'm sorry. I just thought I left you feeling as if you were something I passed my time with, as if I would have only thought of you in a romantic way because Giovanni was gone. You will always have a place in my heart. How I feel for you will exist as long as I do. I will always be there for you."

"Ditto." He pulled me against his chest. "What did she do to you?"

"She did a lot of horrible things, hurt me badly, but she also freed me in a way. She opened my mind and let me see things I'd been denying and lying to myself about. I can't stop my feelings and I don't want to deny them, or be ashamed anymore."

"Me, either. I've never stopped loving you. Coming to terms with my feelings about Micah was such a complicated, confusing time for me. If I look back with honesty, I can say I've been attracted to men for as long as I remember, but it was always overshadowed by how much I loved you. My bond with you was so consuming it was hard to think straight sometimes, and it was definitely hard to be honest with myself. Then Micah came along and I couldn't ignore the truth anymore."

"Do you love me still?"

His eyes burned with conflict. He held my gaze so long I feared the worst before his face softened. "Of course I still love you. Always."

"Then from now on let's make this a source of comfort and inspiration, not something we need to shy away from. We are a part of each other in ways no one else can ever understand, and there's nothing wrong with that. I would give my life for yours without a passing thought."

"Same goes for me." He gave me a genuine, heart-melting Eli smile and, with the burden lifted, everything seemed so much clearer.

"Are we good now? No bullshit. I need to walk away from this moment satisfied, and knowing you're at peace, too," I said, feeling surer with each word.

He stood and pulled me to my feet. "We're good," he agreed then kissed me. There was so much in that kiss—love, lust, understanding, appreciation, respect, gratitude. It was a kiss goodbye and for a fresh start. When our lips parted I was more at peace than I'd been in years. A huge weight had been lifted from my shoulders, one that had been dragging me down and preventing me from having the life I'd been destined to.

We had started back when Eli touched me arm, drawing my attention back to him. "I did need to hear that, Rachel. Thank you."

We laughed and teased each other the rest of the way back

and I was so glad to be at ease with him again. I was aware of Giovanni long before I saw him, and wasn't surprised to find him waiting for me on the temple's bottom step. He stood as we came into the clearing, moving in our direction. Eli stepped ahead of me and I held back as he gave Giovanni a tight hug. He pressed a kiss to his cheek and blew me one over his shoulder with a knowing wink before entering the doorway at the temple's base. I saw movement and smiled as Micah stepped from the shadowy entrance to meet Eli. They stepped into the space together, swallowed by the darkness.

"Everything taken care of?" Giovanni slid an arm about my waist.

"Yep."

"Anything I should be worried about?"

"Not at all. Eli and I needed to settle some things once and for all."

"And you have? Settled things?"

"Completely."

"And that's all you're going to say about it?"

"Yes." I touched my lips to his.

"Okay. Let's get back in before anyone worries."

"There are no more worries. Everything is finally as it should be." I walked toward the entrance, Giovanni following slightly behind.

"That must have been some conversation," he commented, a hint of sarcasm in his tone.

"It was," I agreed. "A very timely one."

Inside the others were settling, breaking off into smaller groups and deciding where to pass the daylight hours. I checked in on Charles and Genevieve, and gave Charles some kind words I knew would not ease his anxiety. I'd done all I could that night.

Giovanni led me to a secluded space far from the others where he'd arranged a makeshift bed. He undressed me, lay me down, and covered every inch of my body with kisses. He stroked and caressed me, the urgency of my desire for him pushing the boundaries of anything I'd ever experienced with him before. My mind swam in a hazy, aching state of lust and need.

When he finally pressed his naked body against mine, I was slick and tingling. I stroked him until he was hard, loving the way his lips parted and his blue eyes darkened as he became aroused. He grabbed my hand, flipped me onto my back, and pinned me beneath his body. I gasped as he slid inside me, letting the waves of pleasure roll over me, drowning me. There was nothing else but our hungry bodies melding, and the sweet words of love whispered in my ear.

The world made sense only when Giovanni and I were together. All other times were just actions, words, and feelings, disjointed fragments of time that never seemed able to mesh. That was why he was the one. The only one.

CHAPTER 26

A commotion outside the chamber where Giovanni and I slept startled me awake the following evening. I jumped up, threw my clothes back on, and stepped out into a flustered, swarming mass of immortals. Saskia brushed past me and I grabbed her by the back of her arm. She looked surprised to find me.

"What's going on?"

"It's Genevieve. When she woke up and realised what happened, she freaked out. Charles is trying to calm her down." Her words were followed by a resounding crash from a source closer to the front of the temple's interior.

Giovanni was at my back by then and the three of us raced ahead. We found Charles and Genevieve in a heated argument on the platform in the desolate atmosphere of the main chamber. Harshika's throne lay on its side, a deep gouge evident in the platform's stone surface where it had been knocked away with significant force. Genevieve ripped the unlit torches from the wall and hurled them at Charles, who ducked and jumped out of their path. Her injuries seemed to have been reversed with the infusion of immortal blood, but that was a minor victory considering the reaction to her newfound state.

"Why?" she howled, throwing another torch like a spear. Charles moved aside, but the torch hit its mark, leaving a thin line of blood across his cheek.

"Gen, there was no choice. If I didn't, you would have died," he cried out.

"Then you should have let me die!" she shrieked, her lips pulled back to expose her sharp white fangs.

I leapt onto the platform, positioning myself between the two of them. Genevieve stopped in mid-throw, realising I blocked her path to Charles. I startled her and her eyes grew wide with alarm, her hair a wild, bushy mass about her pale face. She reached out, pointing an accusing finger in my direction. "Rachel, how could you have let him do this to me?" Her voice was so pained it cut me to the quick.

"Genevieve, Charles is right. There was no choice. We didn't want to lose you."

"But you have lost me. I am not the same Genevieve I was even last night!"

"Charles loves you. I love you. We did what we felt we had to do."

Her eyes widened at my words, understanding dawning. "So it was both of you?"

Charles was at my side by then, Giovanni and Saskia waiting at the edge of the platform. Genevieve stole a look in their direction before turning her attention back to the two of us. Her fury twisted her beautiful features, giving her a harsh, monstrous look that was nothing like the woman I loved.

"Please." I inched forward. "It was my idea. I insisted, and Charles was so upset...if there's anyone to blame it's me."

She sobbed now, bloody tears streaming down her face. "This is not what I wanted...not...why..."

I closed the last few steps between us and she didn't resist when I pulled her into my arms. She continued to cry for several minutes while Charles and Giovanni stood by, silent and helpless. Saskia turned away, leaving us in privacy. Genevieve's hands clawed at my back, her face wet against my shoulder. She shifted her position, her lips now rubbing at my throat as she clung to me. I was not surprised when her fangs brushed my exposed skin. The tension built in her body and she struggled against a hunger she would not be able to ignore for long. "What's happening to me?" she asked.

I pressed my cheek to hers and whispered right against her ear. "You need to feed. You must let one of us help you or the hunger will make you mad and you won't be able to control yourself. Do you understand what I'm saying to you?"

"Yes." Her voice sounded low and strained.

I eased out of the embrace with difficulty. She was strong with desperation and I suspected the blood I had given her during the change had pushed her beyond the typical newling strength we all received upon becoming immortal. I had shared Harshika's power with her through my blood, the strongest and purest to have ever existed, and it was bound to have significant effects.

The men watched us with concern and, in all the years I'd known Charles, I'd never seen him nervous, but he obviously was now. Genevieve finally let go of me, taking tentative steps in Charles's direction. He bit his wrist and, as the bright-red flow came to the surface, Genevieve latched her mouth about the wound and drank.

Charles mouthed "Thank you," over her shoulder and I nodded.

"We'll regroup in town," I said, heading back to the inner chambers with Giovanni.

The others waited. Several pairs of eyes flashed in the darkness as we entered the first passageway out of the main chamber. Saskia stood a stone's throw from the door, talking in hushed voices with Eli, Micah, and Alessandra. She raised an eyebrow as I came nearer and I understood without explanation that they'd all had an earful.

"Give them a few minutes," I said.

We all walked back into the bowels of the temple, encountering a handful of vampires at each twist and turn. By my count about forty remained. The other hundreds must be long gone by now, coping with the events as only the creatures we were could. I imagined them scurrying away into the night like a pack of rats abandoning a sinking ship. At least as we moved through the world from that point on there would be no need to worry about crossing another's territory or provoking unnecessary confrontations. Tolerance would be a pleasant change of pace.

"They've left," David came to inform us. He stepped into the room where Giovanni, Eli, Micah, Emmaline, and Aldous and I sat lost in conversation. We all reacted to the sound of his voice, startled as though he'd interrupted a dinner party and not a group of vampires discussing next steps.

"Thanks, David," Giovanni answered. "What are your plans?"

"Lucy and I are headed back to Mexico. We have a nice set-up there for the time being at least. It will be strange without Solange, though."

"We are sorry for your loss. Solange will be missed, of course we are forever in your debt," Giovanni answered, his sincerity indisputable.

"Keep in touch," I said.

"Will do." And with that he was gone. He and Lucy departed a short while later with a few others I did not know.

Many others peeked in before departing, offering goodbyes and thanks. Some were sincere in their intentions to remain in contact, others we would not hear from again, though they did not mean it as an insult.

Kieran appeared with Daniel and, at the sight of the former rapist, my rage roared like a lion inside of me. I felt Harshika's presence superimposed on my own energy and I imagined her hateful laughter and the petty, spiteful action she would have taken, and recoiled. I forced the anger deep down inside myself, grimacing with the effort it took to keep it in check. My skin flushed, heat simmering to the surface and my fangs were fully enlarged. I forced myself to meet Daniel's gaze and I hoped the expression that emerged was not as menacing as it felt. Kieran plopped down next to me.

"So, Dan and I are heading out, too. He's going to show me around Australia for the next few months and then we'll be back. Maybe we'll finally have the visit that's been put off for so long now," Kieran said, reminding me about a promise made in England. He seemed excited about a new adventure and Australia had many to offer. A warm memory of Donovan crossed his mind, spilling over to me, which helped pacify the volatile emotions I fought against.

"Have fun. Maybe Giovanni and I will make it there ourselves one day," I responded. I turned to Daniel and asked, "What about Clellia?"

He gave a sad smile then dropped his gaze to his feet. "She's found someone."

"I see."

"It's for the best. She deserves to be free of me." He was sad to lose his long-time companion, but knew it was a good chance for her to find happiness and self-reliance.

There was no disagreement, so further comments on the matter were not necessary. Kieran gave kisses and handshakes to all present with Daniel hanging back, his discomfort evident in his hunched shoulders and downcast eyes. They left together, pushing and joking their way out of the space like a couple of college boys. Their laughter trailed them out into the night.

Alessandra and Saskia, and Mengmei and Zhongxing came to us as a group, explaining their intentions to travel together for the foreseeable future. Alessandra and Saskia seemed very close, but I didn't pry. They kept a tight lid on the nature of their relationship, resisting my subtle attempts to touch their minds. Alessandra wagged a finger in my direction before giving me an icy smile. I chuckled and shrugged. As the last wisp of her white-blond hair disappeared from view I knew I would miss her.

Clellia and Billy-Joe came last. She clung to his hand, her shyness perfuming the air about her. I hoped the next time I saw her, her shoulders would not be hunched and she would be able to meet our gazes. She was so lovely I ached looking at her. Billy-Joe was over the moon in love with her and that's exactly what she needed to gain some much-deserved confidence. I asked her to call me and she was surprised and touched by the offer.

"I'd love to have you two visit us. Would be fun to spend some girl time together."

The barest of smiles crossed her lips and, for the first time, I noticed small dimples in her cheeks. "I'd love that. I've never had a girlfriend before." She had the sweetest voice I'd ever heard.

"Well, sleepovers, shopping, and manicures await. Just pick up the phone. And remember Alessandra has promised to help you also." I pressed another thought into her mind. *Call whenever you need something. And if he hurts you, he'll have to answer to me.*

She giggled in response and offered a timid wave goodbye. Once they were gone, their footsteps long lost to the surrounding jungle, an ominous and unsettling presence made itself apparent to those remaining. The specter of Harshika had been forever trapped in the place where her existence on earth had come to a violent, though not unfitting, end. The whisper of her unnatural power sent a chill through the damp caverns. All seemed affected and suddenly anxious to leave.

Personal items were retrieved and outside the warm jungle waited with endless patience. Achyut stood alone in what would have been the site's courtyard in another lifetime. Now there existed only chunks of eroded stone and creeping vines. I encouraged the others to go ahead and only Giovanni hung back to wait for me. I came to Achyut there under the brightness of the moon, humbled and thankful for everything he'd done.

He turned at the sound of my approach and the amulet clutched in his hand swung away from his body, a gleam of polished stone catching in the moonlight. I didn't realise it before, but the piece was a delicate female figurine, so tiny and precise. The stone was cream-coloured with flecks of pale grey, hanging from a thin leather strap.

"You should have this." Achyut pressed the piece into my hand. His touch was frosty fire, sending a spiralling parade of pins and needles up my arm.

"I can't take this. You gave it to her."

"As I did this." He turned his hand to reveal a second charm. It was the wooden tiger goddess amulet she'd worn every moment of her long existence. The features had worn from its long use, but the meaning it held for Achyut remained vivid and unspoiled. "This is how I choose to remember her. The young beautiful girl who danced and sang, and prayed to the tiger goddess for protection. The amulet you hold represents the night the girl I loved died and a horrible monster was born. Keep it to remind yourself of what could have been and what could have been lost." He looked over my shoulder and I turned to find his gaze resting on my beloved Giovanni. He touched a hand to my shoulder and, with his awful, feathery voice he whispered, "Love him every second of every night you may be blessed to exist. Love him as though every moment is your last, and this past month will soon be nothing but a bad dream. You will live forever, she has blessed us with this, but only you can make your love last as long."

"And will I see you again?"

"Of course. For now, I need to go and, if I may be so lucky, love might find me also." He disappeared before my eyes, moving faster than even I could track.

I scanned the darkness, but he was gone. In his place a handsome pair of jaguars appeared. They wandered into the courtyard, and offered no indications they were aware of or cared for my presence. One sat back on its haunches and raised its head to the moon, emitting the most poignant and haunting of sounds I had ever heard. They mourned the loss of their leader, their protector, and from that realisation came a sadness so sudden and deep my inner resolve crumbled from the burden.

"Let's go, Rachel. Sunrise is near." Giovanni snapped me back from the urgent grip of my pain. He brushed a tear from my face, surprising me, as I hadn't been aware I cried.

"I hope the jungle takes this place back, swallows it and buries every trace of what happened here." The vehemence in my words brought shock to Giovanni's face and I was immediately sorry for lashing out at him.

He chose to ignore my tone and concentrated instead on the message. "I think we all want to leave the memory of Harshika here. I, for one, want to look ahead to our future where there will be no more Desmarais, no more conflicts of the heart, and no challenges to the way we live. I want to wake each evening with you and know that nothing is more perfect than our love."

"There isn't anything more perfect. Our love is forever."

San Francisco. Several weeks later.

As I stepped over the threshold into the house that had been my home once upon a time, a cold slithery sensation met me. I stopped dead in my tracks, whispers of my past filtering in from every direction. Harshika's cruel presence lived among the whispers, reminding me of the evil seed she'd planted within me. How easy it would be to give in to the cold comfort of hate she'd exposed me to. Most of the time I could push past, reason with myself that what I felt wasn't real, but even reduced to ash she still managed to lurk inside, waiting to incite and twist my emotions to blackness.

"Are you all right?" Giovanni asked.

When I looked at him, his brow was furrowed with worry. I searched the faces of my companions, finding the same concern, and I made a promise to myself to do whatever was necessary to shed Harshika's influence. I would do it for Giovanni. I would do it for Eli and my friends. I would do it to reclaim the woman I was meant to be.

We'd all survived, in a physical sense, anyway, though the effects would remain within us for a very long time. In addition to my affliction, Micah and Emmaline both carried a new darkness born from a shame they were not even responsible for. From this had sprung an intense and intimate friendship neither could explain nor abandon. They came to each other often, not to share misery, but to escape it and grow stronger for their ordeal. Both Eli and Aldous were supportive and didn't judge or interfere with their partners' path of healing. Eli and I talked about it many times, and I was glad I'd taken the chance to come clean with him, as it had opened a new level to our friendship we both welcomed and appreciated. I shared with him my secret of Harshika's influence, which was to remain between us and Giovanni.

Micah and Eli returned to Micah's house after a few days. I was sad to see him go, but he no longer had a place in the home we'd once shared with Charles. This would be where Giovanni and I would remain for the time being and, though he and Micah were always welcome, they had their own home and lives. Eli and I'd finally cleared the air, leaving the frustrations and misunderstandings of the past year behind us.

Emmaline and Aldous stayed, living in the guest house, but spending the majority of their time with us. It was nice to have a girlfriend with whom I could talk and laugh. Aldous and Giovanni became fast friends, often disappearing together once Emmaline and I were settled with our chosen activity of the night.

Charles and Genevieve appeared one evening, about two weeks after we'd left Peru. I heard the door opening one night and when I came out to the foyer expecting someone else, there they were. Their body language was tense, but their being together gave me hope they would work through the issue and that Genevieve would find a way to accept her new existence. I welcomed them both back, no questions asked.

So, things seemed to be back on track. Past transgressions and conflicts were forgiven, enemies had been eliminated. Yet, a new wrinkle awaited.

Chapter 27

"You're pregnant?" I asked. The word was so foreign and disconnected from the world I had given myself over to. A world filled with death and darkness, not creating new life.

"Yes, pregnant, as in with child. I'm going to have a baby," Danica answered, so happy she looked as though she would burst. Her wide smile made me ache, but I couldn't help but get wrapped up in her enthusiasm. Giovanni, Charles, and Eli were staring at her as though she'd grown a third arm.

"Who's the father?" I asked, discovering I'd been so self-involved since Giovanni's return, I'd been too distant from the people who meant the most to me. I hadn't even known Danica saw anyone.

"His name is Stephen O'Donnell. He's a math professor at the university. I've known him casually for a few years, you know, seen him around campus and at events and such. He asked me out about six months ago and it's been full steam ahead since then."

"Did you know about this?" I asked Giovanni, having been made aware of his contact with her while I was being held captive.

"No. To be honest I was so distracted by everything that was going on I didn't pay much attention to any thoughts or feelings she might have been experiencing. I could only think about you."

"Ditto for me. I was busy with Genevieve most of the time. I only left to feed and all our discussions were about the matter at hand."

"And I didn't offer anything, either, Rach. I just tried to stay out of the way. I only popped in to make sure Genevieve had groceries and check if there was anything I could do to help. My personal life wasn't really a priority." She sat next to me and the warmth radiating from her was so inviting I couldn't resist pressing against her.

"So, when did you find out? When are you due? What does your dad think?"

"Stephen's good. I mean this wasn't planned, but it's not a bad thing. We're both settled in our careers, financially stable. We've told our parents and everyone's very accepting and supportive."

"Well, this is very exciting," Charles offered. A murmur of agreement followed.

Danica's announcement was a big shock for me. I couldn't explain why exactly, it just took me totally off guard. My mind drifted.

"...so I hoped to have the ceremony here. The grounds are so lovely, and there's lots of room to set up some tents for the dinner. What do you think?" Danica asked. Her blue eyes sparkled and her cheeks had the soft, rosy hue of impending motherhood. How had I not noticed before?

It took me a full minute to catch on to what she talked about. "A wedding? Right. Of course you can have it here. We can all disappear for few days."

"What? No," Danica said, getting my meaning. "I want you at the ceremony. I already talked with Stephen about having it at night and he was fine about it."

I was touched and, more than anything, I'd have loved to see her walk down the aisle, but it couldn't be. "And who would you say I am to your relatives? Don't you think your parents and your brother might recognise me and wonder why I look the same as I did almost twenty-five years ago?"

Acceptance of the truth wiped the happiness from her face. Her lips pursed and I read the jumble of thoughts as she tried to work out a way to make it happen. Her shoulders slumped when she realised there was no solution to be found. "You're right. There is no way to explain it without exposing your secret. I guess I let my enthusiasm get the better of me."

"Just because you can't come to the actual ceremony, doesn't mean we can't watch it. We can set up cameras and watch from Eli and Micah's place," Giovanni said, running a hand along my back, the best kind of comfort.

"Yeah, that's a great idea," Eli agreed. "It'll be the next best thing to being there."

So that was how, just shy of four weeks later, a consortium of immortals found themselves about a large screen television in a comfortable living room watching my niece's wedding reception. She elected to keep the ceremony at night, allowing us the opportunity to watch the events as they unfolded. Danica was radiant in an off-the-shoulder cream dress. The presentation was simple but elegant, and touched a soft spot in my heart.

I cried when she appeared, walked down the aisle by my uncle, and again as the camera panned over those in attendance and I saw my aunt, nephew, and other relatives long divorced from my present life. I laughed as cake was smeared across Danica's smiling face and raised a cup of my own with the wedding attendees to toast the happy couple. As the newlyweds' first dance drew to an end, I stepped outside. The effect of what I had witnessed was deep, surprising me.

Giovanni followed me out a few minutes later, closing the sliding door behind him. He found me at the back of the yard on a swinging wooden bench under a canopy of climbing roses. The air was heavy with their perfume. He sat next to me, his weight causing a gentle sway of the swing. I rested my head against his shoulder and we sat in a comfortable silence.

"That was a beautiful ceremony," he said.

"Mmhhm," I agreed, replaying the events over and over again in my head. It really had been lovely.

"I have to say the whole thing's inspired me."

"Really? How so?"

With a smooth grace only the experienced immortals could manage, Giovanni moved from the bench to kneel before me. From the pocket of his coat he pulled a black velvet box, and the sight of it in his pale hand gave me a feeling like a blow to the stomach. The box opened, revealing a gorgeous solitaire engagement ring. My hand trembled as I reached forward.

"Rachel Armstrong, will you marry me?" His eyes were wide with anticipation, so blue they put the ocean to shame.

"Are you serious?"

"Deadly."

That brought a smirk to my face. "You realise this gives a new meaning to the whole 'death do us part' thing."

"I am fully aware of what this means."

The smirk broke into an ear-to-ear grin. "Then, yes."

No sooner had the ring slipped on my finger than Giovanni lifted me into his arms and spun us around, both of us laughing and crying. The door made a gentle swoosh as it opened and the rest of those remaining in the house appeared. They encircled us, arms strong about our bodies.

"You guys knew about this?" I demanded.

Emmaline nodded, joy bright on her delicate face. "Yes, of course. I helped pick out the ring."

I looked down, amazed. "It's beautiful. How did you keep this from me?"

"It wasn't easy. We all tried very hard to keep our thoughts to ourselves."

"I guess that's why I haven't seen much of anyone this week." The group had been noticeably absent in recent days and that, added to the fact we all made a concerted effort not to peek inside each other's minds, had made it easy for the plans to slip by me. The blood we'd drained from Harshika's body had strengthened us all and given us greater control over our minds and bodies. Not to mention how I'd been distracted by Danica and her situation.

Eli leaned in to hug me and whispered, "Just how things are supposed to be."

The group laughed and teased me, and I couldn't remember ever feeling so free. Charles wandered back to the house, reappearing with cups full of our liquid of choice. I didn't ask where he'd found it.

We all raised our cups to toast the happy occasion. "To love," I said, squeezing Giovanni's hand.

"To love," was the chorus of agreement.

EPILOGUE

Finally right

Danica gave birth to a healthy, eight-pound, five-ounce baby girl, whom she named Elizabeth Rachel in honour of her mother and, as assumed by the rest of the family, her deceased aunt. In light of the change in her lifestyle, she decided to cut back on teaching and concentrate more on her writing, which she could do from home. She was happy and safe, and part of my life, and it was a joy to see her embrace her new role of mother. Giovanni and I immediately set up a trust for Elizabeth to ensure she would always be independent and protected.

Charles and Genevieve stayed for a few months before deciding to return to England. Gen had come to terms with her "condition" as best she could, though the anger hadn't entirely left her system, and I didn't imagine it would for many years. Charles treaded lightly with her, giving comfort where he could and staying out of her way when her internal storms brewed. I never doubted the authenticity of his love for her, but the behaviour I witnessed the night of Gen's change and, in the subsequent months, made it irrefutable. They decided to use Genevieve's training and Charles's vast wealth to develop an institute for the research of hereditary and genetic diseases, of which they would act as clinical director and CEO respectively. Vampires helping humans. Who'd have thought it?

Emmaline and Aldous also moved on after a time, heading back to Wales, then on to Germany. Aldous had not set foot on his native soil since his change, and he felt making peace with his past was long overdue. We heard from them regularly, and thought of them as extended family.

Kieran called the other day. He and Daniel were doing well, and enjoying their trek across Australia. Lucy and another vampire named Sandra met up with them, and all were happy with their new "couple" statuses. He let us know he planned to be back in North America in a few months and wanted to visit. Of course, we agreed.

Eli and Micah had been gone for several months. They were on a worldwide adventure, heading off in whatever direction struck their fancy, no clear plan in mind. The timetable was ever-changing and, with our longevity, no need to hurry back. Eli sent me funny postcards and e-mails every so often, to which I always looked forward. I missed him every day, but it was a tolerable pain, as he was only a phone call away, and forever a part of my life. We loved each other in our unique way, and we were both good with the relationship as it stood. We each had our loves, our life partners, but we would always have each other's backs.

Giovanni and I married before Eli and Micah left, in a lovely ceremony at our home in Spain. Emmaline was my maid of honour, Charles the best man. It had been a small, intimate affair, but more beautiful than I could ever have imagined. The moon had been bright and, for the first night after all the months since Harshika's destruction, she didn't speak to me. My happiness, pure and unrestrained, was enough to keep her lingering presence at bay. One day she would be gone forever but, until then, I did my best to fight her influence.

Here I am, in Giovanni's arms, lying on a soft blanket on the damp sand of our private beach. The water laps on the shore, whispering promises of peace and wonder for my future. Giovanni is my passion, my friend, my rock. His kiss is my strength, his touch my reassurance, and being with him is reason enough to want to live forever. Our kind might have been born of blood and retribution, and our existence may border on the edge of evil, but even that cannot take away from the beauty of what we share.

An eternal life, an eternal love.

ABOUT THE AUTHOR

L iz Strange is the published author of ten novels and several short stories. She has also written multiple scripts for both film and television.

Curious about other Crossroad Press books?
Stop by our site:
http://www.crossroadpress.com
We offer quality writing
in digital, audio, and print formats.